T0375572

From Nowhere

Jon Hooks

FROM NOWHERE

iUniverse books may be ordered through booksellers or by contacting:

iUniverse
1663 Liberty Drive
Bloomington, IN 47403
www.iuniverse.com
1-800-Authors (1-800-288-4677)

ISBN: 978-1-4917-8970-4 (sc)
ISBN: 978-1-4917-8971-1 (hc)
ISBN: 978-1-4917-9009-0 (e)

Library of Congress Control Number: 2016902354

Print information available on the last page.

iUniverse rev. date: 02/09/2016

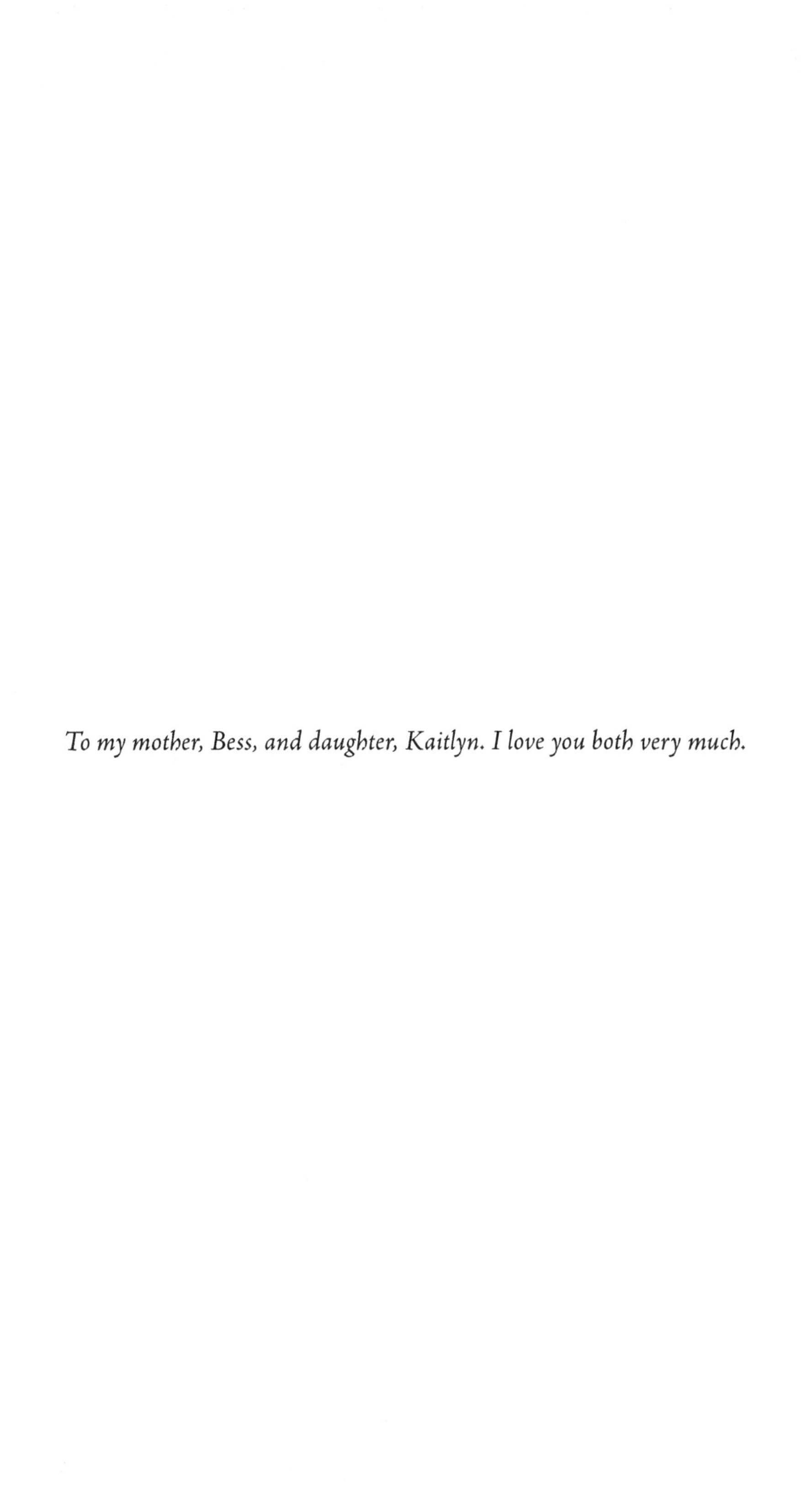

To my mother, Bess, and daughter, Kaitlyn. I love you both very much.

Author's Note

I eagerly went to a movie maybe fifteen years ago. I liked the cast and the storyline conveyed in the movie trailer I had seen. I'd enjoyed the screenwriter's other work, so like a child waiting for Christmas, I anticipated its opening.

The movie started, and I sat there happy, contently enjoying how the story progressed—that is, until the very end.

"Who in the world writes an ending like that?" I asked my friends.

Of course, I couldn't see the forest for the trees, as my mother often reminds me. I was convinced that I could write a better story than what I had just witnessed, but like always, I put it off. In the meantime, I watched the movie again, and this time I saw the forest. I figured out what the story was all about. My faith in the screenwriter now restored, faith in my ability to come up with something better was now very much in doubt.

I procrastinated, if you can call more than a decade procrastinating, and as I began reading another book, I read the author's note for that book. It was his first book, and I decided to take the advice he had given himself. I sat down. Legal pad and pen in hand, I did my best to write a first page that would make me want to write another—and, if someone happened to read that first page, make him or her want to read another as well. I tried to keep that thought in mind as I continued to write.

I want to thank my family and all my friends for their encouragement. Without it, like many other things I have started, I would not have finished. I hope you enjoy the story. Any mistakes were either intentional or mine alone.

My kindest regards,
Jon Hooks

Part 1

Chapter 1

He sat down on the edge of the bed and watched her sleeping. The hallway light drifted through the bedroom door that he had left slightly open. The cotton bedsheet and fleece blanket were bunched up under her left shoulder. She wore one of his oversized gray T-shirts that they had picked up while staying at a bed-and-breakfast on the Outer Banks a couple of years ago. Her foot and calf were exposed, as they always were when she was sleeping. Her skin was deeply tanned, courtesy of a week spent at her parents' cottage in Atlantic Beach ten days earlier. Thoughts rushed through his mind, and he smiled watching her. She was beautiful. Gently, he brushed her wavy brown hair away from her face. It was in these moments that he realized she still made him feel like he had the first time he saw her.

It was at a college mixer. Fall semester, freshman year, and all the students were letting off steam—but especially the freshman. They had survived their first semester of college and were grateful for it. The holidays were a welcome break.

It had been a long first semester for Brad Ford. The challenge of balancing school and golf at the collegiate level had become easier. The pressure of being the latest wunderkind of the historic Wake Forest golf team had not, though. It was a self-inflicted pressure, and he knew it. Spending the holidays with his father would help his frame of mind. He was sitting on a sofa, sipping beer from a longneck bottle his roommate Mark had tossed over. The beer was already lukewarm. Brad nursed his beers longer than most. Quiet in thought, he sat alone staring at his half-filled bottle when the sound of a woman's laughter caused Brad to look her way. It wasn't the typical teenage giggle he was used to hearing at freshman parties.

She was pretty, and her smile was bright and engaging. Her personality seemed to captivate those around her. It drew people to her when they realized she had arrived. She mingled with ease as he watched her seemingly float from one place to another and from one group to the next. The faded Levis clung to her legs but not too tightly. Her Kelly-green sweater and navy peacoat covered a white oxford shirt. The outfit was straight from the preppie handbook. The wavy brown hair came to rest slightly past her shoulders. Her dark brown eyes and olive complexion made Brad wonder if she was Italian or possibly of Latin descent. While she moved about the room comfortable with who she was, Brad was uncomfortable and uneasy. His shyness was intense and almost painful at times. He was hard to get to know, and those who did not know Brad often accused him of being aloof. Mark would know what to do, Brad hoped. *Ah yes, where's my roommate?* he wondered.

He looked up again to find her talking to a woman Brad was certain he'd taken freshman biology with. With no sign of Mark, he thought of what he could do. As he approached them, the woman walked away, and he was able to ask his classmate about the woman she had been talking to. He was informed that her name was Susan Coble. He was also informed that she would not under any condition or circumstance consider going out with a jock. He was almost relieved.

Mark came over to Brad and stood by him. "Well, you look like you're having a blast, bud," Mark said, smiling.

"Well, this isn't my idea of fun. And the first woman I see all semester that I'm attracted to doesn't date jocks. What's that all about?"

"You're kidding, right? She told you that? Where the hell is she? She does realize you're not really a jock, doesn't she?" Mark asked, laughing.

"What's that supposed to mean? No, she didn't tell me that. Some girl from a class I took knows her, and she told me," Brad said in a huff.

"You play golf, and that hardly qualifies you as an athlete. Point her out, and I'll prove my point."

"Kiss my ass. How much playing time are you averaging, basketball stud?"

"Ouch. Low blow there, roomie. Sorry—you're an athlete. Feel better? Now where's she at? I need to talk her."

"Please don't talk to her, and do *not* hit on her. You'll just embarrass me."

"I'm not going to hit on her. You need to meet someone—anyone." And with that, Brad relented and pointed her out. He waited for some snide comment from Mark.

"Atta boy! Well, I've learned two things about my roommate tonight."

"And what might those be?"

"Well, you have great taste in women. More importantly to me, though, you actually like women." Mark erupted in laughter and walked off. Brad flipped him the bird, but Mark didn't see it.

Brad sat there for a few minutes and was just about to leave when he realized *she* was walking toward him. No, she couldn't be! There was no way she would listen to anything his cheesy roommate could have told her. If she did, that would be her first strike, he decided. She stopped right in front of him.

"Are you Brad?"

He was too shocked to answer. He just nodded his head.

"I'm Susan Coble. It's nice to meet you. Is this seat taken?" she said, pointing to the sofa.

"No, no, please. I'm very sorry. I'm Brad Ford. It's nice to meet you." He tried to stand, as any polite southern gentleman is taught to do, but it was much too late for that.

"Is that Mark guy a friend of yours?"

"Well, he's my roommate. That's all I'm willing to admit to right now." *What other idiotic things are you going to think of, Brad?* He took a deep breath and decided he had to regroup, or this would be a very short conversation.

A couple of hours passed quickly as they sat and got to know each other. She slowly sipped a bottle of water. She was from Raleigh and had two brothers and a sister. Her father had been in the insurance business but was now retired, and her mother had stayed at home raising the kids. Brad was from Winston-Salem but never mentioned his parents. They talked about school and what classes they had finished in the fall, what professors to take classes from and who should be avoided. Susan said she was planning to major in English, though she was not sure what that would lead to. Brad was planning to pursue history. It was the only subject that he had ever really enjoyed. When it was time to leave, they promised to meet for coffee after they returned from break. They shook hands, smiled, and wished each other happy holidays.

Watching her walk away, Brad thought about what a pleasant surprise their chance encounter had been. She suddenly turned around, walked back over, and gave Brad a soft peck on the cheek. This time she blushed. As she left for the final time, Mark wondered what Brad could have said to her. He wasn't sure he wanted to know the answer.

Chapter 2

Brad leaned forward and kissed her cheek. Her skin was soft and smooth and warm. Her hand reached for him, and once she found him, she smiled a sleepy smile. "Honey, I've got to go," he whispered. She sat up and wrapped her arms around him. He felt her warm breath on his neck as she nuzzled against him. Her touch was still the most comforting feeling he had ever known.

"When he wakes up, we'll meet you. You start on number one, right?" she whispered. He nodded. "We should be there when you finish the front. I put everything together last night. Tickets, directions, tee sheet. We're good to go. The US Open, baby. Can you believe it? I'm so proud of you. Promise me you'll let yourself enjoy it?"

"I will. I promise. I couldn't do this without you. I love you."

"I love you too." She kissed him good-bye, and Brad left for the biggest day in his professional life.

The condo was part of a massive renovation project by the Lewallen Real Estate Company. The Lewallens owned the largest and most prominent real-estate company in Northern California. They bought, sold, and developed property, and this was another of their ventures. Adrian Lewallen had purchased several rows of abandoned two-story brick stores years ago in what would later be designated a historical area of San Jose. Adrian Lewallen had the clout and connections needed to make things like that happen. The company gutted the insides and eventually transformed them into something close to the beautiful brownstones that made up the landscape of Georgetown. Each unit had three bedrooms and two and a half baths. The original hardwood floors had been restored. The first floor was open and spacious and allowed for creative decorating. The kitchen had every amenity one could dream of having, though his son, Mark, had yet to cook one meal there. They were quite expensive, but Mark had paid nothing. As the only child of Adrian and Natalie Lewallen, it had been given to him. Considering the market they were trying to target, Mark was the perfect first owner prospective buyers might see. He loved it because there was no rent, no payments, just an absolutely perfect place to show himself off to the young ladies of San Jose. Mark was not much of a decorator, though. The walls bore nothing. No paintings, no posters, and not a single picture. He had simply leaned pictures against the walls, assuming he would get to them eventually. Susan had started putting a woman's touch on it while she and Brad were in town.

Mark was waiting for Brad in the kitchen. Mark had the stereotypical California look—blond hair, blue eyes, tall, tan, lean, and fit. He looked in better condition now than he had when he and Brad first met. He was a physical-education teacher at the local high school. Mark was the head coach of the junior varsity basketball team, and the school year was over. His first season as a head coach had been a resounding success. Mark's family was stunned at his success, but Brad wasn't. In college, Brad had been a prize recruit and accepted the Arnold Palmer golf scholarship from Wake Forest University, while Mark had been offered a scholarship because his father was a college roommate of the head basketball coach. Mark was a solid player, but no one considered him a Division I prospect. He was a shooting guard but did not handle the ball well enough, was too slow to play adequate defense—not that he wanted to—and his passing skills were the butt of a constant joke. Apparently the only good pass anyone could count on Mark making was at the opposite sex. He did, however, develop an understanding of the game and how to motivate the other players while spending most of his four years of college on the bench. In the two weeks since school ended, Mark had refused to shave and had done nothing but enjoy the sun and of course a couple of female companions.

Brad and Mark were an odd couple. It was a friendship that surprised almost everyone they'd known in college. The one notable exception was Brad's wife, Susan. She knew the secret of their friendship; it was Mark who had brought Brad and Susan together.

"Morning, sunshine!" Mark said, laughing at his best friend as Brad walked into the kitchen.

"Good morning, Mark," Brad responded with the reserved smile Mark had come to know.

Mark was wearing an old white polo, wrinkled khakis, and an old, comfortable pair of running shoes. He was dressed for duty. He wore a long-billed cap one might see on someone deep-sea fishing, and a pair of sunglasses dangled from his neck. His unkempt look would help him blend right in with the other caddies.

Brad sipped his coffee, and Mark studied his friend. Brad was deep in thought. Mark wanted to know what was going through Brad's mind, but he knew better than to ask. Was he thinking about his mother? Brad never spoke about his mother, and Mark knew very little. Mark remembered seeing a picture of her in their dorm room. He had asked Brad if that was his mother, and Brad acknowledged that it was. He told Mark that she'd passed away when he was fourteen, but he offered little else in the way of details. Was he thinking about his dad? Brad's father had died their freshman year of college. Mark had helped him through it.

The golf team had just returned from their annual trip to the Chris Schenkel Intercollegiate. Georgia Southern University hosted the tournament. The team struggled, but Brad played very well. He started slowly with back-to-back rounds of seventy-two. He caught fire in the third and final round. His sixty-seven vaulted him into a three-way playoff for individual honors with Steve Morrison of Florida and Michael Scott of Georgia Tech. The Florida senior prevailed with a birdie on the second hole of sudden death. The promise of Brad's talent was starting to show. He was subdued on the six-hour ride back to campus. He was excited about his play but felt that it would be inappropriate to be too happy since the team had done poorly. His teammates were happy for him, and all offered their congratulations. He wanted to get home and tell his dad and talk to Susan.

It was nearly midnight when they finally arrived, and the players and their coach were exhausted. Brad looked out the window of the van and saw Mark and the Wake Forest athletic director waiting. Coach Makinney exited the van and walked over to them while Brad gathered his travel bag and clubs, eyeing his coach through the window. He wondered what the two were doing there. He decided Mark had done something stupid and began hoping his roommate was not trying to implicate him in whatever scheme it might be.

Coach Makinney motioned to Brad with his arm. "Brad, come over here, son. We need to go inside and talk."

The three led Brad inside the field house were Coach Makinney's office was located. The small room was cluttered and would stay that way every spring while the golf team traveled. The golf program was easily the most successful program in the school's athletic history, and the pictures that covered the walls like stamps were incredible. Wake Forest had eighteen Atlantic Coast Conference titles and a stretch during the sixties and seventies where the school won twelve in a row. Wake Forest had also won three NCAA championships, and three former players had won individual championships. Legends of professional and amateur golf played at Wake Forest.

It was in this office that Brad learned that his father, Frank, had suffered a massive heart attack and passed away while the team was coming home.

Breaking the silence, Mark said, "Ready to go, Sparky?"

"Ready as I'll ever be."

"You got everything?"

How and when did Mark become the responsible one? Brad thought.

Brad laughed. "This ain't my first rodeo."

"Well, it's your first Open!"

"You're right about that. But focus on what I need you to do, and I'll focus on what I need to do."

"And what am I supposed to do?"

"When we get there. We'll talk then. Let's get on the road." He winked at Mark and hugged him. "Thank you for everything. I'm asking a lot of you."

"No way would I miss this," Mark replied as he pulled back.

They hopped in Mark's SUV at a little after four in order to be there plenty in advance of the 7:00 a.m. tee time. In the darkness of the early morning, Brad enjoyed being a passenger for a change. The drive from Mark's condo in San Jose to San Francisco gave him time to think. Mark knew exactly where they were going, and this was no time to be making a wrong turn. In the past three and half years, he and Susan had traveled roughly two hundred thousand miles roaming the mini-tours, the minor leagues of professional golf. It was not the life he had expected when he left college, but it was all he knew right now.

Brad thought of his dad and mom. He wished they could be there with him and his family. He was the only child of only children. Susan, his son, Will, and Mark were really all Brad had.

Brad's thoughts bounced from one to another. His dad had taught him everything about the game he loved and hated. He had taught him everything he knew, not just about golf but about life and being a man. He always reminded him that an honest and decent man was a rich and blessed man. He could still hear his dad as clearly as if he were in the backseat.

Brad was lost when his father died. His mother's death had changed their father-son relationship. They were more than just father and son. They had become friends and leaned on each other. When Brad left for college, it was hard on both of them. He hoped that he would be half the father to Will that his father had been to him. He could not help but think how his parents would have doted over Will. His father would have spoiled him rotten, and Brad hated that Will never met him. He loved his father, thought of him every day, and was grateful that he had been raised by him.

He tried to forget the pressure he was feeling. After another dreadful performance at the final stage of qualifying school, he decided that this year would be his last. He was tired of living like a gypsy. Will was about to start school, and he would be there for him. Susan never complained. She supported his dream, but enough was enough, he had told himself. He had an open offer to become the teaching professional at the Old State Club. The Wake Forest golf team practiced there, and a group of prominent alumni had all but adopted Brad into their collective families. He spent his holiday and school breaks with them, and then they welcomed Susan and Will.

Susan had spent the week being wife, mom, and executive assistant. She returned phone calls and handled all the e-mails from well-wishing friends. She wanted Brad to relax, enjoy, and savor this week.

Brad came out of his deep thoughts as the lights of San Francisco came into view. They were dimmed by a scattered morning fog coming off the bay. Mark exited onto the 380 and then north onto the Junipero Sierra Freeway. Brad took a deep breath and tried to relax. Until he was there though, the effort would be in vain.

They finally arrived at the players' entrance of the San Francisco Athletic Club. Like all players, they were greeted by event security. Mark lowered their windows.

"Good morning, guys. Need to see your credentials please," the security officer said.

"Yes, sir, right here. Players badge and ID. I'm Brad Ford, and this is my caddie, Mark Lewallen. Here's his paperwork and ID as well," he said, handing over the information.

"Thank you, Mr. Ford, and good luck this week."

"Thank you."

Mark parked the car. They both yawned and stretched. It was cold, and the wind made the air crisp. Brad opened the door to the backseat and grabbed a pullover and slid it on. "Grab the clubs, and

I'll meet you at the players' clubhouse entrance. Need anything to eat or drink?"

"No thanks. I'm good. I still can't get over how damn heavy your bag is."

"It's awesome. The guys gave it to me when I qualified. And stop whining. Susan's caddied for me before and never complained." He smiled at Mark.

Brad walked into the players' locker room. Once inside, he spotted Malcolm Jefferson putting the finishing touches on a pair of golf shoes for one of the other players. Malcolm was close to seventy years old and looked every year of it. His hair was short and graying. He wore an apron to keep the shoe polish off his club uniform. He was a short and small-framed black man, but his smile lit up the locker room, and Brad was glad to see his smiling face.

"Good morning, Mr. Ford. You're the first one here."

"Hey, Malcolm—and please stop calling me mister. By the way, how long have you worked here?"

"Not really sure. Fifty years at least, I guess. I wanted to caddie when I started, but I was too weak to carry a golf bag. Caddie master felt sorry for me, so he let me clean clubs and shag balls for the members. Folks here have always treated me good, so I stayed. Son, how much golf history do you know?"

"A little ... my dad loved it and would tell me stories. I know that two of the biggest upsets in Open history happened here. Why do you ask?"

"That's right, boy." Malcolm smiled in approval of Brad's knowledge. "That Fleck fellow beat Ben Hogan in 1955 and then Billy Casper in 1966. He beat Arnie. I just wanted to cry. I love me some Arnie. He's still the king, you know?" Malcolm's eyes were sad, as if it had happened yesterday. "Come over here a minute." Malcolm walked Brad over to his locker. Brad was still trying to get over seeing the other names. Woods, Singh, Mickelson. Those names belonged there. As they reached his locker, he read his name and thought how out of place it looked with the others.

"That was Mr. Fleck's locker in 1955," Malcolm said as he pointed at Brad's locker. "This place is full of miracles. Look at me, boy." He placed his callused hand on Brad's shoulder and gently patted it. "This place is full of miracles," he repeated as Brad looked into Malcolm's eyes, which were no longer sad. "Believe in yourself, and you go shock the world." He turned and walked away.

Brad opened his locker to find his shoes looking as if they were brand-new. As he was lacing them up, he couldn't help but feel like his father had somehow borrowed Malcolm's body for a few minutes so he could give his son one last pep talk. He wasn't sure how much of the story was true, but it was a great story, and he appreciated Malcolm sharing it with him. He looked for Malcolm as he left to thank him, but he had slipped off somewhere. *After the round,* he thought to himself. He met Mark, and they walked to the putting green.

"What the hell took you so long in there?" Mark impatiently inquired. Brad shrugged and kept walking. It was time to focus. He grabbed his putter and a couple of balls. The putting green was roped off for a good distance in every direction. It was a place of solitude for the players as well as the caddies. After putting for a few minutes, Brad grabbed his sand wedge and hit a few chip shots. Next he grabbed his lob wedge and a few more chips. Convinced that he knew how the greens would react to the variety of short game shots he would play, he headed to the practice area.

The morning air was still damp and chilly, and the fog they had encountered on the drive had barely lifted. Mark threw on a Wake Forest windbreaker he had stuffed in Brad's bag. It was now wrinkled to match the rest of his attire. Dew was clinging to each blade of grass they walked on, depositing small grass clipping on their shoes. The sun was working its way up into the sky, and the club was coming to life. The last-minute details were many. Volunteers must be in their places, and rules officials had to be stationed. They doubled-checked the walkie-talkies used to communicate. The maintenance staff put the finishing touches on the course. Brad could hear the sound of mowers in the distance and smell the freshly mown grass. The fairways would be firm and fast and appear striped from the mowers.

Gone were all the tractor-trailers from earlier in the week. Every major was a Mecca for the endless golf equipment companies. They came in on the prior Sunday night to set up shop. The trailers were mobile workshops so players could get grips changed and clubs fine-tuned or try the latest and greatest club head or shaft claiming to be the longest on tour. The tour representative's biggest job was to make sure his or her staff players were happy and to make sure they had the strongest presence possible when the Darrell Survey was released. It was an advertising coup if their company was perceived to be number one on tour. And to this end, guys ran around soliciting all players, including Brad. One company promised Brad a thousand dollars to have their driver in his bag, and another offered a thousand dollars for wearing their hat and golf gloves and using their wedges and putters. He was thrilled to do it. The money meant his expenses were covered for the week, and he would be able to give Malcolm a really nice tip, the thought of which made him smile.

The United States Golf Association had renovated the practice area prior to the Open. Brad was still in awe at how perfect it was. He walked over to get a bucket of balls. Because tour players were under contract, the ball manufacturers provided a sufficient number of balls for the players to use from each manufacturer. Every day, brand-new balls were opened. The majority of players used Titleist, and Brad fell in that group. He stared at the bucket of new balls for a moment. It was a far cry from the overused range balls they hit on the mini-tours. Brad was told that after the tournament the balls were donated to local junior golf programs.

Mark followed Brad to his designated spot. He found his name placard, *Bradley Ford, Winston-Salem, North Carolina*. Brad laid the bucket on its side and went to his golf bag. He pulled out his golf glove, a few tees, a tool to repair ball marks, and a couple of coins he used to spot his ball on the greens while he waited for his turn to putt. When he was done gathering the essentials, Brad noticed Mark studying another caddie. He had no doubt that Mark was determined to be as professional as possible for his friend. Brad smiled as Mark imitated the actions of the other caddie, grabbing the towel and quickly walking over to a water cooler. He wet the bottom third of it and then hustled back to his place beside Brad. He then grabbed the bucket and stood it upright next to his feet, copying what he had witnessed. Brad took gentle swings, trying to loosen up his back and shoulders. Each time, the club brushed the grass just enough to disturb its position. The dewy blades splashed water onto his clubface.

Brad stretched and then looked at Mark with amusement. He just had to know. "What are you doing?" Brad asked, laughing.

"Being your caddie. Why?" Mark answered, looking perplexed. Brad laughed again.

"Okay, why are you wiping off brand-new balls?"

"Well, since you haven't exactly given me a lot of instruction on this whole caddie deal, I decided to watch and learn."

Brad smiled again and shook his head. "Okay, it's time."

"Time for what?"

"Your responsibilities. I'll go slowly. Wanna take notes?" Brad was enjoying that for once he was able to give Mark a hard time instead of it being the other way around.

"No, I don't need to take notes!"

"Relax. I'm just busting your chops. You've been doing it to me for years. It's not complicated. Caddies have three rules they live and die by. Show up, keep up, and shut up. You're already here, so worry about the other two. If I say something out loud, I'll be talking to myself. Just nod in agreement. I don't wipe off practice balls, nor do I expect you to. I have no idea who that guy is you've been copying, but I'm willing to bet you dinner tonight he's an ass." With that, Brad patted Mark on the shoulder, they shared a quick smile, and he went back to his routine. The routine had been the same for years. He started with his wedges and then slowly went through his irons. He would hit even-numbered clubs one day and odd ones the next day. Fairway woods always followed the irons, and then finally his driver. Once he was convinced that his swing was in order, they went back to the putting green, which was on the way to the first tee. Again he grabbed a couple of balls and dropped them onto the green. He paced off a distance of forty-two feet and then worked on the pace of his putts. He then moved closer. He always practiced six-foot putts from north, south, east, and west of the hole. Once he made them all, he was ready.

Chapter 3

Mason Randolph and Nathaniel Monsees were cousins growing up on tobacco farms in Emporia, Virginia. The War Between the States had ended. They were each the youngest child of their families and now the only surviving males. Mason's father and two older brothers had given their lives defending the Commonwealth, while Nathaniel lost three older siblings. Nathaniel's father died from grief. He could never get over the deaths of his children. The only reason Mason and Nathaniel had been spared was, as the only males, they were needed to tend to what was left of their families and their farms. Their families treated their slaves well, and they were reluctant to leave, but when freedom was offered, they headed north in hopes of a better life. The burden of running the farms without any other males was overwhelming.

Mason and Nathaniel both had brilliant minds and ambitious dreams. Neither had ever had a desire to toil away in the dirt of their family farms; it was just expected of them. They jumped when they had the opportunity to sell the farms. They now had the money to pursue their bigger plans. Together they studied carefully the many options they had before deciding to move to Winston-Salem, North Carolina.

Winston-Salem and the neighboring city of Greensboro were quickly gaining fame for their railroad systems. The cousins took their money, purchased as much land as they could around the depots, and quickly started erecting warehouses. The trains gave them access to many rural areas in North Carolina, where tobacco was the most important crop any farmer could have. It gave the farmers another option for selling their crop, and they were grateful for the competition for their golden leaf instead of feeling like they were being held at gunpoint in smaller local markets.

Mason and Nathaniel lived frugally and reinvested their profits. Their warehouses followed the expanding rail system and by 1890 dominated the tobacco business in North and South Carolina as well as Virginia. The R&M Tobacco and Trading Company later would be shortened to the R&M Tobacco Company.

As the twentieth century rapidly approached, Mason and Nathaniel decided it was time to start enjoying the rewards of hard work and years of tight-fisted living. Their company had purchased a thousand acres of rolling woodland not far from the ever-expanding downtown of Winston-Salem. It was time to show the world what their hard work had provided their families. They would build the grandest homes in the grandest neighborhood the South had ever seen. They both built houses that bordered on being mansions. The style was renaissance revival. They stood on two of the highest points of The Park, standing guard and protecting it. The houses were built to remind others what was expected in The Park. Mason and Nathaniel would determine who would be allowed into The Park. Some of their employees would be rewarded with lots. Doctors, lawyers, and the local textile magnets would purchase the rest.

The game of golf was also starting to find its way onto the American landscape. All cities of consequence were building courses and starting country clubs, and the proper society of Winston-Salem would be no different. It was decided that they too must have such a club, and the Old State Club was built. It would run through the heart of The Park and was opened in 1914. Bill McKnight, Tom Rhodes, and John Hicks grew up there, lived there, were for the most part retired there, and would die there. There was no other place they would rather be. There was no other place they would have wanted to raise their families and now live out their lives.

Brad received e-mails and calls from all of them. Bill McKnight, Tom Rhodes, and John Hicks were nervous "fathers." His adoptive fathers were in their fifties and sixties. Brad was the son all of them had wanted. Polite and well mannered, even at his young age he understood that grown men have their secret lives to help them cope with the stresses and pressures of high-profile lives. They had old family money and political interests to control. One was a lawyer, one a doctor, and one a retired CEO. Brad could learn more in a few hours with them than in ten years at Wake Forest. Give his fathers a couple of good, stiff drinks, preferably a single malt scotch, and the secrets would come pouring out.

Bill McKnight was the lawyer. He was sixty years old and semiretired. He, along with Jim Edwards, had started McKnight and Edwards thirty years ago. His specialty was tax law and estate planning. Anyone who was anybody went to Bill. At fifty-five, he informed Jim it was time to start grooming his successor. He still handled a very select group of clients, one of whom was Brad. Brad did not come from old money, but his father had been a very successful sales representative with a large pharmaceutical company. When Brad's father passed away, Bill helped Brad through all the legalities of his father's estate. Bill simply would not let Brad be taken advantage of. His mostly gray hair had once been almost black when he started his firm, and his waistline had been much smaller. His cheeks stayed a reddish color, giving his face the appearance of a man who had enjoyed a drink or two over the years. He refused to wear suits unless he had to attend a funeral. His favorite ensemble was a golf shirt with the Old State logo, khaki shorts, and Top-Sider loafers with no socks. Unless he was playing golf, his reading glasses hung from his neck or were perched on the end of his nose.

Tom Rhodes could pass as Bill's brother, though they were not related. Similar in build and looks, Tom was a retired orthopedic surgeon. When he was still practicing, Tom had been without peer in the state of North Carolina and among the top three in the southeastern United States. Knee and hip-replacement surgery were his specialties. Tom and Bill had been good golfers in their youth but never as good as John Hicks.

Two years younger, John Hicks was a retired CEO with one of the many tobacco companies based in Winston-Salem. He was much taller and much thinner than Bill and Tom and was often seen with his trademark bucket hat covering a head that had balded over the years. Through hard work, he had risen the corporate ladder. His success as a CEO was attributed to the fact that he knew the responsibility of each employee. He had been trained about the business from the ground up. He had been a buyer and a seller, vice president, and president of sales. He had traveled the world and had played golf all over the world. He owed much of his career to his stellar golf game. He also had an uncanny ability to provide his clients anything and everything they might want. Whatever it took to close the deal. It was a part of his job that he detested. The business could be dirty at times, but he knew it. He spent most of his career in a private conflict with himself. The perks and the pay were too good to walk away from, so he made peace with it by making sure he could retire early. Bill helped him plan it. At fifty-one, he finally freed himself from this life. He now led a relaxed life that centered around his beloved club. He, Bill, and Tom had grown up together at this club.

Someone from their families had been a member since it had been founded. Over the years, John Hicks had won the club championship twelve times, and with Bill as his partner, the Chairman's Cup nine times. He had competed in the Unites States Amateur while in his thirties and still relished the competition with the younger members. He worked hard on his game. His immense pride had made him determined to not go down without a fight. The young guns were coming, and he knew it. He practiced and played with Brad. He enjoyed this time and was convinced that he felt much younger because of it.

After their usual Wednesday afternoon golf match, the fathers had agreed to meet Thursday morning at the club. ESPN was starting its broadcast at eleven, and they would retreat to the men's lounge where there would be no nagging of spouses, no phone interruptions, no disturbances of any kind.

They arrived at the first tee, where the starter introduced Brad and Mark to the other players and their caddies. Tom Crocker was from Houston, Texas, and Vince Lewis was from Tucson, Arizona. All three played the mini-tours, and other than an obligatory "good luck, play well" and a handshake, nothing else was said. Each player's nerves were on edge, as their opening shots would soon be upon them. Pin sheets were given to each of them, and Brad quickly checked it and neatly folded it in such a manner that he could see three of them at a time without folding and refolding. He then reached in his back pocket and pulled out a bright orange yardage book. The pin sheets simply showed the players the length and width of each green, how far on the green the hole was located, and how close it might be to a given side. The yardage book was not the typical graphically enhanced book found in pro shops. Tour books were hand drawn with immense detail. A former caddie, a real character referred to as Rickie Lee, was the supplier. He had made a small fortune following the tour from tournament to tournament, selling his goods.

The starter grabbed his microphone, as if he needed it. There were no more than five or six people watching their threesome as they were about to tee off. "Please welcome the seven o'clock starting time. On the tee now from Houston, Texas, Tom Crocker," he announced. Vince Lewis would be next, and finally, "and from Winston-Salem, North Carolina, Bradley Ford."

Brad's hand trembled as he placed his tee in the ground and then his ball on the tee. He reached for his driver and then stood behind the ball. He picked his target line and took one last deep breath, and with it he forced the nervousness out of his body. "It's show time," he muttered to himself. He took his stance and gave the target one last look. His swing began, as if in slow motion. The club worked its way over his right shoulder, and then as his body started moving back toward the ball, his arms led the club head as they dropped around his waist and with perfect rhythm and timing seemed to connect back with his torso. Working as one, it all delivered a powerful blow to the back of the ball. The ball screamed off the tee it had been perched on and like a bullet raced for the target. It was absolutely perfect as it rolled slowly to a stop in the right side of the fairway nearly three hundred yards from its starting point. The USGA had converted the first hole from a par five that the members played to a brutal par four for the greatest golfers in the world. The United States Open is a test, an examination of golf skill, and what an opening test this would be.

Even with a perfect drive, Brad was still left with nearly two hundred yards for his second shot. It was playing even longer because of the uphill angle from the fairway to the green. He determined through careful calculation that his shot should play two hundred yards just to the front edge of the green, and armed with that knowledge, he pulled out a four iron. "Solid four iron should be right," he said, and Mark nodded and backed away. Another flawless swing, and Brad walked toward the green watching his ball in flight. It landed in the fringe and gently rolled past the hole, stopping fifteen feet away. Brad smiled, handed his club back to Mark, and with a confident stride continued toward the green. As good as his shot was—and it was a great shot, as no one would hit it closer in the opening round—it still left Brad a very fast downhill putt that broke from his right to his left at least five feet as he looked at the hole. *Welcome to the US Open,* he thought. He circled the hole from all angles as he waited for his turn to putt. Crocker and Lewis were now finished, and Brad was ready. His stroke barely started the ball moving. It crept its way on the line Brad had chosen. It moved so softly you could see the dimples on the ball and read its logo. An eternity seemed to pass as it trickled into the center of the hole. With a deep sigh of relief, he bent down and retrieved the ball, excited and grateful for his good fortune on his first hole.

Brad followed his birdie on the first hole with another one on the second. He then birdied the third and the fourth holes and headed to the fifth tee. He was completely focused and unaware of the growing crowd watching him. Gone were any of the nerves he displayed when he began. He grabbed a bottle of water and took a long sip and handed it to Mark, who was pale and staring at all the people lining up and down both sides of the fairway.

"I'm scared to death!" Mark whispered to Brad.

"Scared of what? I'm the one playing."

"Scared of screwing you up."

"Then shut up and keep up. Remember? You're doing just fine."

"Sorry."

"No worries. Just let me play."

"Just stay out of his way," Brad heard Mark quietly remind himself.

Brad split the middle of the fairway with his three wood. As he waited for Tom and Vince to play, he stood beside Mark. He put his hand on Mark's shoulder and felt him take a deep breath. Brad walked tall and with a purpose. His approach landed fifteen feet from the hole. He tapped in a short par putt after a lackluster first attempt. His drive on sixth just missed the fairway but avoided the thick rough just a few more feet to his right. The ball nestled down in the grass just enough to cause Brad to second-guess himself. The indecision showed in his swing, and the result was going to be a bogey. Brad was livid at himself. "Total lack of commitment. Damn you!" he scolded himself. He promised himself not to let it happen again. Pars on seven and eight, and he and Mark had made it to number nine at three under par. The leaderboard by the eighteenth green read, *Ford minus three.* He had no idea he was leading the tournament.

Chapter 4

It was just after eight Thursday morning when Walker White arrived at the San Francisco Athletic Club. With him were sons Tyler and Cameron. At forty-nine years of age, Walker stood out in a crowd. Tall and still very athletic looking, his hair was thick and white, and stylish horn-rimmed glasses covered his dark brown eyes. The boys both looked like their father—tall and strong and handsome—and all had engaging smiles and soft southern accents that made anyone talking to them feel comfortable. Walker was a successful attorney at a small law firm in Wilson, North Carolina, a town of roughly fifty thousand people and thirty-five or forty minutes east of Raleigh, the state capital. He had graduated from the University of North Carolina at Chapel Hill and then completed law school, graduating with honors. He was now the senior partner at the firm his father started. Tyler and Cameron had followed their father to Chapel Hill, where both played golf and helped lift the golf program to successes not seen since the Inman brothers roamed "Finley Flats." Walker had played there as well and was still considered a top amateur player. Tyler and Cameron kept his competitive fire going. He enjoyed his boys' successes, but he still relished the times when he beat them. Those times were rapidly dwindling.

San Francisco was one of Walker White's favorite cities, and he brought his entire family. His wife, Lynn, and daughter, Lauren, were busy taking in the sights and shopping for Lauren's upcoming wedding. Walker refused to dwell on that subject. He did not mind the shopping and the spending of money; he just had no desire to ruin his week and vacation thinking about his future son-in-law. He was determined to enjoy the time with his family, San Francisco, and the greatest players in the world playing the game that he loved.

Walker and the boys headed to the information center to get tee sheets and then headed for the merchandise tents and refreshment area. It was to be a long and exciting day that all of them had been looking forward to.

Walker and Tyler were heading to the eighteenth green when Cameron informed them he wanted to watch golf's greatest player warm up. "All right. We're leaving here around four, so let's meet back at the information center around three thirty. Agreed?"

"Agreed," Cameron said.

"Let's go check the leaderboard," Walker said to Tyler.

When they saw the leaderboard, Walker mentioned the traditional no-name was leading early in the first round. Tyler checked his tee sheet, trying to believe what his eyes were reading. "Damn, how about that!" He looked up at his dad.

"What is it?" Walker was anxious to know what had his son so excited.

"I know him. The Ford guy that's leading, I know him."

"How in the world do you know him?"

"My freshman year during ACC championship. Second round, I was paired with him. I played over my head the first round and got paired with Brad Ford. He was the one seed at Wake. I think he was a junior. He never missed a shot, Dad. Not one. It was the easiest sixty-five I've ever seen."

"What happened to him?"

"Long story and not really sure how much is true. Nothing awful, but he's close to making the turn. I'll give you the details when we find a place to watch from. I wanna see him come up nine."

They found a small knoll to watch from. The crowd was in full force to watch the no-name leading the Open come to the ninth green. The big names—the legitimate contenders—were teeing off soon, so there was time to watch. Tyler stared at the crowd as it swelled around them. "How many people do you think are watching this?"

"Five or ten thousand. It's a sea of people out there waiting for him to fall back to earth. They always do. People just love the carnage,"

Walker said, remembering disasters in previous majors. "Do you see him?"

"Yes, sir. Yellow shirt. Looks like he's laying up." Tyler was enthralled, watching closely every movement of his former foe. He began going through Brad's story. Brad and Susan became engaged the Christmas of their junior year. Their plan was to wait until the June following graduation, but when Susan became pregnant, that plan was abandoned. Brad turned professional. Susan finished her degree and tended to Will. Brad struggled with his game. He finished his degree with the help of Susan and some understanding professors.

Chapter 5

They met in the pro shop and had a quick word with their pro and his secretary, a large-breasted, young Italian girl by the name of Gracie, whom they were certain was more than just a secretary. Then they quietly retreated to the men's locker room. The gold plaque beside the door reminded everyone who passed that door that beyond it lay a sanctuary. It was sanctuary for men, adult men. Once past the door, the corridor turned right and then sharply back to the left. The walls on each side were adorned with framed, original sketches. Nine hung on the left wall and nine on the right. Donald Ross, the famed golf course architect of Pinehurst number two, was also the designer of Old State. These were his sketches, his drawings of each hole at Old State in perfect detail, showing how he expected each hole to look. They were placed on the walls to remind those who passed them that this was no ordinary club.

The narrow hallway led to the men's lockers and showers. Large, solid mahogany lockers provided enough storage for everything imaginable. Nameplates and numbers told which locker belonged to which member. The bottom of each locker had two pullout drawers for shoes. The showers looked like works of art. The mosaic tile was breathtaking. The individual showers were oversized, allowing for each to have a tile seat strategically placed so that the large sunflower-shaped showerheads could soak and soothe any type of strain.

Past the lockers and showers was the men's lounge. Multiple televisions were on the side walls, allowing one to check the stock market, up-to-the-minute world news, and any sporting event. The far wall was glass from ceiling to floor, allowing the gentlemen to stare out at their treasure. The view started at the eighteenth green and spread across the golf course. Someone many years earlier had the foresight to make sure the clubhouse was built on the highest part of the property. Opposite the window was an elegant bar supplied with virtually every concoction desired by the members. If they developed an appetite while relaxing, "Tiny" and the staff would make the proper arrangements.

The fathers were alone. It was early Thursday morning, and they would not have been there if the Open wasn't on. Their plan called for brunch, a little gin, and the hope that Brad was—if nothing else—at least surviving in his first major. Their nerves were a bit more alive as they waited for news of how Brad was doing, and they decided a good drink would be appropriate. Bill and Tom ordered Bloody Marys, and John settled for a vodka grapefruit. Two decks of new cards were opened when the drinks arrived. A silent toast was made, and ESPN was back from commercial. The announcers went through their usual opening remarks as cameras from all over the golf course flashed. They did a five-minute history of the past Opens held by the famed San Francisco Athletic Club, and then finally the leaderboard flashed on the screen. The moaning about the delay in showing the leaderboard stopped. They stared at the screen in silence and then at each other. They all checked the screen again.

"Well, I'll be damned," Bill muttered in disbelief. "How about our boy?"

Tom made some kind of grunting sound. He never said much unless he was ripe from drinking all day. This of course angered his dear wife, Nancy Jo, to no end.

John quickly regained himself and reminded Bill and Tom, "It's early, guys. He's only played seven holes."

Because of Brad's incredible start and his two-shot lead, ESPN's highlights started with his birdie rampage over the opening holes and his lone bogey. They told the viewers the leader was on the eighth green with a three-foot putt for par. The men had quickly finished the first round of drinks watching Brad. It was almost more than they could comprehend. Tiny was already at the table with the next while they watched Brad take his stance for his putt. His stroke was perfect yet again, and the ball found its home at the bottom of the cup.

"Nine's a par five, right? Unbelievable," Bill muttered.

In the ninth fairway, Brad and Mark reached his ball. After laying up, Brad had left himself exactly eighty-seven yards. The pin was located in the back left portion of the green. Normally it would be a routine lob wedge but not today. Brad was certain a lob wedge would impart too much spin on the ball. There was a ridge just short of the hole. He could see the ball spinning and racing away from the pin and toward the front of the green. The putt would be impossible and another bogey.

"Be committed," he told himself as he pulled his sand wedge out. "Soft hands, open the face a touch, ball back. You've hit this shot a thousand times. See the shot," he told himself. He stood behind the ball, carefully placing his hands on the club. Watching the pin, he rehearsed the swing he needed to make. On a parallel line left of the ball, he took his stance. Brad held his finish and stared at the ball.

The crowd noise grew as the ball made its way to the flag.

"Be right!" Mark shouted.

"It's perfect," Brad replied calmly. And it was. The ball landed into the slope and hopped forward toward the hole. It was trying to spin and grab to the firm grass covering the green. For a second it appeared to stop, but then it started moving again. Brad heard the crowd screaming for it to go in. Finally it stopped, and the crowd groaned but then roared in approval. Six inches away. It was a formality. Walking with Mark by his side, Brad approached the green. Mark handed him his putter, and Brad finally tugged the bill of his cap to acknowledge the crowd. He wanted to finish but knew the crowd would start rushing around and moving, so he waited. He stared into the crowd searching for Susan and Will, but there were just so many faces. Maybe she was waiting on the next tee.

Mark nudged him. "It's your turn."

"Thanks."

Brad carefully remarked his ball and tapped it in. His fifth birdie on the front nine and a total of thirty-one. He glanced at the leaderboard for the first time. He had a two-shot lead as the crowd gawked and cheered for the unknown leader of the United States Open.

Brad scanned the crowd again. "Where the hell are they?" he said.

"Who?" Mark asked.

"Susan and Will."

"You've got God knows how many thousands of people watching you, and you really think you're going to see them?" Mark reminded Brad. "They're here somewhere, but you might want to focus on what you're doing right now."

"Okay, time to focus," Brad said as he slid his glove back on.

Tiny returned with yet another round of drinks. The card game had been abandoned for the time being. Who could concentrate on anything other than Brad? The sports section of the *Journal* listed all the tee times and pairings. Bill quickly glanced up from the paper and announced, "Well, I doubt our boy is gonna get much more air time. He's about to tee off."

"That's just great. They'll show every damn shot he hits. It never matters how he plays. When he hits it all over the place, they show every swing, every putt. Makes me sick," Tom added.

"Well, you—" John began.

"Don't start, John. I know. We all know. Everybody wants to see him, but I'll be damned if I gotta like it!" Tom was sick of the reasons. He wanted to watch the leader play, whoever it was, and right now it was their boy, their son, and nothing else mattered. No one had dominated golf like him since the glory days of Palmer and Nicklaus. They set the precedent for television coverage, and now half of those watching were simply watching to see the great one play.

The first and tenth tees were both buzzing with activity. The majority of the first-day crowd was now on the grounds of the San Francisco Athletic Club. The congestion was intense, and the crowd spread across the club like an avalanche. People jockeyed for position wherever they were. The ample spaces that lay around the massive clubhouse under normal conditions were gone. Hosting the United States Open took every last inch of it. The information center seemed to be under siege. The necessities of hosting a major championship were grabbing up chunks of ground. The corporate tents, concession stands, and merchandise tents took up a great deal of space. The media center was enormous. The USGA had requests for all over the world.

Writers and reporters needed instant access to send articles back to their home offices, and this was also the site for post-round interviews with the leaders and top players. Broadcasting trailers and satellite dishes littered the parking lot, and electrical cables ran everywhere. The San Francisco Athletic Club looked like a circus and would continue to look like one until the Open was over.

Adding to the frenzied atmosphere was timing. The greatest player in the world was starting his first round on number one, and the leader was making the turn and on his way to the tenth hole. Bradley Ford was leading the Open, and he was a nobody from somewhere in North Carolina. Besides Mark and Tyler White, not a soul had ever heard of Brad, but when you shoot a thirty-one and have a two-shot lead, curiosity grows.

The crowd wanted to see. Who was he? What did he look like? Could he keep it going? Would he realize what was going on, where he was, and collapse from the magnitude of the situation? Golf, unlike team sports, is a lonely and sometimes painful adventure. The solitude of it and the time between shots allow players' minds to wander. Negative thoughts can undo any player. The crowd knew carnage could be just a hole or two away. Greg Norman and Ed Snead collapsed at the Masters. The king of golf himself, Arnold Palmer, had blown a seven-shot lead over the final nine holes at this very place, in this very tournament, to Billy Casper. If it could happen to Arnie, it could happen to anyone. Golf's history was filled with these stories, and whatever the outcome of Bradley Ford's round, historic or disastrous, the majority wanted to bear witness.

Brad tried to regain the focus he displayed on the first nine holes, but it was clearly a struggle. Every free second, his eyes searched the crowd, never looking at any one person very long. Mark caught him again and again. His tee shot managed to find the fairway thanks to a fortunate bounce. He handed his driver back to Mark and looked again. After Tom and Vince hit their shots, they walked toward his ball, and Mark confronted Brad.

"You gotta stay focused." Mark's voice was shaky.

"I am."

"The hell you are! You didn't even look at me when you answered. You keep staring into the crowd. Man, I'm begging you."

"All right, all right. Enough already. I know what I'm doing."

Brad attempted to collect his thoughts, and as much as he hated to admit it, Mark was right. But Brad was a natural worrier and had been all his life. Brad had an eight iron left to the green and managed somehow to hit it ten feet from the hole. The putt was makeable. He knew it, Mark knew it, and the crowd knew it. Five under after ten holes was impossible to fathom.

Brad again went through his routine and then gently placed the putter behind the ball. The stroke was a quick stabbing motion. The ball never had a chance, sliding by the hole, and Brad walked up and tapped it in. Gone was the flawless, silky stroke he displayed earlier. It was a pattern that would continue. The par at ten was followed by near-miss birdies at eleven, twelve, and thirteen. Every miss was followed by the groans of a crowd growing restless for something to happen. With every miss, the moans grew louder and louder. Brad needed something to happen, and fourteen was a hole that had to be birdied.

"Watching this is too damn much for me to stand. What the hell is wrong with him?" Bill snarled, "Tiny, I need another drink!"

"He's holding together just fine. Nearly every round has a lull in it, much less a round in the Open. He just needs one to fall, and he'll be back in business." The calmness John showed came from experience but wasn't comforting to Bill and Tom. Watching Brad was leaving Tom at a loss, though it was not as apparent as it was with Bill.

They sat there and suffered through every minute and every shot. They were helpless, and for men who reveled in power and control, being helpless was simply unacceptable.

The USGA decided to dangle a carrot at the players on fourteen. Playing as long as they could make it, fourteen was only 344 yards. When setting up the course, the USGA ordered the rough around the green to be a minimum of six inches. For the first round, the tees were placed forward, allowing players the opportunity, with a perfect drive, an eagle putt. Wayward drives would be punished severely, though. From no more than twenty or thirty feet, the rough was so thick and sticky even the greatest players in the world would have trouble getting their ball on the green and no chance of getting it to stay if they did.

Brad did not have the length to carry his tee shot onto the surface of the green, but during his practice rounds, he was convinced there were three options. The first was trying to make the green, and the second was to lay up off the tee and try to hit a short iron close. The third option would be to purposely drive the ball into the front bunker and play from there. Brad needed to jumpstart his last nine holes, and a birdie would do it. His lead was still two shots, and if he didn't pull it off, his lead would be gone. Standing with Mark at his side, Brad pulled out his pin sheet and yardage book and studied them closely. He paced back and forth on the tee, waiting for the group ahead of them to clear. Brad never looked up at them. His focus was back and just in time.

"What are you thinking?" Mark asked.

Showing Mark the yardage book and pin sheet, he said, "Well, we know I can't drive the green, and even if I could, it would be a dumb play."

"Yeah, you should have seen—"

"I don't care what those guys in front of me did. The pin is front right, five yards from the front, and six yards from the edge. Other than a couple of guys, trying to fly on the green isn't the play. The ball will bounce long, and the rough is brutal. Like I said, I don't care what those guys in front of me did, but I know what they did. Two made fives, and the other a six. Right?"

Mark nodded, the expression on his face not hiding his shock at Brad's accuracy. "So what are you gonna do?"

"The front bunker, just like in the practice rounds. If the pin was on the back of the green, I would just lay up, but since it's on the front, it's a no brainer. Splash it out and let it roll. But if—"

"But nothing," Mark interrupted. Brad was ready. "It's golden, Sparky."

Brad smiled at Mark, now confident that he would indeed play for the front bunker. He placed his tee in the ground and again rested the ball on top of it. The crowd waited to see whether the leader would lay up or not.

Bill and Tom sat staring at the television. They saw Brad reach for his driver, and Bill could not help himself. "Don't do it! Don't hit that damn driver, son! You can't get there!" Tom shook his head in disgust.

"He's not going for it," John said, assessing Brad's club choice.

"How the hell would you know?"

"He knows he can't get there. We talked about his practice rounds last night. He's gonna play for the front bunker, and it's a great play where the pin is."

"This is a disaster waiting to happen." Tom took a long, hard sip of yet another drink.

Bill and Tom watched Brad tee the ball up. They shook their heads at the screen and then sat there and watched as he lined up and waggled and settled into his stance. The ball left perfectly again, and the analyst described its flight; if Brad's objective was to hit his drive in the front bunker, it was almost certain to happen. The ball landed and skidded forward. Just short of the bunker, the fairway rose to meet the front edge of the bunker. The ball darted off this rise, trying to clear the bunker, but hopped into the thick grass on the front lip. It nestled out of sight into the grass, and the crowd collectively gasped in horror. As their gasp came to an end, the ball somehow wiggled free and dropped into the bright, grainy, white sand, perching itself perfectly on the upslope just thirty-five or so feet away from the hole. The crowd erupted when they saw Brad's good fortune. They finished their drinks again, and John said the three needed some ice water.

Brad wasted no time over his bunker shot, lifting it softly from the sand to a mere two feet from the hole. The putt was uphill, straight, and just a formality. Tom and Vince completed the hole, and quickly and with no reservation, Brad banged the ball squarely in the cup to go five under and increase his lead to three. Just four holes left, and the word spread quickly.

The next three holes were all easy pars, and Brad reached the final hole of his opening round. He felt the confidence surging inside him. It was a feeling he had not known in years, and he was letting it sink in. The eighteenth was a par five even Brad could get to. His mind was set, and he would go for it. There was no water, and even if he missed the green and was trapped in the rough, he could make a bogey and still have the lead, but Brad was certain there was no chance of that happening. The tee shot was uphill and moved to the player's right, curving and working its way to the clubhouse and to the amphitheater that the metal bleachers and seating had created around the massive green. The green measured over seven thousand square feet, and the edges were littered with sand traps of all shapes, sizes, and depths. The rough around them was wild and thick and very much like the fourteenth hole.

Brad's tee shot bounded its way up the left half of the fairway. His ball striking had been nearly flawless. Just 241 yards left, but it would play fifteen or so yards further he figured. Brad pulled his three wood and readied himself for the second shot. The on-course reporter and cameraman were hovering close to Brad, too close for Brad's comfort level.

"Hey, guys, if you could stand back a bit, I'd really appreciate it. I'm having enough trouble breathing on my own," Brad said with a smile. They nodded and backed away.

Mark took the hint and backed away as well.

Brad heard a noise of some kind and backed away himself to regroup and think. He closed his eyes and pictured the flight the ball should take and then slowly opened them. He focused on an imaginary tunnel the ball needed to travel through. He took a deep breath and finally asked the marshal to help quiet things down. The crowd was enormous and maneuvering for a good place to see what Brad had left.

The ball hissed as Brad's club made contact, and the crowd's heads turned toward the green.

"Come on, baby. Be as good as you look," Brad pleaded. "Come on, get there!"

Mark leaned against the bag, trying desperately to see.

The ball landed and rolled with the contour of the green bending left and slowly heading for the hole, narrowly missing it, and the crowd erupted again. It finally stopped six feet from the hole.

"Damn it! I'm so glad this is almost over with." His face was red, and his emotions were starting to show. He took his hat off and covered his face and turned away from Mark. Tom and Vince had hit their third shots onto the green and waited for Brad.

"Lead us up there. The fans are waiting for you." Vince swung his arm as if opening the door for Brad. Golf is filled with traditions, and this was one of them. The leader of the tournament leads his group to the final green. Mark handed Brad his putter, and Brad pulled his cap off again. He placed his arm around Mark, and his eyes began to get teary. Mark helped him steady himself, and they started toward the green.

"What's wrong?"

"My dad ... I wish Dad could have seen this."

"He did. Every shot. And you're not done yet, so try to hold it together."

"I know. I'm trying."

"You're fine. Don't you need to wave to these people or something? Smile and take some deep breaths. I can't have you choking up on me now." He laughed and smiled and pushed Brad ahead of him.

"Thanks, Mark."

"I didn't do a damn thing, bud. This was all you. Now make that putt so I can call it a day."

Brad acknowledged the crowd. His face was still flush from emotion and the embarrassment all the attention was making him feel.

The Whites had walked every step with Brad on the back nine. They had lived and died with each shot. Tyler felt a certain sense of pride. While none of the people crammed around the green knew who Brad Ford was, he did. He had played golf with the leader of the United States Open. He had walked and talked with him. He felt connected to him and could not help but ponder whether Brad remembered him as he smiled proudly and cheered loudly.

"He's played a helluva round," Walker said.

"I wonder how he's feeling. He's gotta be out of his mind. I mean, a chance to shoot sixty-three in the Open is incredible," Tyler answered quietly.

The group finally reached the green. Tom and Vince realized the magnitude of the moment and treated Brad with immense respect and curiosity normally reserved for a final round. This could be a historic moment. He had only six feet left, and they wanted out of the way.

"You're away" is a polite way for one player to tell another player it is his or her turn. They say this because golf etiquette requires the player farthest from the hole to play first. There are times when this ritual is suspended, and for Tom Crocker and Vince Lewis, this was one of those times. It was unusual for it to happen in the first round, but Brad's first round was not the usual round. They finished their rounds to get out of Brad's way. Six feet away from a round of sixty-three, if he could manage to make this putt, Brad would tie the lowest round ever shot in United States Open history. He would tie San Francisco's own Johnny Miller nearly twenty-five years after his final-round sixty-three won him a national Open.

Cameras were positioned at all angles surrounding the green, and while one showed Tom and Vince completing their rounds, the others stayed on Brad. They showed on a split screen his every emotion, look, and nervous tick. Everyone waited anxiously for Brad to play what all hoped would be his final shot.

Brad diligently tried to slow himself down. "Slow your walking. Slow your breathing. Stay calm," he quietly told himself. He went through his normal routine and did so without a sign of discomfort. He gripped his putter as softly as he could and let his arms hang free and loose from his shoulders. For the last time, he hoped, he placed his putter behind the ball. The silence was chilling, and even with all the people watching, you could hear the click his club made against the ball. Tumbling end over end, the ball rolled. Brad seemed frozen in time. He refused to look and chose to listen. The crowd would tell him what he needed to know. His concentration was so deep; he did not realize the ball had stopped. Mark dropped the flag and nearly knocked Brad over grabbing him. The crowd screamed and jumped up and down. Brad finally turned and looked. He saw only the hole.

"Oh my God, it went in."

"You're damn right it did. Son of a bitch, Brad!"

Brad fell to his knees. He could feel the ground rumble beneath him, and his emotions took over. Tom and Vince made their way to him while Mark helped Brad to his feet.

"Thanks, guys. I appreciate all of the courtesy," he said, shaking their hands and wiping his eyes.

"Man, don't sweat it. That was an awesome thing to watch."

"Yeah, I just need a beer. Are you always this good?" Vince asked with a sly smile.

The crowd waited for Brad to acknowledge them one last time. The scene was like a concert, and the fans waited for their encore. With his emotions under control, he reluctantly turned to the crowd and, like he had seen his heroes do, waved his right hand and mouthed a silent thank you to them while walking off the green.

A roped-off walkway led the players from the green to the scoring tent. The group would check and recheck their scorecards and totals. After all the cards were signed and attested, they turned them in for inspection and posting by the USGA. A man near the end of the walkway stood out from the crowd that was pawing for Brad's attention, waving programs and hats in front of him to sign.

Brad said, "I know you, don't I? Tyler, right?"

"I can't believe you remember me."

He grabbed a hat from a small child and signed it, and another kid asked so politely he could not refuse. He signed the oversized hat and then placed it back on his head. The child smiled broadly, and Brad felt good about that.

"Are you gonna be here for a bit?"

"Yeah."

"Well, hang tight. Let me finish this, and I'll be right back."

"Great round."

"Thanks." Brad turned to Mark. "Please find my wife and son and some aspirin. My head is killing me."

"You got it."

Chapter 6

Brad entered the scoring tent and shook hands with the officials inside. Tom, Vince, and Brad checked their cards and asked the officials to review their cards and totals. When all were in agreement, the signatures took place. Tom and Vince again conveyed praise and were told they needed to proceed to the media center.

"Brad, if you could stay here while they go, we would appreciate it," the official said while looking at Tom and Vince as they exited.

"Is something wrong? Please tell me there's nothing wrong with my card."

"No, son, nothing's wrong with your card."

"Then why can't I leave?" Brad asked.

The official stood up and left and quickly returned with Wallace Fay, the president of the USGA and a detective with the San Francisco Police Department by the name of Ward Messeke. Mark had also returned. He handed Brad a Diet Coke and some aspirin.

"Did you find them?"

Mark shook his head slowly.

"Where are they?"

"Brad, I don't know."

Wallace introduced himself to Brad and Mark but didn't introduce Detective Messeke.

"Brad, I need you to come with us."

"Who the hell is he?" Brad asked.

"I'll tell you everything you want to know, but right now you need to come with us," Fay answered.

"What's going on? Would someone tell me what the hell's going on?" Brad responded, his voice gaining in pitch and concern.

"Brad, just go with them." Mark grabbed Brad by the arm and made his friend follow Mr. Fay.

Fay and the mystery man led Brad and Mark to a courtesy cart, and they sped away to the trailer that served as the USGA headquarters.

The news spread like a tidal wave across the course, and ESPN brought it to the rest of the world. The announcers were clearly shaken, having to relay the somber events that had taken place earlier in the day while Brad Ford had been racing to a first-round lead and taking his place in golf history. Susan Ford and Will Ford, the wife and four-year-old son of Brad Ford, were dead. Details of deaths had not been released, but the deaths had been confirmed by the San Francisco Police Department.

The news instantly sobered Bill, Tom, and John. They sat in total disbelief. Seconds later, their pro raced into the bar to find the three staring blankly at the table where they sat. They needed to find Brad, Mark, and Susan's parents. They called their wives first, and all began shrieking and sobbing, making them all more emotional than they already were after watching Brad on television. Susan and Will were family. Their voices and bodies trembled as they tried to grasp what and why and how this could have happened. John called Thurston Cox, his former right-hand man and his hand-chosen successor as CEO, and informed him what had happened. He said that he needed the company jet readied and on standby. John was still on the board of directors, and Thurston said he would make the arrangements.

"Call my house and tell Mary Nell when it's ready. We have to grab a few things. She's packing now."

"Consider it done and call me if there's anything else I can do," Thurston answered.

Bill and his wife, Martha, had lifelong friends in the Bay area, and Bill asked her to find them and explain the situation and that they were needed. Bill needed Martha's help, and Martha needed to be busy. After the initial shock and outburst, Mary Nell and Martha went to work. Details needed their immediate attention. Bags needed packing, calls needed to be made. They were truly at their best when there was a crisis, and that dark hour was at hand.

They entered the room Wallace Fay used as his office. It was certainly nothing like his lavish office back east. No, this office was not adorned with historic photos, golf trinkets, and antique furniture. The air was stale in spite of the best efforts of the window unit, which provided a constant humming. The carpet was worn and stained. He sat in a rented cloth office chair behind a cheap used desk. The clapboard walls bore nothing but a cork message board that was used for reminders and pressing matters than needed attention. A computer and phone sat on the desk, and a fax machine sat idly behind him on a smaller table. Mark was asked to wait outside, and Brad vetoed that immediately.

"That's not gonna happen. Mark is part of my family and will be in this room with me regardless of the consequences."

Mark followed Brad, and they were instructed by Fay to sit in the black vinyl chairs positioned in front of the desk facing him. The unintroduced stranger stood silent next to Fay. He looked at Messeke and then turned to Brad.

"Brad, this is Detective Ward Messeke." Fay stood long enough to pull another chair to the edge of his desk, positioning the chair so it faced Brad and Mark. "Detective Messeke, if you would join us please." With a simple gesture, Messeke sat down.

Messeke looked at Fay, who nodded and then with an empty, disbelieving stare looked at his desk. Messeke glanced at the notepad he had retrieved from the inside of his suit coat.

"Brad, this morning the 911 operators were contacted at 8:57 a.m. about a shooting incident. Police in the area responded to the call. There's no easy way to tell you, but they're gone. Your wife and son are gone."

Brad's eyes widened with shock. It had to be a mistake, he thought. He looked at Wallace Fay and then to Ward Messeke and realized that no one would make that kind of mistake. He lowered his head as his mind filled with a realization he wasn't ready to accept. Some tears dripped from his nose, and some passed his nose and made it to his creased, tightly closed lips. He wrapped his arms across his chest as a pain he had never felt before ripped through and seized his body. He moaned and screamed, and Mark grabbed him. Wallace Fay broke down watching him. Wallace stood and touched Detective Messeke's arm. Messeke stood as well and followed Fay.

Brad wept like a small child, gasping for air between sobs.

"Brad, I'm going outside to speak with those guys. I'll be right back," Mark said.

"Just go ... just leave me alone. All of you."

Mark left and found Fay and Messeke alone just outside the office. Mark was at a loss, but he wanted to know what had happened. Fay explained that he wanted Messeke to handle the media and would escort him there.

"I'll be very brief and then return. Detective Messeke will also return, and if Brad is up to talking, then we'll be here for him. While I'm gone, please think of everyone that needs to be notified, and we'll work on that when I get back," Wallace Fay said.

The media center was a temporary structure set up at all major golfing events. For the United States Open, it appeared on the landscape like a warehouse. Walls were erected, and a few rooms were formed. It was quite an eyesore. For the 1998 Open, over three hundred media credentials were granted to reporters in over seventy countries. One large room had rows and rows of folding tables butting up against one another. The floor was nothing more than thick, industrial plywood stacked on cinder blocks. Electrical wires and plugs were running under the tables. The seating was assigned. Laptops covered the tables, and in the front corners of the room, televisions were placed so writers and reporters could sit lazily and offer their very learned and experienced opinions without having to break a sweat. A small room near the front served as a cafeteria of sorts. One of the walls erected ran lengthwise and divided this room with another of equal size where the press conferences and most post-round interviews took place. There was a podium at the front of the room with some more desks. On top of the desks, for the players' benefit, was a layout of the course to refresh their haggard memories of the day's grueling events. Several microphones were positioned, and the backdrop was a sateen curtain bearing the USGA logo printed all over it on a back wall. Behind this wall was where the players and anyone who would have reason to be interviewed entered and waited their turn. It was a green room of sorts for the players.

Fay led Messeke through the maze. They entered the small backroom were Fay grabbed a bottle of water from a freshly iced-down cooler. His mouth was dry, and he hoped the water would help him keep his voice from cracking. Messeke declined the offer for water, something he would later regret.

"Ward, I wouldn't be surprised if every media member here is on the other side of that wall. I'll introduce you, and then I'm going back to my office. I would appreciate you being as brief as possible, but I have to warn you. They'll keep asking and asking, so when you're done, leave. I'll be waiting in my office."

Messeke nodded, and with that, he and Fay walked around the corner of the wall, and the chatter among reporters abruptly stopped, replaced by flashes erupting from every direction. With so many people in such a small place and the lights facing them, the room felt like it was a hundred degrees. They took seats next to each other. Fay's eyes were puffy, swollen, and bloodshot. Adorned in his navy USGA blazer, he looked at the tabletop. His fingers smoothed the collar of his white pinpoint oxford, and then he fidgeted with his ever-present bow tie. He pushed his glasses to their correct resting place and ran his fingers through his graying brown hair. He finally looked up when the flashes stopped, but they immediately started again. He gave Messeke one last look and then looked at the reporters.

"By now, I'm told, all of you know of the tragedy that has befallen the Ford family. We feel—and when I say we, I mean the USGA as a whole—that it's imperative and in everyone's best interest that I make myself available to Brad. Having never dealt with such a horrific occurrence, protocol isn't something we can rely on. Whether right or wrong, Brad is our number-one priority, and we'll be of any assistance that he needs. We feel strongly that this tournament will play out the way it always does, but right now we can't think of anything more important than Brad, his wife, Susan, and their son, Will. With me is Detective Ward Messeke for those of you with questions." As Fay stood, there were flashes again from every possible angle. He left without fielding a question. He wiped the perspiration from his forward and left Messeke to deal with the mass of humanity.

Messeke waited for Fay to leave. This was not his first press conference, but it was certainly his largest one. He was immediately bombarded with questions and quickly raised his hands.

"Do you have any idea how difficult it is to try to listen to fifty people ask fifty questions at the same time? I'll take one question and then another, or I'll leave."

Many questions he avoided for a variety of reasons. Some questions were so inane he would simply respond "next question" or tell the reporters he could not answer that yet. He finally ended the chaos by telling them that he could confirm two deaths had taken place earlier in the morning and that the decedents had been identified as Susan and Will Ford.

"I feel confident that there'll be a press release, and we'll make that release available to you. Thank you for your time and patience." Messeke was gone, leaving the media with what they felt was very little information—not that he gave a damn.

Fay called the onsite medical center while he and Mark waited for Messeke to return. He spoke with Dr. Hugh Schweiger and requested his presence at his office. He would explain further once he arrived.

Messeke and Schweiger arrived together. Schweiger had the silver hair of someone who had grayed years earlier. His usually pleasant smile and manner did not show. He carried a black bag and stethoscope around the neck of his dress shirt. Mark slipped back inside Fay's office to be with Brad, who was sitting up staring blankly. He was emotionless. He was no longer crying and sat with his arms hanging limp by his sides, his hands resting on his thighs. Mark recalled the night Brad found out about his father's death. He looked eerily similar now.

"What am I supposed to do without them, Mark?" His voice was dry and raspy. "I can't believe they're gone."

"Brad, there's a doctor outside, and he wants to speak with you."

"Tell him to go away," Brad said calmly and softly.

"I won't do that. I think you should see him."

Mark emerged from Fay's office. He was introduced and repeated his most recent exchange with Brad. "I'm not sure now is a good time for this. He said he wants to be left alone. I have no idea what to do." Mark rubbed his temples; his head was throbbing because of the stress.

Fay suggested that Mark and Dr. Schweiger go in together, and Schweiger agreed that this would be as an acceptable way of approaching Brad as anything else they could come up with. Brad was not going to be very responsive to another stranger, but with Mark there, he could excuse himself if and when the ice was broken with the doctor.

Dr. Schweiger followed Mark in to the office, and they pulled another chair up closer to Brad. The doctor quietly observed for a few moments.

"Brad, I'm Dr. Schweiger."

Brad didn't budge. Mark tapped Brad on his leg. "I know you don't wanna do this, but we're not leaving until you talk with him."

Brad nodded but barely.

"No one can imagine what you're going through. No one should have to go through this, Brad. I just want you to talk to me. You can yell, scream, say anything—"

"I've got nothing to say. What can I say? My world died today."

With Brad at least responding to the doctor, Mark leaned down to Brad and whispered that he was leaving him with the doctor and would be waiting in the other room. He walked quietly to the door and left. Mark needed to let go of his own emotions but knew it would be a long time before that opportunity presented itself.

Mark sat down with Wallace and the detective. His head was killing him. He was drained mentally and physically. He was hurting for his friend and hurting because of the tragedy of Susan and Will's deaths. He explained that Brad's parents had both passed away and that he had no other true family. He gave the details of Brad's relationship with Bill, Tom, and John. Wallace decided that Mark should call them first.

The private hangar sat to the far left of the main terminal at Smith Reynolds Airport. Chris Baker, one of two pilots employed by the R&M Tobacco Company, greeted the trio. He, and only he, flew John Hicks. He walked briskly to the car and greeted John with a crisp but genuine handshake. He acknowledged Bill and Tom and then moved to the rear of John's black Suburban to handle the suitcases and bags Mary Nell, Martha, and Nancy Jo had hastily organized.

The men boarded the jet while Chris managed to load their belongings into the cargo bay in two swift and efficient trips. He closed the bay door and handed an attendant John's keys so he could moved his vehicle to a secured parking area on the front side of the hangar. Chris climbed the steps and joined his passengers while another attendant walked onto the tarmac to help Chris shut and secure the door. A quick glance, followed by a hand gesture from his pilot let John know that tower and takeoff information would be forthcoming.

Baker started his taxi and informed Hicks that once they reached the runway they would be third in line for takeoff; they should be in the air within fifteen minutes. The flight would take six hours or so, depending on winds and other factors.

As Chris predicted, the flight left within the time he had anticipated, and as soon as they reached their cruising altitude, he signaled with two soft chimes that they were free to do as they pleased. John stood and walked to the bar not to have another drink but to brew coffee. French roast was his personal favorite, and he preferred it strong. It had been a long day and would get longer. Bill and Tom gazed out the windows, lost in thought and hoping for some divine guidance.

Chapter 7

All three resided in the house in which they were raised. The McKnight family home was a corner lot formed by Cornwallis Drive and Lafayette Place. The Rhodes lived three houses down on Cornwallis, and the Hicks lived three houses down on Lafayette, where their backyards met to make a rather large play area for the three boys while they were growing up. As kids, Bill would walk down the street and meet Tom and John and either play basketball or football with other children or head to Old State. During the summer, it was golf and the swimming pool, and as they grew into teenagers, the young ladies in bathing suits were too much to resist.

Bill and Tom were accepted to Wake Forest the first year it held classes in Winston-Salem after moving from the small town where its name originated. John joined them two years later.

The McKnights' home was a one-and-half-story brick Cape Cod style house built in 1928, across the street from the seventh hole of Old State. The brick was painted an oyster white, and the windows were accented with black shutters. Bill never liked the color of the brick and thought the paint made the house look clean and more modest. It was the only decorating decision Martha allowed him to make.

The large lot was perfectly landscaped and manicured and was maintained by a service. Bill was thoroughly convinced that the man who owned the service and gave his personal attention to their yard, under Martha's watchful eye, was a homosexual. Any time Bill felt the need to remind Martha of his opinion, she quickly reminded him that she had no concern for such private matters. He was nice, reliable, and her yard looked fabulous, and in The Park, that was all that truly mattered.

The half-circle front driveway used by visitors was lined with boxwoods perfectly matched in size. Dogwoods and magnolias added splashes of color during the spring, but as summer came, the color was gone, and the trees leafed out. Decorative flowerboxes with seasonal flowers accented the grand double-door entrance on the front of the house, and Martha's roses were the envy of every wife in The Park.

Martha and Bill had spent a small fortune on the backyard. The sides were lined with pines and made the area very secluded. Only their closest friends knew of the private back driveway, and the pines made it virtually unseen by passing traffic. The porch was wide and had four columns for support. Four rocking chairs sat idly under two ceiling fans that were used to circulate the muggy air the summer brought. The porch led to a patio that was all brick and extended from the porch to a wall on the other side of the gas grill. The wall had built-in flowerboxes, and holly bushes were planted on its outer edge. The hot tub was built into the patio and was concealed nicely so as not to be an unseemly distraction. More flowers added color, and a short wrought-iron fence served no more purpose than to add to the privacy of the area. It was the tranquil haven Martha had intended it to be.

The inside of the house was stunning. Throughout the years, the McKnights updated one part or another. The front two rooms were a parlor area and a formal dining room. All the furniture pieces were perfectly conditioned antiques that were either inherited or patiently purchased by Martha when—and only when—she found a perfect piece to add to their collection. The floors were hardwood and covered with intricately designed Persian rugs, whose collective cost Bill refused to think of. The hallway was wide and L-shaped and contained an ornate bar. The first doorway past the dining room led to a kitchen that would be a dream for any gourmet chef. Granite countertops were covered with top-of-the-line appliances and gadgets. Bill and Martha both loved to cook, and it was a thrill to be invited to dine at their home.

Past the kitchen and alongside the porch was a large den for less formal settings, which Martha preferred. As the hallway turned, stairs led up to a pair of bedrooms, a full bath, and a small room Bill used as an office. Further down the hallway were two more bedrooms, one of which was the master, and another bathroom for the guestroom.

The master bedroom was spacious, with two large walk-in closets that were filled to capacity with clothes needed for any occasion. Martha had remodeled the bathroom with white marble sinks and counters, tiled floors, and a tiled steam shower that Bill loved.

The house had one of the few basements in The Park, and Bill had convinced Martha to have it finished. The cave, as the men referred to it, served as a card room, a game room, and the place where the three watched their beloved Deacons play football and basketball games, screaming and cursing at officials, coaches, and players and smoking an occasional cigar. Bill insisted the cave have a full bathroom downstairs, and Martha still had no idea why.

Martha McKnight, Nancy Jo Rhodes, and Mary Nell Hicks were all the eldest daughters of prominent families in Kernersville, Lexington, and Thomasville, North Carolina, respectively. They were small towns west and southwest of Winston-Salem. Like most daughters of such families, they were sent to a private preparatory school for young ladies. Salem Academy shared the same campus with Salem College since the turn of the century. They were all debutantes and followed the traditional paths that young ladies of their background would follow. They continued their education at Salem College for the same reasons that most women in the South who had family money did. The first was their families had the means to educate their children, and the second was that college was where educated young ladies with family money met their husbands. Dances and other social events were held between Salem and Wake Forest, and eventually all paths crossed.

The wives had spent their lives like every woman in The Park. They were mothers, and they were perfect partners for their husbands, dutifully raising children and making their husbands' lives run smoothly. Over the years, their spare time was spent volunteering in the PTA, the Junior League, at church, in bridge, book, and garden clubs, at the art museum, and at the symphony. If it was a social endeavor, they participated. What they enjoyed most was doting over their families and spending time with one another.

After receiving the news from their husbands and expediently preparing their travel bags, they decided to gather at the home of Bill and Martha. At Bill's request, Martha called Nolan and Olivia Beecham. Bill and Nolan were law school classmates, and the couples stayed friends over the many years that had passed. They had heard the news and would make themselves and their home available. Nancy Jo and Mary Nell met in the backyard and walked arm and arm quietly up the street to meet Martha.

All three had aged far better than their husbands. Nancy Jo had shoulder-length blonde hair and now colored it to hide the gray that she detested. She loved the sun, and it showed. She enjoyed golf as much as her husband and was still a fine player. She was in her usual outfit—a sleeveless polo and pleated shorts and sandals.

Mary Nell was tall and thin and still managed to turn heads. She was the youngest of the three, with natural blonde hair, slightly longer than Nancy Jo's. She was wearing one of her trademark sundresses and matching flats.

Martha was the lone brunette, and like Nancy Jo, she enjoyed the sun immensely. She was shorter than the other two but had maintained her figure with a lot of hard work and the help of a personal trainer at Old State.

Nancy Jo and Mary Nell walked up the back driveway and let themselves in, finding Martha waiting in the kitchen with a bottle of chardonnay chilled and breathing. Hugs were exchanged, and tears were shared. They sat around the large island in the middle of the room. Nothing was said because no one knew what to say. They all felt like they had lost their own child and their own grandchild. After a few minutes of silence, Mary Nell suggested they move outside to the patio for some fresh air.

Martha grabbed the portable phone, Nancy Jo the wine, and Mary Nell grabbed glasses and napkins. As evening approached, the sun was starting its descent away from the backyard toward the front of the house, and with it went most of the humidity.

They gathered around one of the two wrought-iron tables that matched the fence, set in the middle of the brick. Martha lit a trio of tiki torches positioned perfectly around the patio to help with pestering bugs that liked to prey on people and to provide enough light to see yet not be overbearing. They waited to hear news from anyone. The waiting made a difficult time even more unbearable. They could not imagine the suffering Brad must be going through.

Dr. Schweiger emerged from the office Brad had been hiding from the world in. The good doctor joined the others, looking far worse emotionally than he did when he first arrived. It was easy, even as a stranger, to suffer along with Brad. Mark walked over to the doctor.

"How is he?" Mark asked.

"Not well, but no one would be doing well if they were dealing with the shock of what happened to his family. He's been on an emotional ride no one can imagine. He plays the greatest round of his life in the most stressful conditions, only to find out his wife and son are dead. I still can't believe it. Mark, are you familiar with the stages of grief?" the doctor asked.

"Yes, I think so. There's something like three of them?"

"No, there are five."

"Five?"

"Denial and isolation are what he's going through now. Initially, he mentally absorbed the news and reacted to it. He was overcome with emotion and now subconsciously is probably in denial. He wants to be alone and is now more unaware of who and what's around him. Anger is the second stage. It will more than likely be triggered by an event or situation. Does he have a temper?"

"No, I don't think so. I've never seen it if he does. He's the biggest worrier I've ever known."

"Well, it *will* surface and is almost always the longest of these stages. You can't take anything personally he might say or do. He'll then start bargaining, bargaining for anything that might bring them back. He'll suffer from depression and will need professional help with this. As his friend, when the time is appropriate, encourage him to seek help. Acceptance is the final stage. There's no time frame for acceptance to occur. It's different for everyone. I gave Brad a Valium to help settle his nerves. Here's the bottle. Under no circumstances do you give him this bottle. Proper directions for its use are on the label. Understand?"

"Why can't he have the bottle?"

"I have no way of determining his state of mind, and there's no need to take any chances."

"I understand, and thank you, Dr. Schweiger." Mark shook his hand and watched him leave then turned to Wallace, looking more helpless and lost than ever.

"Mark, go make the rest of your phone calls. I'll sit with Brad."

A warm evening breeze swept through the pines. It kept the remaining soggy air from settling in and was steady enough to allow the wind chimes hanging from the ceiling of the porch to dance against one another. It rustled the corners of the napkins their glasses sat upon. The sounds the chimes produced were similar to the bells heard on Sunday mornings from the First Presbyterian Church just down the road from The Park. The chimes and the distant sound of children's voices were all that interrupted the silence. When the phone began ringing, it startled all of them from their individual daydreams. They looked at one another as Martha reached for it. Nancy Jo and Mary Nell watched her push the talk button and raise the phone to her ear.

"Hello?" she answered with her soft, elegant, southern tone.

"Martha, it's Mark." His voice was strained.

"Mark. Goodness, darling, how is he? How are you holding up?"

"He's not good. I'm not good. He just saw a doctor. He gave him some Valium. Is Bill there?"

"No, sweetheart. He, Tom, and John are on a plane going there."

"Thank God. I'm so lost. I have no idea what to do." His voiced cracked, and he sniffled. Tears formed in Martha's eyes. She cleared her throat to make sure her voice wouldn't give in.

"Just be there for him. He'll need you even when he doesn't think he does." Nancy Jo and Mary Nell watched Martha and hung on her every word.

"When do you think they'll get here?"

"John told Mary Nell it would take six hours or so. I would say seven at the earliest. Mark, I need you to listen to me. Bill and I have friends in San Francisco. Do you have something to write with?"

"Yes, ma'am."

"Mark, do you know what happened?"

"No, ma'am. Just before I called you, I overheard the detective telling someone that Brad would have to go downtown and identify them."

"Oh my, that's just awful. He has to do that today?"

"I'm not sure about that. I was hoping Bill would be here before that. Please don't think I'm being short, but I need to make some other calls. Do Susan's parents know?"

"Yes. Bill called them before he left. They were in Florida visiting Susan's brother. Their flight will be arriving shortly. Anna's picking them up. They'll be staying with us." All the children had volunteered to host any family and friends that would be coming to town.

"Okay. Thank you, Martha."

"You're welcome, honey. Please give our love to Brad. Please keep us informed. Don't worry about the time, just call."

"Yes, ma'am. Good-bye."

"Bye, darling."

Adrian and Natalie, Mark's parents, agreed to meet Brad and Mark, reminding Mark it would be an hour or so depending on traffic. They would be waiting. Adrian's voice was sincere and concerned, wanting to know if there was anything else they could do. Mark just needed someone to be there when they went downtown.

Mark called Nolan and Olivia next and introduced himself. He explained he had spoken with Martha and that she had given him their number. Olivia said they had been waiting for his call. Bill was on the way, and Mark had no way of coordinating everything that was going on. Bill and those guys were coming. His mom and dad were on the way. He had Brad to worry about. They still had to go downtown. Mark's brain was going to implode with everything going on around him. He needed help. Olivia asked what she and Nolan could do.

"I guess if you could wait for them. Brad doesn't know he has to go downtown to identify the bodies. I hope Bill gets here before that happens."

"I understand how you feel. We'll stay here. Call us, and we can exchange information. Let us know when and where you and Brad are. We can get Bill up to speed when they arrive. It'll be seven or eight before he gets here. We have plenty of room at our house. Just take care of Brad and plan on staying here as long as you need to. Bill can handle things when he gets here."

"Okay. Thanks for all your help."

Wallace had been sitting with Brad while Mark made his calls and spoke with Detective Messeke. He offered to listen if Brad wanted to talk. Brad said nothing. He asked Brad about his record-tying round and right away realized the inappropriateness of its timing.

"Like that matters now. Nothing matters."

Mark and the detective rejoined them, and Messeke walked over to Fay and whispered that Mark knew that Brad would have to go downtown. Wallace removed his glasses. His fingers started in the middle of his forehead and tried unsuccessfully to smooth the wrinkles the tension he had been under were causing. He slid his glasses back on.

"Brad, I spoke with Martha. Bill, Tom, and John are on the way here."

Brad looked at Mark and looked away.

"My parents are on their way too. I spoke with Nolan and Olivia Beecham. Martha said to call them. They're—"

"I know who they are," Brad answered.

"Bill and the guys should be at their house by eight. They want you to come to their house. They said they have plenty of room."

"What about our stuff? Susan and Will's stuff, my stuff, it's all over at your house."

"Don't worry about the stuff. I'll get it later. Okay?"

Now the moment they had all dreaded. It was time to tell Brad what his last duty of the day would be. Mark looked at the detective, and that was his cue to tell Brad.

"Brad, I need you and Mark to come downtown with me."

"Why?"

"We need a family member to make an official identification."

"Before I go, tell me what happened."

Chapter 8

He was in his midforties but looked much older. The job could take its toll. The stress and the long, unpredictable hours being a homicide detective had caused a divorce he had never wanted. To those who knew him well, it showed on him. His appearance was sloppy and of no concern to him. His shirt and pants were wrinkled. He tried daily to iron them, but it was a skill he did not possess. After five minutes, he would become frustrated and simply don them as they were. He had only two jackets—one navy and one black. He purchased new ones each year at Christmas. A local dry goods store ran a special each holiday season. Buy one and get the second free. The tie that hung loosely from his collar was several years old and showed many stains, coffee here and mustard and ketchup there. A haircut was overdue, and he had not once contemplated changing the style in his twenty-plus years with the police department. His mustache was bushy and covered most of his upper lip. He could have grown a beard in less than a week, but it simply left a shadow on his face.

Detective Ward Messeke had been with the homicide squad for eight years. He had delivered the awful news of someone's death many times, but it had never become any easier. Some wanted details, and others did not. He had never given much thought as to why. Sometimes it was the overwhelming grief that kept them from asking. Sometimes a family member was guilty of the crime, but something else would always trigger his suspicions if that was the case. Messeke just wanted to solve the crime and give some form of closure to the victim's family.

When Brad asked what happened, he instinctively reached for the inside pocket of his navy blazer. He rolled his eyes when he realized he had lost one of the cheap gold buttons from its sleeve. The pocket was where he kept the little notepad carried by detectives.

He had no use for it at the moment. He could recall every gruesome detail. His recall had served him well during his career. He pulled it nonetheless, as a matter of professionalism.

"Susan stopped at the Gas Mart. She never went inside. She used a debit card or credit card at the pump. The Gas Mart was in the process of being robbed at gunpoint by a Bryce Erickson. Erickson has a history of drug problems, arrest, and theft." Messeke spoke as softly and slowly as possible. His voice rang of confidence because of the unquestionable facts that had been gathered. Several shocked bystanders had given identical accounts of what they had witnessed. Brad didn't look at Messeke once. His eyes were fixated on the wall just past Messeke.

"After the robbery, Erickson appeared panicked about what he should do next. Witnesses stated he raced to the car and was heard telling your wife to get out of the car. She refused to do it because your son was in the backseat." The story was now reaching its most difficult point. Messeke stopped for a moment. He filled his lungs slowly with a deep inhale to help settle his nerves and finish.

"Erickson reached in the car, trying to pull Susan out. They struggled, and during the struggle, the gun discharged, striking your son in the chest. Your wife was screaming, and he snapped when he realized what had just happened. He fired two more shots and appeared to push your wife over the center console and into the front passenger seat. Then he raced away. Witnesses said the sound of sirens were close by. Within three blocks, he had been cornered. He fired at the officers at the scene as he tried to flee on foot. They returned fire, striking him twice in the chest. As they moved in closer, Erickson pulled his own gun up to his head and fired."

Mark and Wallace Fay left the room in a hurry. Mark vomited into a trash can just outside the door.

"Brad, do you have any questions?"

He shrugged his shoulders. "What do I do now? I mean, what's the next thing you need for me to do?" he said, finally looking toward the detective.

"Well, we need you to come downtown for identification. I know that's not something you want to think about right now, but the sooner we do that, the sooner we can release them to you so that you can go home. I'll take you, or you can ride with Mark and just follow me."

"I'll ride with him."

"I understand."

Brad followed Messeke out of the darkening office for the first time since he arrived. Mark had gathered himself. He was embarrassed at his own weakness and angry at Bryce Erickson. Not only had he robbed The Gas Mart but he robbed Brad of his wife and son. He had also robbed Mark of two people he dearly loved. Brad walked listlessly to Mark. When their eyes met, the tears returned for a moment. Mark looked at Brad and felt his pain. He could not help but contemplate how much more his friend would have to suffer and endure. Brad was only twenty-five years old. In the last dozen years of his life, Brad had lost both his parents and now his wife and son. The more Mark tried to grasp the reality of what had happened, the more his own carefree spirit died inside him.

"I have to go see them," Brad said.

"I know you do."

"He said I could ride with him. I'd rather you take me, but I understand if you don't want to," Brad uttered with a flat, empty intonation.

"I'll do whatever you ask me to, Brad. I'm not leaving you. My parents will be waiting for us when we get there. I hope you don't mind. You know how much they think of you." Wallace Fay had Mark's SUV brought close to the rear of the building. The media was loitering around the front, hoping to get a glimpse of the pain, maybe a picture for tomorrow's edition or a comment from someone who had been inside and witnessed all the turmoil and emotion. Fay would have none of that. They allowed Brad to elude the hoard through a rear door that was never used, and they met Messeke by the entrance they came in that morning.

The Hall of Justice on Bryant Street-North Terrace served as the home of the medical examiner and the morgue for the city of San Francisco. The building looked like many of the city's other municipal buildings. The sides of the rectangular building looked striped. The corners were stone-pebbled stucco from top to bottom and then a row of tinted glass windows. This pattern repeated itself around the building.

The morgue was housed in the basement of the Hall of Justice building. Morgues reek of death. The finality is overwhelming. The basement hid this from the many people that came and went over the course of a day. The three entered a service elevator where Messeke used his thick thumb to push the B button. The doors closed slowly, and they felt a momentary jerk before it started the descent. Brad flung his exhausted body into the corner and looked away from Mark and Detective Messeke. The elevator seemed to slow before it even started and finally came to rest after another less noticeable pull. The doors open reluctantly to a bright hallway. The fluorescent lights that lined the ceiling glared off the freshly waxed, square tile floor and the glossy, white finish on the empty walls on either side of the floor. They passed various offices and departments with large windows. The glass zigzagged with embedded fire-safety wire. They walked past another detective who was speaking with an older couple.

The on-duty medical examiner was Dr. Jane Cho, an attractive Asian woman in her late thirties. She was tall and slender with a warm, compassionate smile. Her eyes were almost black and gave her a mysterious quality. Her white lab coat covered a black turtleneck sweater and black skirt that revealed only her calves. Her shift was nearly over, and her green scrubs had been abandoned. She exchanged handshakes with Messeke and Mark and then motioned for Brad to follow her.

Dr. Cho led Brad through a metal door with a push bar across it into a large open room. Four tables were spaced evenly apart in the center of the room. The left and right walls when facing the tables looked like enormous file cabinets. From top to bottom, there were three doors, and from side to side, they numbered fifteen. Forty-five on each side of the room and ninety total. Brad scanned all ninety doors, contemplating where Susan and Will were.

Brad had neatened himself as much as he could. His shirt was back in place, and he put his hair back as best as he was able. He could not bear to have Susan seeing him a mess.

Dr. Cho walked him to the left side of the room. Her slender fingers wrapped around the handle, and with no sound to speak of, she slid the metal conveyor tray from its womb. She pulled the thin, white sheet back just enough to reveal Susan's face. Brad knew it was her immediately, though she did not resemble the woman he had gazed upon earlier that morning. Her cold, lifeless body was seemingly frozen before his eyes. Her pretty, full lips that took the breath from him when they kissed were now a drab blue shade. Her warm, soft, tan skin was now ashen. He wanted to reach down and hold her but could not bring himself to disturb her. He looked at the doctor and nodded his acknowledgment that this was in fact his wife. It was real. This was not a dream, and he quickly realized that Will was there as well.

Dr. Cho took a step to her right and opened the conveyor tray next to Susan. Will's tiny four-year-old body only occupied about a third of it. Again she pulled back the sheet. Even in death, Will looked so innocent and sweet and vulnerable. From the day he was born, he looked like his mother, something Brad had always been grateful about. Now, with no life left in him, he was the very image of her.

Brad began to writhe. His face turned red again, and his jaw clinched. His face creased as he forced the emotion back deep inside his body.

"Oh God, Will. I hope you know how much I love you." His hand brushed the top of his son's head, feeling his soft brown hair and the chill of his scalp. He stared at his little man and then turned to the doctor and gathered himself. He nodded, and she covered their faces. With one hand on each tray, she pushed Susan and Will back into the dark belly of the morgue's cooler.

Dr. Cho escorted Brad back to the hallway and gave him one of her cards. He would need to make arrangements for the bodies. She scribbled her home and mobile numbers on the back and insisted that he call her, and she would help him with every step of what could be a very complicated situation without the help of someone with knowledge of shipping bodies and the necessities that were needed.

Mark and Detective Messeke stood together silently. They were leaning against the wall, and both had their hands in their pockets. Brad shook his head as he tried to make the images of Susan and Will go away.

"Thank you for all you did for me today," Brad uttered as he offered his hand to the detective.

"It's just part of the job," he said as he accepted Brad's hand.

"You certainly didn't need to waste your time catering to me the way you have, but I'm grateful for it."

"You're welcome. Thank you for saying so. I gave Mark my card. If you need anything at all, call me."

"Thank you."

He made a departing handshake with Mark and then meandered down the hallway and around a corner, disappearing from their sight.

"Mom and Dad are waiting in the parking lot," Mark said. "I'll pull the car up to the door."

Brad leaned against the wall and nodded.

The older couple they had passed was still down the hallway conversing with the same detective they had been with earlier. Brad watched Mark walking past the three figures. His eyes were dry and itchy. The glare was harsh and did not help. The water fountain was nearby, and Brad's mouth was arid and his lips on the verge of cracking.

He had eaten nothing all day and was feeling a bit lightheaded. His stomach ached and churned, and he felt the knots as they shifted from one place to another. He stood up as best he could and raised his arms above his head, stretching his torso and breathing as deeply as he could the chilly air that filled the hallway. The other conversation seemed to be finally coming to a conclusion, so he felt better about making his way to the water fountain. He did not want to intrude on their privacy. He bent forward, pushed the little knob, and watched the water start flowing. His mouth and lips gulped down the stream of cold liquid.

Brad slurped away as the detective began parting ways with the older couple.

"If you or your wife has any questions, feel free to call the department, Mr. Erickson," the detective said.

"We will," the older man answered softly as he wrapped his arm around his wife.

Brad turned his mouth away from the water, and the cold stream hit the side of his face. He studied the couple watching the detective walk away. He turned back to his water and closed his eyes, trying to replay the words his mind had somehow trapped. *What did he just say? Did he say Mr. Erickson?* Brad replayed the words rapidly until he was certain he had heard them correctly. He looked at them again as they started to inch their way to the exit. The man was subdued, using his arms to support and help his wife with each step she took. He followed them, obsessed with the words that were now echoing inside his head.

"Excuse me, sir," Brad said with a sense of urgency. They stopped and slowly turned to him. "I'm sorry to bother you. I wasn't trying to eavesdrop while I was getting some water, but did he say your last name was Erickson?"

"Yes, he did," the man said.

"You're Bryce Erickson's father?"

"Yes ... and you are?"

The word yes was all Brad needed to hear. His face reddened, and as he grinded his teeth, a vein bulged on the side of his neck and throbbed. He grabbed Joe Erickson with both hands, nearly knocking the man's wife to the floor. Brad's clinched hands each held a wadded combination of the man's jacket and shirt.

"I'll show you who I am, you son of a bitch!" Brad screamed as he dragged the resistant man down the hallway while the wife begged on deaf ears for help.

"You wanna know who the fuck I am? Do you know?" Brad slammed the man's back against the push bar of the metal door. Mr. Erickson winced in pain.

"Come on, let me show you. You said you wanted to know!"

Dr. Cho opened the door to the autopsy room that Brad had the man pinned against. As the door opened in, Brad held tightly to the man, pushing him past Dr. Cho, who was clearly startled and yelling, "What's going on?"

Brad turned to her, and then his focus quickly snapped back to the man. "He wants to know who I am!"

"No, please don't," the man started. "I know, I—"

"You know *nothing*! Don't you *dare* say another fucking word!" He turned back to Dr. Cho. "Take them back out and pull the sheets back!"

Turning to Erickson, he screamed, "Look at them! I said look at them!" The man stood rigid in front of Brad, looking the other way, trying desperately not to see what lay under the sheets Dr. Cho had pulled back. As Brad released his grip on Erickson's shirt and placed his hands on the sides of the man's face, Dr. Cho raced out of the room.

"Are you looking?" Brad screamed again.

"Yes," he answered, his face trembling in Brad's hands and his body trembling against Brad's.

"That's who I was! They were my life, and that fucking coward you raised took them from me!" He released his hands and moved away. Mark charged through the door and grabbed Brad.

"They're gone, Mark. They're really gone. Did you see them? What am I gonna do without them?" He was exhausted from the energy spent from the tirade. The only thing holding him upright was Mark.

"Let's get you out of here."

Mark was still clutching Brad as they emerged. Mark's parents were trying to comfort a near hysterical stranger. Dr. Cho was just returning, with Detective Messeke in tow. Messeke placed his hand on Brad's shoulder, but he felt nothing as Mark helped him to the car.

Chapter 9

Mark had given the Beechams' address to his parents. Brad would ride with him as his parents followed. Brad crawled into the backseat and lay quietly staring at the dome light on the ceiling of the car. He was oblivious to the various turns and hills and traffic both cars negotiated on their way to Russian Hills.

The gothic Tudor mansion had been built less than ten years after the 1906 earthquake that destroyed San Francisco. It was a corner lot perched atop a hill, allowing for some of the most incredible sights in San Francisco. Panoramic views from every level of the house showed some of the city's famous landmarks. The bay, Golden Gate Bridge, Fisherman's Wharf, and the Rock and its infamous Alcatraz were easily seen. When Olivia told Mark that they had enough room for everyone to stay, she meant it.

The Beechams welcomed their guest. Olivia gave Nolan his instructions, and he quickly helped Mark and his parents settle in. She clutched Brad by the arm and quickly ushered him away to the room she had prepared for him on the second floor. She doted and pampered the young man in a way only women are capable of doing. He might as well have been her own son. The back right bedroom had a large window overlooking the bay. You could sit up in bed and gaze comfortably out of it. The full bathroom was just a few steps from the bed, and a mini-fridge was filled with bottled water and assorted juices.

"Brad, why don't you take a nice, long shower and change. It'll help you rest, dear. The towels are in the cabinet behind the door, and if you need anything, you can just call me."

"Yes, ma'am. Thank you."

Nolan had just placed the phone down as Olivia made her way back to the sunroom. Bill and his group had arrived and were going to use the shuttle service so they would not force anyone to leave, even though Mark had volunteered. The last thing he wanted to do was sit there as his father and Nolan discussed real estate and business issues. Nor did he care to listen to his mother and Olivia go on about the beauty and history of the house. He also did not want to sit there and give detail after detail about everything that happened and then be forced to do it again when Bill, Tom, and John finally got there. He needed some space. He needed to be alone to deal with his emotions. Nolan finally asked Mark about what happened. Mark's eyes were fixated, watching the light reflect on the crystal tumbler Nolan had just placed on a stone coaster beside his chair.

"Mark, Nolan asked you a question." His father's voice aroused him from wherever his mind had drifted.

"I'm sorry. I'm just tired."

"It's okay. I was asking if you knew any of the details."

"More than I ever want to know. I hope you understand if I want to wait until everyone's here. I really have no desire to go through it any more than I have to."

"That's very understandable," Nolan replied.

Olivia asked Mark if he would like a drink and to get cleaned up, and his mother encouraged him to go ahead. He followed her to the room across the hall from where Brad was resting. It wasn't exactly what he had in mind for space, but it was better than nothing. Once Mark had cleaned up, he went across the hall to check on Brad, who was sitting up in bed staring out the window. Mark heard commotion downstairs and headed down to meet everyone. *So much for the peace and quiet,* Mark thought.

The flight made better than expected time thanks to lighter than normal headwinds usually encountered on trips from east to west. All three were exhausted and running on nothing but adrenaline. Their only concern, their only focus was Brad, Susan, and Will. Bill hugged Olivia and quickly reminded her how lovely she looked. He loved needling Nolan. Nolan married over his head, Bill was fond of telling him. Nolan reminded them all that they all married well. Bill shook hands and shared a manly half hug and swat on the back with Nolan. He reintroduced Tom and John. They had all met years ago at an alumni function. Tom and John exchanged pleasantries with everyone while Bill put his arm around the lanky frame belonging to Mark, and they retreated from the rest.

"How are you, son?"

"Just glad you're here. I feel like an idiot. I don't know how to help him or what to do next."

"You're doing everything you can. That's all you can do. Where is he?"

"Upstairs resting. Bad scene at the morgue."

"I can only imagine."

"No, it gets worse. I'll tell you about it later. You guys need to go see him. He's seen my face enough today."

Bill nodded, and they walked back to where the others had collected themselves. Bill motioned for Tom and John. They followed Bill up the stairway to the corner room. Bill rapped a knuckle lightly three times on the door.

"Come in," a voice wearily answered.

The door creaked slightly. He was still perched against the wall. His knees were pulled close to his body, his bare feet near the pillow, and his forearms on top of each other, resting against his legs. His sharp chin rested against his arms, and his eyes, dazed and frozen, looked out the room's only window. His hair was still wet on the back of his head from the shower earlier. They stood silently at the door watching him, and finally he turned to look their way. He stood slowly, gathering himself, and walked to them. The normally tough, hardened men were now seeing and feeling firsthand the damaged soul of their beloved young friend. The three opened into a semicircle and collectively embraced him.

"Brad, we're so sorry, son. We couldn't get here fast enough," Bill offered in order to break the uncomfortable quiet of the moment.

"Thank you. I'm glad you guys came. There's so much to do, and I have no clue where to start. Do her parents know? I can't believe I haven't thought to call them. I can't think of anything right now, to be honest. The doctor gave me something. My head feels like it's in a fog."

"I called them. They should be at the house with the girls by now."

"I need to call them. I'm sorry for being such a bother."

"You're not a bother. We're family, and families are there for one another. We'll get through this," Tom softly replied. Tom's hand brushed over Brad's ear, putting a few out-of-place strands back in place.

John reached a long, lanky arm out, and his hand wrapped around the back of Brad's head. He pulled him close the way a father would and wrapped his other arm around Brad. They both fought their emotions.

"Tom's right. We'll get through it." He felt Brad's head slide up and down across his chest, though he doubted Brad believed a word of what they were saying.

The Beechams were busy being gracious hosts to Mark and his parents when the men finally returned. Tom was temporarily back to his normally gruff self when he reminded Mark that a haircut and a shave seemed long overdue.

"You know you looked like a damned hobo on TV today?" The comment drew approval and smiles from Adrian and Natalie.

"Yes, sir." Mark ducked his head down, a bit embarrassed by Tom's frank assessment.

It was time for Mark to take them through all of it. John stood by the doorway. He wanted to make sure Brad did not overhear what was being said. Mark spared no detail. He went through it all step by ugly step. The group, individual and as a whole, took turns shuttering, wincing, and groaning. Heads shook, eyes were covered, and the women clutched arms to their chests as they gasped thinking of the horror Susan must have felt trying to protect Will and then seeing her child shot, the blood leaking out of his small chest and staining his little shirt with a crimson hue. Their senseless deaths hung in Mark's trembling voice as he struggled to get it all out. His parents had never seen him like this. His face was strained, exhausted, and had lost its gleeful ever-present display most found so charming.

Mark then recounted Brad's confrontation with Joe Erickson. He explained the timing, which like everything else that day had been dreadful. If Susan had been five minutes later, they would still be here. If they had waited until Friday, they would have missed the Ericksons.

Mark gave Bill the card Detective Messeke had given him. Bill had spent the entire flight making a detailed plan of the various tasks that had to be handled before leaving. He wanted things done quickly so that he could get Brad back to North Carolina. He needed to get Susan to her parents. Even Bill was having trouble accepting the reality that in just a few days, Susan and Will would be laid to rest.

Brad gathered himself before heading down to return the phone to Bill. The stress of telling her parents the details proved to be as hard as anything else he had encountered that day. They did not blame him, but he felt guilty. He had brought them to San Francisco, and had he not, they would still be alive. It was not the first time he had thought this, but it was the first time he felt it while talking to someone else. The hour-long conversation sapped what little strength he had left. He gave Bill the phone and relayed Martha's request to be called in the morning. Mark managed to get Brad to take another Valium before turning in.

Brad thanked everyone for their help and support and love. He would have been lost without them. He excused himself and headed back to his room. Nearly twenty hours after he had started his day, his eyes finally closed. He prayed they would never open again as he drifted away.

Chapter 10

Friday morning came much too soon at the Beecham house for everyone concerned. Unaware that anyone else might be milling around, Brad walked as quietly as he could. The hardwood floors creaked here and there as he searched for the kitchen in an unfamiliar home. He had a fitful night trying to rest. He had tried and tried but never could get comfortable sleeping alone. He could not feel her curled up next to him. He could not feel her leg lying on top of his own. Her head did not rest on his chest, and her arm was not draped across him with her fingers grazing his. He had never slept well without her.

The Beechams were early risers but made a point to make sure they got to the newspaper first. The murders and subsequent suicide dominated the front page of the paper, and for that matter the front page of sports section. No less than five staff writers contributed various columns and storylines. Pictures of the crime scene and convenience store accompanied the articles. There were pictures of Brad playing, and stories overlapped other stories. Quotes from one article showed up in another. The television was worse. Local and national news, ESPN, and the Golf Channel covered it ad nausea. CNN actually showed footage of Brad leaving the Hall of Justice. Nolan turned off the television, disgusted with such a blatant violation of privacy. As they heard Brad approaching, Nolan stealthy departed, newspaper in hand.

Brad was surprised to see Olivia and apologized if he had disturbed them, which she immediately denied.

"Not at all, dear. We're always up early here. Breakfast to make, things to do." She smiled and walked over. She gave him a motherly hug and rubbed her hand up and down his back. She placed her hand on his cheek and offered to make him breakfast, but he declined. Food was the last thing on his mind despite not having eaten since Wednesday night when he and Mark picked up Chinese takeout on the way back from his last practice session. Will loved lo-mein or Chinese "skeggiti" as he called it.

"I would love some plain old black coffee if you have some." He walked to the sunroom and waited as the coffee brewed.

Nolan woke Bill. Still groggy from a long previous day, lack of sleep, and now a touch of jet lag, they rushed through the articles and multitude of photos while they were still in their room. He would glance up now and again, shake his head in disbelief, and then continue.

"Bill, if you think that's bad, you should watch the television."

"Oh, I can imagine." Bill folded the paper neatly and left it on the bedside table and turned the reading lamp off.

When Bill joined Brad, he was holding the cup with both hands. Brad was oblivious to the steam drifting from the mug as he stared out at the morning fog that shrouded the bay. His face devoid of expression, his body spoke to Bill in a wordless exchange. His shoulders sagged, his torso and legs nothing more than a lethargic clump. Bill knew another long day was ahead of him as he joined Brad. He knew there were no words to comfort him, so he just sat there. Brad felt the cushions shift as Bill sat. He turned just enough to see him and then turned back.

"Would it be better if I leave you be?"

"No, sir. I'll be alone soon enough." The words pierced the air. They rang with a truth Bill could not stop mulling over. Most men Bill's age could and would use any excuse to get away from the house and family. It wasn't a lack of love but just the way it was for that generation. Brad was not like that at all. His father had always been there for him, and maybe if his mother had not passed away, it would have been different, but his father was a softhearted, caring man who was involved with his son, and Brad was his father's son when it came to family. Brad gazed out, looking for answers to questions that had none. Bill just helplessly sat by his side.

Mark had always slept as late as humanly possible and even later during the summer when he had no place to be. He was a night owl by nature and always had been. He tried in vain to sleep in. He slept off and on during the night. He thought he heard Brad scream once, and his own nightmares woke him other times. The morgue, their faces; his body sat straight up, unnerved by the images he had witnessed. He tried to convince his mind it was nothing more than a dream, only to realize this was not his bed. This was not his room. His eyes opened wide to the strange room that reminded him the images were real. He struggled as he placed his feet on the cool hardwood. His back and legs ached from his work the previous day. He had a splitting headache and hoped someone had aspirin.

One by one, the kitchen became more crowded. Olivia bustled about, pouring juice and coffee. She made egg whites, turkey bacon, and wheat toast for those who were hungry.

Mark kept Brad occupied so Bill could start the unpleasant tasks that lay ahead. Bill called Detective Messeke, and they agreed to meet at nine. Messeke would help Bill coordinate with the medical examiner's office the release of Susan and Will's bodies and transportation issues. Tom would accompany Bill to decipher medical terminology and to get away from the house.

Dr. Cho came in early to help the detective with the meeting. She was also very concerned about Brad's mental state and was eager to talk with the people who knew him the best. Bill was introduced as Brad and Susan's attorney, and Bill explained Tom's presence was simply for any medical dialogue that might transpire.

"I'm sorry we have to meet under such circumstances," she offered upon her introductions to Bill and Tom. She admitted that she had no idea who Brad was until she returned home and her husband, an avid golf fan, informed her.

Bill was anxious to get through the formalities and down to the important details. He still had to meet with the rental car company, contact the airlines, make arrangements with Mark concerning what was at his condo, and contact the funeral home in Winston-Salem.

Dr. Cho explained the pertinent laws regarding autopsies in the state of California. Virtually all homicides required an autopsy, but it was not the case for Susan and Will. Autopsies were performed for investigative purposes, and since there would be no investigation, there were no plans to do one unless requested by the family of the victims. Bill reached inside his attaché case and removed a copy of his power of attorney form for Brad and handed it to the doctor.

"The family doesn't wish to have one performed. Just a few more questions if you don't mind?" Bill asked.

"Not at all, please go ahead."

"How long before the bodies will be released? What's the best way of transporting them? We have a private plane available and would prefer to transport them ourselves."

She said the plane would be just fine for transporting. The bodies would be released when they were ready to leave, and arrangements would be made to deliver the bodies to the airport. She would have them stored in cooler cells, which were designed for air travel. Her only request was to make sure the funeral home returned them to her upon completion of their needed use. Bill sighed, grateful that it would not be any more complicated than what she had explained.

Bill then discussed the desire of everyone to leave Saturday morning. She said that there would be nothing preventing that from happening. She expressed her concern for Brad and briefly mentioned the incident involving the Ericksons.

"Yes, Mark mentioned that to us privately. It's nothing like the Brad we all know. I'm not sure any of us have ever seen Brad lose his temper. It doesn't sound like we want to either. I think he's caught in an emotional state right now that renders him a bit helpless in his decision-making process. He lost his mother when he was fourteen and his father at nineteen. Susan and Will were all he had as far as true family. Mark is as close to Brad as any brother would be, but he has no siblings and no other family except for us and our families, and it just makes this all the more devastating. At some point, Brad will realize his interaction with Mr. Erickson was wrong, and he'll want to apologize. If there's some way to obtain contact information for them, I would really appreciate it."

"I'm sure we can work something out. I would have to speak with them before I do anything."

"That's understandable. Once we've dealt with everything, I'll call. Thank you so much for your time. I'll call later today to give you a more specific flight schedule." The three exchanged handshakes and bid good-bye.

After completing several hours of tasks all over San Francisco, Bill and Tom finally arrived back at Nolan and Olivia's home. Bill quickly cornered Mark and gave him a brief update. Bill thought it would be best for Mark to discuss what was left at his condo with Brad. The last thing Brad needed to see were Susan and Will's belongings, but the decision would be Brad's. It was a conversation Mark wasn't looking forward to but one he knew must be done. Mark's mother had mentioned that she would go over and pack things and have them shipped back to North Carolina. Bill thought the idea was perfect, but they had to check with Brad.

Mark hustled upstairs to Brad. The door was half closed and creaked as he pushed it open enough to see Brad lying on the bed.

"Brad, I know you're dealing with a lot of things right now, but Bill wanted me to talk to you about some stuff."

"What stuff?" His pitch was as lifeless as his body.

"Well ... man, I hate talking about this."

"If Bill said we need to talk, I'm sure he's right."

Mark pushed ahead. He said that the plan was to leave in the morning. Bill had covered everything that needed attention except for one last thing.

"What's left?"

"What do you want to do about the things at my place?"

"Oh yeah, that sorta slipped my mind."

"Well, we didn't think you needed to drive back over there and pack everything. Mom volunteered to go. She has to grab some things for me because Bill wants me to fly back with you guys. She said if it was okay with you she'd grab your things as well, and before she and Dad fly to Winston, she'll get things packed up and ship them back to you. Would that be okay?"

"Damn, I do need to go back. I'm sorry. I totally forgot."

"No you don't. Mom doesn't mind. She wants to help, so let her."

"I hate putting your mom and dad out. Hell, I'm putting everybody out."

"Brad, you've gotta stop saying that. This wasn't part of a plan. When are you going to understand that everybody cares about you and wants to help? Bill and those old farts ..." Mark's flawless timing showed again as John Hicks walked in.

"Old farts, huh?" John replied, smiling.

"Sorry. I didn't mean it like—"

"It's okay," John answered. Brad cracked a small smile. Mark knew there were few things in life more enjoyable to Brad than Mark making a fool out of himself.

"My parents love you. They're thoroughly convinced the only reason I made it through college was the good fortune of having you as a roommate, so let them do what they can."

"How have your parents put up with you?" Brad asked.

Mark just shrugged his shoulders. He was as confused as anyone when it came to the answer to that question. His older sister, Julie, was a pediatric neurosurgeon, and his younger brother was starting law school in the fall.

"Well, they're right. I probably would have flunked out."

"I doubt that. There was always someone willing to do just about anything you asked them to do. Should I go through a list?" Brad was actually enjoying himself, if only for a moment or two.

"I really wish you wouldn't. Can we get back to what we were talking about?"

"Yeah, I guess so."

"Like I said before, with your permission, Mom will get everything packed up and ship it back. She's going to bring the rest of your stuff over today when she packs for me. Is that okay with you?"

"Yeah, that's fine. If I don't tell her when she's here, please tell her I said thank you."

"Oh, you'll see Mom for sure. They're both worried about you. She won't leave without seeing you. She already called to say they booked their flight for Winston."

The plane and its pilot were ready and waiting when Bill, Tom, and John arrived with Nolan and Olivia. Brad and Mark were right behind them in another car with Mark's parents. Dr. Cho had kept her promise to Bill; the bodies were already on board. Chris expected a routine flight that would take no more than five or six hours. Getting home would be a relief on one hand and dreadful and emotional on the other. The wives would be waiting, as well as Susan's parents and all the friends who were still trying to grasp the shock of all of it. Constant phone calls, well-meaning souls who would feel a duty to not only call but come by and visit, send flowers, bring food, and pay more attention to Brad than he would care to have.

Brad confided in Mark and John the guilt he was feeling. He could not accept their fate. He asked again and again the questions that would always haunt him.

"Why didn't I just make her stay home Thursday? How am I going to face her family?"

"You couldn't have forced her to stay home. She would have come with or without your permission," Mark answered quickly.

Brad glanced out of the window as the plane slowly picked up speed. He turned away as the wheels raced faster and faster down the concrete runway. The wheels, one at a time, lost contact as the nose of the small jet lifted up and turned eastward toward home. When the plane reached its cruising altitude, Brad laid his head on the armrest of the leather sofa and closed his eyes. He would sleep the rest of the trip. The group woke him as they started their descent. John joined Brad on the sofa as Brad came out of the deep sleep he had managed. John reassured Brad that no one held him accountable but himself. Everyone waiting for their return mourned with Brad.

Chapter 11

Anna steered them in the narrow driveway. The wheels finally crawled to a stop. She turned the keys, killing the engine while the four doors opened and closed as her passengers filed out. It alerted all those present that they were finally home. Anna unlocked the bay door on the back, and Brad, Mark, and the rest grabbed what belonged to them. One by one, Martha, Nancy, and Mary Nell appeared, ready to welcome their husbands back home and to see Brad. Bill whispered back and forth with Martha. She walked over and wrapped her arms around Brad. Her hand touched his cheek softly, and before he could see the tears form, she retreated hastily. She gathered all the guests and led them to the patio.

Brad reluctantly climbed the stairs that led to the kitchen, where Susan's parents were waiting for him. His feet felt numb and heavy, and his body felt weighted down; it was taking all his energy just to move forward. His eyes met theirs, and as he inched his way in their direction, he tried mightily to maintain eye contact, breathe deeply, and hold in his emotions. The pained faces did Brad in, and he broke down in front of the two of them. Victor's normally steely demeanor was not present at all. He was a hard man to read unless you knew him well. His black and white hair was parted neatly from right to left, and his mustache was perfectly groomed. His wife, Rita, was an older version of Susan in every respect. She had a warm and happy demeanor that all who knew her loved. Her wavy, almost curly, brown hair had a few scattered gray ones among them. She looked as though she had aged greatly in just the last two days. They clung to one another, each opening an arm to invite Brad to join them and grieve with them. His knees buckled for a second, and he quickly reached for the edge of the countertop to catch himself. They lunged forward, expecting him to fall. He was overwhelmed with grief and guilt. His body felt like it was being assaulted from every angle. The three sobbed quietly.

Bill came in and said, "I'm sorry to interrupt, but I know you all could use some time alone. Brad, you know where my office is. There's plenty of room. Please make yourselves at home. If anyone needs anything, just let us know."

"Thank you," Victor replied, nodding deliberately. Brad, clutching Rita's hand, led them down the hallway to the staircase, where every step would feel like two. The office was small but had more than enough room for the three of them. The walls were covered with all kinds of things. Some had to do with law, some were framed newspaper clippings, some were Wake Forest trinkets, and there was a framed picture of Brad playing golf in the United States Amateur championship. A desk stood against one wall, and a loveseat sat across from it. Victor and Rita sat there. Brad turned the well-used leather chair toward them and sat down. The moment was quiet and awkward. Sitting in Bill's chair seemed inappropriate, but it was his only choice. Brad's mind splintered away. He could not help but remember the last time he had sat with the two of them alone like this. Brad could still feel the lingering fear he had when he went to them when Susan became pregnant at the end of their junior year of college. He begged for their forgiveness and spent hours convincing Victor how much he loved Susan and of his intention to marry her if they could see past the mistake and give him their blessing. Brad knew he had little hope of Victor blessing it, but Rita knew how much Brad loved her, and more importantly, she knew how much their daughter loved Brad. All of those fears and anxieties seemed beyond trivial now.

"I don't know what to say," Brad mumbled in a barely audible voice. "I'm sorry. I know that's not enough, but it's all I can say. I should've made them stay ..." Rita reached out and grabbed Brad by the arm. She held it tightly, stopping the words. His voice was raw, and his head was congested from crying.

"Brad, please don't do this. How could you have prevented any of this? We hurt like you and with you, not because of you." Victor, looking on, patted Brad on the head and gently put his hand under his chin, lifting his face up. When their eyes met, Brad saw Victor nodding in agreement with the words his wife had just spoken, but Brad did not believe Victor agreed with Rita.

"Just tell us what happened."

"I'll try." Brad wiped his eyes and did his best to recall every detail possible. He of course had practiced every day. Mark drove him back and forth so Susan had a car to use. She wanted to shop and do a little sightseeing. Mark's mother was more than happy to show her around. Natalie doted over Will, not knowing when she would have a grandchild of her own. They went shopping and each day spent a little time trying to organize and decorate Mark's condo.

"Tuesday or Wednesday night, we discussed my tee time for the first round. It was 7:00 a.m., and we both agreed that dragging Will out that early wasn't a good idea. So we decided that Mark and I would just go and they would get there when Will woke up. We were pretty sure that if he was up like he normally was, they would be there when I made the turn. Friday, I was playing late, so they would ride with me. Anyway ..." Brad then started giving them the details. Susan stopped for gas and the robbery and how everything just went wrong. He talked about having to identify them and hoping they were wrong but knowing in his heart that he was going to find them. He talked about Joe Erickson and how he lost control of his temper. He recounted forcing Mr. Erickson to look at Susan and Will. He admitted that part of him regretted what had happened with the killer's father, but for the most part, the only thing he regretted about the confrontation was that Mark had kept him from killing the old man.

Victor and Rita talked with Brad about the arrangements. Brad had no idea what to do. It was something he and Susan had never discussed. *Why would we at our ages?* he thought. Brad wanted them to make the arrangements. He assured them he would agree to whatever wishes they had. His defeated voice had no words left to say. He just wanted to rest, but with a house full of people, there was no chance of that happening anytime soon. He told Victor and Rita he wanted to sit in Bill's office and collect his thoughts, knowing he would be wanted downstairs soon. They hugged him and left.

A few minutes later, Mark came into the office, sat down across from Brad, and said, "We don't have to stay long. My parents' flight will be getting in soon. Just go down, tell everyone thanks for all the concern, and we'll bolt. Once we pick up my parents, we can hide at your place."

"I don't care if I ever see that place again," Brad said.

"I've got no clue how he's gonna be when we get him home, but I don't think he needs to be alone whether he wants to be or not." Mark's observation met with his parents' agreement while they waited at the baggage claim. Mark spotted his mother's things and pulled them off the carousel. His father's bags followed shortly afterward.

Brad was waiting at the curb when they went outside. "Hello, Mrs. Lewallen. How was your trip?"

"It was lovely—no problems whatsoever." Brad held her hand as she stepped off the curb. She gave him a soft hug and a small peck on his cheek. "Always the gentleman, aren't you, Brad?" Mark enjoyed that Natalie's smile brought a small smile to Brad as he blushed, something that always happened when he received a compliment.

"I want to drive. Hop in on the other side. Besides, I don't feel like telling you the turns."

"Okay. You sure?"

"Yep."

The drive, depending on the traffic, would take thirty minutes or so. Then Brad would be home and be one step closer to arriving at the end of this journey.

Their home was the one Brad grew up in and inherited after the death of his father. It was the only home he had ever known. Nothing much on the outside had changed. The roof and windows had been replaced. Susan added a little color to the landscape of the front yard but nothing that would cause someone to not recognize it. The interior of the home was uniquely Susan. With Brad's blessing, she slowly changed things to make it their home. Brad's room was now their office and the trophy room, though Brad did not like them being displayed. Susan was his unofficial manager. She helped organize his schedule, travel arrangements, bills, and all the other nuisances of working on the road.

One of the guest rooms had become Will's room. The corners of the room were littered with all the toys and stuffed animals a four-year-old could dream of having or want. Will's set of golf clubs leaned against the foot of the bed with a basketball nearby. A baseball glove with a ball and a small football lay on the covers. The walls were adorned with a variety of Wake Forest posters announcing to all who his favorite team was. His favorite poster was centered on the wall above his headboard. It was a picture Brad had blown up of "Uncle" Mark dunking a ball against the Duke Blue Devils. Will loved it, and Brad was thrilled because it might have been the only highlight of Mark's career, and he loved making sure Mark saw it every time he visited.

Susan slowly changed colors, updated the furniture and appliances, and made the house their home. The changes had taken time, but Brad had welcomed and helped with the changes. Her decorating style reflected a perfect relationship of their personalities and their partnership. The rich earth tones blended seamlessly through the rooms. When Brad was home, painting had become a welcome distraction from golf. When the painting was complete, he felt and saw the achievement, and it was a feeling he was finding less and less on the golf course. Every day Brad walked in it, regardless of his day, he felt at ease. That feeling would come to an end now at this very moment.

He grabbed Mrs. Lewallen's bags as Mark tended to his father's luggage. As they reached the door, Brad fumbled with the keys until they dropped, clanking against the brick stairway. As he bent down to pick them up, Mr. Lewallen bent down as well.

"Let me get them, Brad." His words were soft and met with a barely noticeable nod from Brad.

"It's the one next to the car key. It opens the dead bolt and the knob."

As the door opened, they faced a wall filled with framed photos.

"She was quite the picture taker, wasn't she?" Brad wasn't asking. He knew, but merely pointing out the obvious would get it over with. He paused for a moment and panned the room, taking all of it in. It would serve as a reminder every day of what had happened. He would have to learn to live with these images. He would feel as if he were drowning each night he would go to bed, only to wake up and realize he had survived yet again to deal with his loss.

"Sorry, let me show you to your rooms," Brad said as well as he could.

Mark's parents spent early Sunday morning in the kitchen. Adrian sat at the table reading the paper, which was again littered with stories and pictures and quotes from people claiming to know the entire story and having inside information. Natalie joined her husband while Mark dealt with a phone that rang incessantly. Some calls were unavoidable, like the one from Victor and Rita wanting to come by, but most were people looking for a scoop. Brad had not taken a call, and he had no plans to start.

Natalie opened the door for Susan's parents. She offered coffee, but they declined. They were both clad in dark clothing, and their faces had an ashen tone.

"Brad's in the back. Mark's with him. The only time he left the room was when he tried to sleep. He just lay on the sofa and watched movies until he drifted off." Her voice was laced with concern. "I'll let him know you're here."

She motioned them down the hallway and then left. Brad was sitting in a chair beside the nightstand. Mark excused himself and joined his parents, leaving Brad alone with Victor and Rita. The phone rang often, but Brad just let the answering machine collect more messages. Once in a while, he would listen to the messages, delete some, and write names on a notepad.

"Am I supposed to send notes to these people for calling? I don't remember doing that when my dad died. And how do these other people get an unlisted number? Isn't that the point of having one?" His tone was showing a lack of patience bordering on anger. They looked at his notepad and the list of names. He hit the play button so they could listen, skipping some messages to get to the ones he had been referring to. Local papers and television, national news—it was absurd, he pointed out. He could not comprehend the morbid fascination and had no desire for the attention. He mentioned Mark's idea of having Bill come up with "one of those press-release things," as Mark called it, but Brad thought if he ignored them, eventually they would go away, or he would just turn the ringers off and never answer the phone again.

"I just wanna be left alone. Why is that so hard to understand? What could possibly make someone think that I'm interested in being interviewed about the death of my wife and son? That's just sick."

Rita grabbed the pad from Brad and sat next to Victor on the edge of the bed.

"You have no obligation to talk to any of those people. Don't worry about those things. Everything will eventually settle down," Victor told Brad.

"We made most of the arrangements yesterday. Martha was a big help. We just wanted to make sure what's planned is okay with you and see if there are any additional things you had in mind," Rita said.

"Whatever you've chosen to do is okay with me. I'm such a mess right now I wouldn't know what to do, where to start. One thing I've begun to realize is this, though: I'm as inept at day-to-day life as anyone you'll ever know." His speech faltered as his voice cracked with each word.

"Don't say that, Bradley!" Rita scolded him. "I know you think that right now, but it's just not true. You have so many people that care about you. We care about you. We want to help you, not out of pity but out of love."

They sat and talked for a few hours about the funeral home, the church, pallbearers, caskets, and every detail possible. They would need ten pallbearers—six for Susan and four for Will. Her parents exuded strength, which should have been comforting for Brad, but instead it made him feel inadequate, weak, and ashamed. The visitation was scheduled for Monday evening, and Brad needed to pull himself together for the next couple of days. He was not sure how he would be able to do it given the way he felt.

Chapter 12

The parade of cars left Brad and Susan's home so they could arrive at the church thirty minutes early. Brad donned the same dark charcoal suit, shirt, and tie he had worn to his father's funeral. Mark rode with Brad, Victor, and Rita in the lead car provided by the funeral home. It was going to be a long and difficult night. Everyone knew it would be. Brad had been insulated from the outside world with the help of those closest to him. Though he had no other desire but to stay hidden, his privacy was about to end for the next day and a half.

As he rode, he calmly stared out the window. Sunglasses covered his eyes as he thought about the endless line of people who would come tonight. He thought about his parents and their funerals and how those days had been so long and draining. His parents would have loved Susan and Will. He thought of what a wonderful grandfather his dad would have been. He was momentarily comforted knowing that his parents were with Susan and Will now. He fretted about forgetting names and faces that he would see tonight. He wasn't sure why because he was confident that he would not see many of them again. He took deep breaths and quietly reminded himself that this would be over soon. He wanted to be alone, and in order to be alone, he would have to endure what was ahead of him. The speed bump on the side street behind the church brought his wandering mind back to the present.

They were met in the parking lot behind the church by the minister and two suited gentlemen from the Edmonds and Steed funeral home. The cars emptied efficiently, and the shutting car doors echoed through the spaces not yet filled. Richard Lofton greeted Victor and Rita, and he then turned to Brad and shook his hand as well. The reverend's demeanor was calm and his voice compassionate, its tone deep, warm, and rich with just a trace of his southern upbringing. His hair was an even silver shade, and not one strand of it was out of place. His dark suit hung comfortably on his angular frame. He looked like a man born to be called by God to do His work. He led the group to a large room behind the sanctuary used by the choir for rehearsals and storage of their robes. He briefly went over a few details with them. He expected a large turnout for the visitation because of the family's request for a private graveside ceremony; the visitation would be the only chance for some to pay their respects. The church's deacons would handle the parking and ushering of guests, and the two gentlemen with the funeral home would handle the other issues.

"Brad, if I could have a word in private please?" the reverend discreetly asked, leaning over. He followed him over to the piano, placed his hand on the edge of the shiny, black surface, and looked at Brad.

"I've called to see how you've been, and I do realize that you don't feel like talking right now. I just want you to know that if or when that time comes, call me. Day or night, I'll be there when you need me to be."

"Thank you."

They walked back over, and he led the group into the massive sanctuary lined with row upon row of solid oak pews with deep maroon, almost purple cushions. Majestic stained-glass windows decorated the sides. The largest window was behind the pulpit and choir. It was intricately detailed with a depiction of Christ and the Last Supper. The family was seated in the front row just feet from their caskets. The flowers that had been sent wrapped around the walls at least two deep, and their fragrances mixed and lingered throughout the room. The rest took their places directly behind the family. Reverend Lofton asked them to bow their heads, and as they did, Rita, who sat between her husband and Brad, grabbed one hand from each of them and clutched them tightly.

"God, I ask that you be with this family tonight, to show them your strength, lend them your strength. Help them realize that

Susan and Will were a gift from you. Help them through and guide them, oh Lord. Please be with those who come tonight to show their support and love for this family. We ask this in thy name. Amen."

The reverend then addressed everyone present. "Is everyone ready?"

They turned and looked at one another.

"Yes," Rita answered quietly.

He motioned to the back, and the far right doors opened. The long line of people slowly made their way down the aisle. His golf coach was the first one to reach him. As he realized who it was, his eyes glazed with tears.

"Hey, Coach." His voice trembled as he looked at Coach Makinney.

"Brad, I'm so sorry. I have no idea what to say. I hurt for you. I really do."

Brad realized how difficult this night would be for those who came to pay their respects. Maybe it was Reverend Lofton's prayer, maybe it wasn't. Maybe his dad was giving him the strength, but his mind calmed, and he realized he would get through this night. He was grateful that Susan and Will were so loved, and if only for tonight, he would be strong and understanding. No one would know what to say to him or the rest of the family. No one ever does.

They came and went, one after another, for nearly three hours. Memories were shared, and Mark—being Mark—flirted with every attractive female that slinked past. His mother was livid, but Brad actually smiled the few times he caught his friend in action and laughed when he showed him a piece of paper with Sara Jamieson's number on it. Only Mark could find a way to pick up a girl at a visitation.

The next morning came with a brilliant sunrise typical of June in North Carolina. The orange glow would slowly give way to a sky filled with blue and dotted with white clouds. A gentle breeze came from the north, making for the most ideal of conditions. Susan and

Will deserved such a perfect day, Brad thought as he peered out of a window.

Brad took a long shower, trying his best not to think of what was awaiting him. He tried to take his time getting ready, but it did not help. He sat on the sofa while the others readied themselves and waited for everyone to meet. The funeral home sent enough of their large, black sedans for everyone to ride without feeling crowded. They would follow the hearse to the cemetery.

They exited the cars and paused while the pallbearers unloaded the caskets and started toward a large portable tent the funeral home had placed there for shade. Folding chairs had been placed in a semicircle under the tent, and after the caskets were positioned in their proper places, Reverend Lofton motioned for the family to take their seats. Victor and Rita and then Brad were followed by their sons and their wives. Rita's mother was the only grandparent alive and was too ill to attend. The others quietly found places behind them. It was as intimate as Rita had hoped for. Everyone was in the shade.

He started with a prayer as they again bowed their heads. A collective amen ended his opening prayer. His message was clear to all of them.

"Many times in life, the plan God chooses for us is hard to accept and even more difficult to understand and fully comprehend. It can at times make us question our resolve, our faith, our beliefs, and everything we have come to know and expect in life. This is one of those times. It is in times like these that only our faith in God and his strength gives us that which can sustain us. This is something that shakes us to the core, but your faith in our Lord will make you strong and help you withstand the pain and loss you feel now. Only God knows of his plan for Susan and Will, and we must accept that his plan would take them from us, and they are surely with him now ..." He continued for just a few more minutes and paused. Anna walked around to the front and joined the reverend. Her voice was pitch perfect, almost angelic as she sang the first verse of Susan's favorite hymn. Her audience, every last one of them, shed tears. Bill held Martha, Tom held Nancy, and John held Mary Nell. Victor held Rita, and their sons held their wives. Brad sat alone staring at the caskets. Bill and Tom each placed a hand on one of his shoulders. Anna walked over to Brad.

"I hope she would have approved," she quietly said to him.

"It was wonderful. I'm sure she would have been as moved as all of us were. She would have been grateful to you for having agreed to sing. I know I am," he told her, and she leaned forward to kiss Brad on his cheek. She finally broke down as well and went back to be with her parents. John's arms were now full with two sobbing loved ones.

One last prayer was made after some of the emotion ebbed. Brad sat calmly waiting in his chair. One by one, they passed the caskets, placing a flower on each before saying good-bye. Brad finally stood clutching the two long-stem roses that he had been holding in his lap. He placed one on top the others already left on Will's casket. He chose a white rose for Will because such young children are so pure of heart and spirit and love. He leaned down and kissed his casket.

Daddy loves you.

He turned to Susan and placed the red rose with the others.

I never deserved you. You're the most amazing person I'll ever know. I ache without you. I'm empty without you. His lips moved, and inside his head he could hear his words, but no one else would.

Every day I woke up, my life was better because of you. I hope I showed you my love for you every day. I hope you never had to doubt it. I hope most of all that I was the husband and father you expected me to be.

He kissed her casket as well. He touched it with his fingertips, which slid off one by one as he forced himself to walk away.

As he left the shade of the tent, the sun's glare reminded him to place his sunglasses back on as Mark waited for him. Brad leaned against his friend as the two walked slowly back to the car. Brad had no tears left, but they were being wiped away by most everyone else.

Off the back of the house, a large wooden deck protruded into the grass. Brad and his dad had built the deck together on and off over one summer when he was in high school. Every night they were in town and not away at a junior golf tournament, they would work for a couple of hours or until the darkness forced them to stop. He could still see his father every time he stepped onto its surface with his bare feet. He could see them both hammering away that summer. He missed his father every day. He wished Will had known him. He wished his father were there for him now as he stared out past the edge of the yard, seeing Forest Pine Country Club and the backdrop it created. The fifth hole ran perpendicular to his house and was where his father began teaching him the game. He sat down under a green and white striped umbrella that jutted out of the center of the glass top of the picnic table. His suit was off, replaced by frayed cotton shorts that he saved for chores around the house. Little splatters of paint decorated these from the times he had spent working inside the house. The dress shirt remained with the top button left open. The starched sleeves he rolled up, and the shirttail was hanging loosely past his waist. He took one of his pale white feet and with his toes dragged one of the other chairs closer so he could prop both his legs up. It was shear habit. He did it every time he sat outside. He tried to distract himself by watching some kids walking and playing golf, but it was useless. They registered as nothing more than some dots moving in the background. His eyes never made it past the thick, green grass that needed some attention and the hand-built wooden jungle gym and bright yellow, plastic slide that Will loved to play on. No one else could see what Brad was seeing, nor could they feel what he was feeling.

He took a long, deliberate sip from the can of beer he was holding. The afternoon heat was starting to make its climb to its apex, which occurred in the middle of the afternoon. The sweat of the can dampened his fingers. The beads eventually dripped to his shirt. He felt their coolness soak into the threads of his shirt, causing him to glance down to realize the pocket of his shirt was still starched together. Susan loved running her hand into the pocket of his dress shirts when they were like that and when she could manage to get Brad to wear one of them. He closed his eyes, and his head, shoulders, and torso tilted slightly as though he was merely adjusting his position in the chair. A warm breeze glided over the deck toward him. He could still feel her. From behind him, she would wrap her arms around his neck, kiss him softly, and slowly slide her left hand down his chest to his pocket. The tips of her French-manicured nails would gently work open the top edge of the pocket until her fingers could slide down the rest of the way. He detested wearing dress shirts, but she would gush over how handsome he looked in one, and he could not resist. Most every night he would wear one, she would wait for him to change and then wear it herself to sleep in next to him. Brad saw that image as well, his eyes still shut and knowing he needed to stop. He could hear cars coming up the road and stopping; he would be needed inside. He preferred to be alone with these thoughts because he was afraid that they would soon go away. He feared he would forget the things that made his life so wonderful and that they would be forever replaced with the reality of what had taken place.

Mark waited patiently by the back door, watching Brad closely and looking for the right moment to interrupt him and the private moment only Mark knew his friend was having. Brad appeared to be finishing his beer—and in record time for him—when Bill and Martha approached Mark.

"Hey there ... just keeping an eye on him," Mark said. "I guess we're starting to have some arrivals?"

"Yes. Do you mind telling him?" Martha requested politely of Mark.

"Yes, ma'am, I'm on my way." He leaned into the laundry room just far enough to reach a refrigerator that had been placed in that room to hold beer and wine. He grabbed two more beers and walked onto the deck. Brad turned to him when he heard the door close.

This was one of the few times Mark appeared neater in appearance than Brad. He had tossed his jacket on the bed he was sleeping on, but the shirt, tie, and slacks all remained. His normally wild locks were neatly gelled into place, and he was clean-shaven for the first time all summer. He did not know if Sara Jamieson would be coming by, but he had no intention of taking any chances. Brad smiled at his friend as he approached.

"I guess people are here?"

"Yeah, Bill and Martha said I should come and drag you back in."

"Why are you still wearing that?"

"You're kidding, right? My mom would kill me if I changed."

"And that's the only reason?"

"Yeah, why?"

"You're so full of … you think Sara is coming by, don't you?"

"Well, would that be a bad thing?"

"No, not really. She looked like your kind, didn't she?"

"No, I was thinking she looked drop-dead gorgeous, and I think she's had a little work done. Don't you?"

"How would I know? You two were always hooking up in college."

"Well, all I can tell you is … well, let's see how I can put it exactly … she just didn't have that kinda lung capacity back then, if you get what I'm saying."

"Gotcha," Brad answered while looking down and shaking his head.

As they walked back inside, there was Sara waiting. They turned and looked at one another and smiled again.

"How does she know where I live?" Brad said.

"I gave her directions last night on the phone. It's not the hardest place in the world to find, you know," Mark quietly replied.

Brad said hello to Sara, and once he did, he looked past her to find everyone from the funeral had arrived. Through the bay window in the den he could see cars finding places to park up and down the street. A few neighbors that had watched Brad grow up were there as well. Reverend Lofton was there holding a box containing all the cards from the flowers that had been sent. He handed them to Brad, who then walked down the hall to his office and placed it on his desk.

He looked around the room, and their pictures looked back at him. Their pictures were everywhere. The memories surrounded him. He sat down in the chair she used when she was helping him with his schedule and everything else, and as the air released from the cushion, the faint smell of her perfume escaped and hung momentarily in the air before disappearing. He instantly felt a burden, as if someone had sat on his chest to crush the air from his lungs. He could only hope for such an ending. He knew somehow it would pass.

Chapter 13

January came quickly; it was only seven months later. Time passed quickly for most people but not for Brad. The holidays were a long and seemingly unending reminder of them. Seven months of grief, loss, and regret had taken their toll. Brad was even thinner than normal. His hair was longer, and a goatee had appeared covering his mouth and chin. He was certain that he had answered all of those who had sent flowers, cards, and e-mails. He had refused anyone's help and was making his first effort at doing things on his own—and for him and him alone. As much as he did not want to, he forced himself to go about his normal holiday routine. Thanksgiving came and went, and he visited Bill, Tom, and John and then went to Susan's parents. He spent very little time there before speaking privately with Victor and Rita and telling them he had to leave. He could not handle being there without Susan and Will. He would rather be alone than ruin their time with the remainder of their family. As much as they wanted him to stay and realized that he needed to stay, they could not convince him of it.

Christmas was worse because Brad loved showering them with gifts. He loved surprising them with odd things from the road. Susan loved T-shirts, and any time he could find one from somewhere that he knew she would like, he would buy one. Will had a collection of golf balls from everywhere he played, but Christmas was special. Brad would spend September through the eve of Christmas picking out small, what most would consider inconsequential trinkets most would not appreciate, but Susan and Will did. He knew how forgetful he could be at times, so he made notes reminding himself of the things Susan and Will had mentioned wanting. Susan begged him each year for a list of things he wanted, and she always got the same answer.

"I want you and Will to be happy, and if we could just have a night alone … maybe your parents could take Will for a night. I just want to spoil you one night," he would reply, smiling, and her blushing acknowledgment of what he was truly requesting was answered with a simple kiss.

This was not one of those holidays. He shopped only to realize how much thought and time Susan had put into the gifts for everyone. He was inept at finding things for his friends. He was humbled once again at Susan's thoughtfulness. He conceded his lack of knowing what family he had left might want by getting them gift certificates for things from places he was certain they would use. He reluctantly visited everyone, and just like Thanksgiving, he was bombarded with questions and love. He expected the attention and hated every second of it. He had been hard to reach since the funeral. He had always been dependable when it came to returning calls, but since June, his friends were lucky to find him or talk to him. Usually not a week went by that Brad and Mark didn't talk, but since Mark had gone home, Brad called rarely and let all but one of Mark's calls go straight to voice mail. Brad knew Mark was concerned, especially after Mark flew in for Christmas. Brad found out that Mark's parents had wanted to come too, but Mark had insisted that things would be better if he came alone.

Mark spent most of his time trying to convince Brad to go back to California, and Brad became cold and distant. How could he not at the idea of staying with Mark? And not because of Mark's lifestyle but because it was too close to what happened. Brad was afraid of himself and his emotions.

Brad also realized that he needed to move forward in some way. The hardest part was taking the first step. The comfortable life he had known with her was over, and his future was uncertain. Even though he had his friends, he was alone, and the one unrelenting thought he had was to get out and get away. It was time to start over, and being there was not the place to start over. He needed to get out of that house. It was once a haven to him but now was nothing more than a shrine to the memory of the people he loved and had lost. He needed to get away from Winston-Salem and go somewhere and start again. He felt guilty because his friends worried about him so much, almost too much. He wanted to be out of sight and hoped that would lead to being out of mind. He owed it to Bill and the rest to tell them of his intentions. He could not just disappear. Bill was still his advisor, and there were things to deal with, and whether Bill wanted to or not, he would have to help Brad with those. Good, bad, right, or wrong, he was moving forward. His plan was to deal with Bill first and then speak with Susan's parents.

Martha always greeted Brad, and this day was no different. She hugged him and gave him a motherly kiss on the cheek. She gently tugged at his longer than normal hair, ran her fingernails against his goatee, and gave him a disappointing look.

"I thought you were going to clean all that fuzz up, sweetheart," she said while she locked arms with him.

"I am. I've just been distracted with a few things. I know how sloppy it looks."

"Well, I wouldn't say that, but it just doesn't suit that handsome face of yours, dear." She led him to the stairs. "He's in his office, and he's in a foul mood. Did you watch the game last night? It was just God awful, and he's still acting pissy about it. Ugh. Men and their teams."

"No, I didn't watch, but I read about it this morning. Thanks for the warning." He headed up the stairs, knowing that if she thought he was mad now, she was about to see him become downright livid.

He found Bill sitting at his desk. The sports section was spread open across its surface. The phone was plastered to his ear, and he was spouting out one obscenity after another. Brad sat quietly and listened. Bill raised a finger over his head to let Brad know he was just about done. Bill peered through his glasses, looking at the paper and shaking his head.

"Okay, I need to run. Brad's here. I'll call you later. Uh-huh ... all right ... bye. I thought you said you were going to get a haircut. You know you look like shit, don't you?"

"Good to see you too. I am as soon as I leave here."

"While you're at it, shave that crap off your face too. Don't forget about that!" Bill snarled, pulled his glasses down, and stared steely at Brad. "Did you watch that damn game last night? I hate losing to those damned Heels!"

"No, read about it this morning."

"Well, good for you. I just wanted to throw up. What's on your mind, son?"

"Well, a few things actually." His tone was assertive. He had made up his mind to be the one in control of the conversation.

"Well, let's hear it."

"I'm leaving." He leaned forward and looked Bill straight in the eye. His upper body braced against his legs with his forearms supporting him.

"Leaving? For where?"

"Not sure yet. I sorta have something in mind, but I'm leaving. I just have to."

"Well, that's a helluva a plan ... not sure ... sorta ... you need to come to your damn senses. Have you lost your mind?"

"Well, this isn't what I came to ask advice about. I'm here to tell you that I'm leaving out of respect for you and everything you and Martha and everyone have done for me. This is something I have to do. Please understand I'm not changing my mind. I need to do this. I have to get away. I might be right back here with my tail between my legs, but I have to do this. Ask yourself this: would you want to wake up every morning to what I see? Live my life before you tell me to come to my senses." His voice was assertive, calm, and determined.

"That's fair enough. Tell me what you have in mind."

Brad leaned back against the cushion and crossed his legs. The initial confrontation with Bill now over, he became more relaxed on the inside.

"I want to sell the house. I can't live there, and I'm not going to live there. I'm going down east for a while. Dad grew up down there, and I still have the farm, not that I'm going to start farming. I just don't know where else to go, so I'm going."

"And what on earth are you planning on doing there?" Bill asked.

"That I'm not sure of just yet. I haven't thought everything through yet. I still have to sell the house and take care of a lot of things, but I'm sure I can find something to do."

"What about staying and working at the club? That's the best solution, son. You can sell the house, get an apartment or condo, but don't move. We want you here with us."

"Teach golf? You gotta be kidding me. No way. I'm through with golf. It's the last thing on my mind. I haven't touched my clubs since the Open, and to be honest with you, I'm not even sure where my clubs are and don't really give a damn."

"Okay. What else?"

"Nothing I can think of right now. I'm sure I'll have lots of questions before I leave, so I'll be calling. I won't leave without everybody knowing. I promise. Susan's parents are coming over later so I can tell them. I want them to go through all the things in the house and grab things they might want, like pictures and that kind of stuff. I'm going to rent a storage unit and start moving things into one of those."

"I think this is a mistake, Brad."

"I know you do, but if it is, I need to find out for myself. They're going to be coming over soon, and I need to get back to the house."

Bill and Brad went downstairs. Brad thanked Bill and said goodbye to Martha. Brad then left, knowing how disappointed Martha would be as soon as Bill told her what Brad had come over to tell them.

As he turned into his subdivision, Brad thought he spotted their car just ahead of him. He sped up briefly, finally getting close enough to confirm it was Victor and Rita making their way to the house. He was right behind them as they turned down his street. He followed them up the drive, pulling under an old pecan tree that shaded whatever was under it or parked nearby. He invited them inside, where they gathered around the table in the kitchen. It had been several months since they had been over to visit and the first time Brad had invited anyone to the house.

"Do either of you need anything to drink?" he asked politely as their eyes wandered about, obviously noticing the drastic changes around the house. There were taped-up boxes scattered around, with labels neatly detailing the contents.

"No, nothing for me," Rita finally answered, turning back to Brad and nudging Victor, who shook his head no.

"I need to talk to you both about some things I've been thinking about. I asked you to come here because I always feel so intimidated when I need to speak about something serious, and that's not the fault of either of you. It's mine, and I know that." Brad had meant to be amusing but missed the mark completely. "I'm selling the house and moving."

"But—" Rita started to say.

"Please let me finish. This is hard enough. Just please let me get it out, and you can ask all the questions you want. I promise."

Victor looked at his wife and patted her knee. Her expression was one of confusion, but Victor told Brad to continue.

"Thank you. I grew up in this house and watched my mother pass away here in the same room I shared with Susan. My father and I survived by leaning on one another until he died and I had the luck of meeting Susan. Susan and Will made this a home again ... they made it our home. For nearly seven months, I've been here alone. Alone by choice, but I would've been alone no matter who was here. I've been alone with all of them. My mom, dad, Susan, and Will. I've been alone with them and their ghosts and all of the memories I have of them. I'm living with their ghosts, and it's more than I can take. I want you to follow me for a minute. I know this seems silly, but please just indulge me."

They all stood, and Brad led them around the house. He stopped at picture after picture and never had to say a word. He had left the pictures up to help make his point. It was like the world shut down around them, and they all relived the memories of those pictures. They could recall the conversations that had taken place around each picture. Brad could still smell her perfume; he could remember everything, and so could they. It was not one thing or the other; it was all of them as a whole. He watched her parents and waited. He invited them to come back over and sit down. Rita laid her head on Victor's shoulder while he wrapped his arm around her. It was clear they understood how Brad felt.

"I'm sure you've seen the boxes, and the only things in them are trivial things that mean nothing to anyone but me. I wanted you to come over so you could take anything you want. I'm sure there are pictures you'd like to have. Just take whatever you want. What you leave I'm boxing up and moving to the storage unit. I've gotta get out of here. I can't do it anymore."

"Where are you going?" Victor asked.

"I'm going to the small town where my dad grew up. The only person there that knows me is the guy that looks after the farm. I won't have to answer the same questions over and over. I don't have to stare at things that remind me of what my life was like or wonder how it could have been."

"What'll you do?"

"I have no idea. I really don't. Hopefully I can find something."

They sat in awkward silence, all knowing there really wasn't much else to say.

It would take Brad almost a week of constant loading and unloading his truck. One trip after another to the You-Rent-It storage unit facility had been grueling, but the task was complete. He was left with nothing more than the basic essentials he would need to take with him. He met with Vicki Culpepper, the real-estate agent that Bill had told him to use. She would handle anything that pertained to the house. She knew landscaping and cleaning services, and she would handle everything while trying to sell the house. It was one less thing to worry about, he thought while booking his hotel room. He reserved a room at the closest place he could find to the family farm, not that there were a lot of choices.

Chapter 14

Brad loaded a couple of suitcases into his truck and hung a garment bar for his hanging clothes. He went back inside to take one last look around. It was the only home he had ever known. First with his parents, then with Susan and Will, it was the only place he had memories that mattered. It was finally time to leave, and his intention was to make sure he had not left anything, but he lingered in each room. He closed his eyes, and his mind raced backward. It did not matter what room it might be, images reluctantly overwhelmed his mind and body. He watched them as though someone was standing on his chest, forcing the air from his body. The pressure rested squarely across his sternum, and he tried to breathe slowly to relieve it. He came to the den first, which was an open area where he had no reason to linger but did anyway. Because of the Christmas that had just passed, his mind pictured a tree from when he was a child. He could see his mother decorating it, and of all the things he could have remembered, his mind could only wrap itself around two. He remembered making popcorn in an old metal popcorn maker his parents had received as a wedding present, and then with his mother, making strings with the popcorn and decorating the tree while sharing the leftovers. He could remember the Christmas when, at age five, he received his first set of golf clubs from Santa Claus. He watched himself as if watching a movie. He watched his parents smiling and holding hands as he squealed in absolute delight as he opened his gift.

His memory accelerated to the Christmas only one year prior, watching Will opening his last present. Brad, with Susan's permission, wanted this gift to be from him and Susan and not from Santa Claus. He saw himself struggling to hide his smile as Will tore through the wrapping paper to realize it was his own set of clubs, and he, like his father, squealed with pleasure. Brad had kissed her quickly before young Will ran as best he could for a child of his age to interrupt his parents' little moment. Brad was thrilled his son was as excited as he was.

Part of him now wanted to smile, part wanted to cry, and part wanted to take a golf club and start smashing the walls of the empty room. It would do no good, and he knew it as he made his way to the kitchen where other memories waited for him.

Whichever memory he relived determined what else he recalled. When he watched his mother cooking dinner for him and his father, he watched her at the stove and how she greeted his father upon his arrival. The food she prepared flooded his senses and thrust his mind forward to a memory of him cooking for his family. He could see Susan getting their son settled down and then joining Brad in the kitchen and Will always coming in at just the wrong moment, causing them to laugh at his inexplicable ability to come in wanting to show mom and dad something precisely when they were trying to steal a second of intimacy.

He walked down the hall and reached his son's room first. The door was the only one on the left side of the corridor. He could see Will asleep in his bed, a sight he didn't want to think about, so he shut the door, hoping it might end his thought, but that was not going to happen. His memories of Will were like those of all the people he had lived with here. Some were joyous, some amusing, and some were sad. He walked into the master bedroom and wanted to cry. His mother died in this room, and he hadn't slept there since returning without Susan in June. A sofa in his office had served as a bed, and he used the hall bathroom to shower. He avoided their room for all he was worth. He could not sleep without her next to him. He slept only when his eyes were too heavy to stay open any longer.

He grabbed his carry bag, the only item left, lying next to the door. He draped the strap over his shoulder and turned the brass knob, allowing his exit from the house. He paused a moment, realizing this would be the last time he opened or closed this door. He knew it needed to be done. He checked to make sure he had secured the lock and then deliberately shut the door. It rattled as he tugged at it, making sure it was tight, and then walked down the driveway to his truck. Halfway down, he paused and reached for the collar of his worn leather jacket and pulled it upward to cover his exposed neck. The January day was overcast, windy, and cold, but the forecast predicted sunnier skies once east of Raleigh. Once he reached his truck, he crammed the small bag in the passenger's floorboard and walked his way around the front, never looking up. He opened the driver's side door and pulled his body in to the cab. He grabbed his sunglasses from the console. He then took the seat belt and pulled it across his chest until it was tight and checked his mirrors. He had nothing but clothes stuffed everywhere there was room. He turned the key, and the engine rumbled to a start. The tinted glasses turned toward the empty house and then back. He pulled down on the handle until the dash displayed he had made it to D. His foot lifted off the brake, and the truck tumbled forward. He was moving forward to something new, he hoped. He prayed it would be something new, a new life, as he went to the end of the road and turned around in the semicircle of the cul-de-sac and made his way past his house, this time not giving it a last look.

The three-hour drive would start on an interstate bustling with cars zipping past him. As he entered it, he was greeted with a wall of bright red taillights filling every lane he could see. He waited cautiously until one kind person was nice enough to let him merge. He waved gratefully as he positioned his vehicle in the stream of traffic. Brad could not decide if his pace was one of contentment or fear as he watched a frenetic pack of the cars zipping past him. The interstate eventually led to a smaller highway, and the traffic and pace lightened, as did the skies. Just past Clayton, he took Highway 42, which was nothing more than a two-lane road. The drive was uneventful if not boring, but he was heading to a new life, and that kept him focused. The road was lined with trees barren of leaves, save a few pines that grew among them. The sun was now bright and below any clouds that were left, making its afternoon descent. The rays fired bright flashes through the scattered thickets of trees. Brad fiddle with the visors as best he could. He was occasionally distracted by a house here and there; each seemed to have a gathering of one sort or another. The number of people varied from place to place, groups mostly made up of older men attired in work clothes. He guessed they must be farmers gathering to discuss the always-dim prospects for the upcoming season. Brad laughed before catching himself. If they only knew what dim prospects were, he thought.

The town of Kenly was where his father had grown up as the son of a local farmer. The city limits focused around Highway 301, which had been rendered basically useless since Interstate 95 plowed its way by the edge of the town. Businesses once thrived up and down the highway until it came by and made a nearly twenty-mile stretch from Kenly to Wilson a modern-day ghost town. The 1,500 residents for the most part had no opinion about the effect it had on their town because their main concern was farming, and Kenly did only as well as its farmers fared.

The Kenly Inn sat right off the main street, if it could be called that. The town had only one stoplight, and that seemed an excess. The inn, as it was known, was the converted log cabin home of Hinson Scott, the town's most successful farmer at the turn of the century. The cabin itself actually predated the Civil War and had been purchased for nearly nothing, as it sat rotting for years as the Scott family moved into more rural locales as the town grew closer to their original homestead. The tobacco barns and chicken houses behind it had been renovated, and an even dozen hotel rooms had been made from what was left of them. Hinson Scott's old house was now the main lobby and housed the town's only upscale restaurant, and "upscale" was pushing things for anyone who had ever been to a metropolitan area.

The atmosphere was quaint and what would be expected in such a location. The lighting was just dim enough to provide the privacy for those looking for it and not so dark that a dinner party would be uneasy trying to converse and socialize with the members of their group. The menu was limited, but what was served was of the finest quality. The inn had a very loyal following of the town's small upper crust, a surprising number of people from bordering counties, and Wilson's large tobacco market. They needed somewhere nice and nearby to entertain their big-money clients.

The inn had been the brainchild of a local self-made man. This was one of many different business interests for him, and like this one, all had been successful. He was a childhood friend of Brad's father. Brad unknowingly chose the inn based on nothing more than its proximity to his family farm.

The gravel grinded, cracked, and rattled under the rubber of his tires. He carefully pulled up to a small wooden sign that denoted where guests should go to check in. The ride had left him a bit stiff but no worse than any other trip of that length normally left him. As he opened the glass door, he entered a small, open area used as a duel lobby for both the inn and its restaurant, which sat to the far right of the front desk. The lobby was decorated with farmhouse antiques. It did not matter if they were furnishings or tools; nothing strayed from the theme.

A cherub-faced woman at the highly glossed, solid oak counter that served as the front desk greeted Brad. She was short and had a thick build and rosy cheeks from the obvious overuse of rouge. Her brown eyes were sharply contrasted and framed by a week's worth of blue eye shadow. Her smile was wide, and her demeanor gushed with enthusiasm, and he was removed from the distraction that her less than perfect makeup presented.

"Welcome to the Kenly Inn—or the inn for short!" she exclaimed with a thick North Carolina accent. "How can I he'p you?"

"I have a reservation. It should be under Ford."

She rifled through a small box containing three-by-five cards and quickly found it.

"Got it right here. For five nights. Is that correct?"

"Yes, ma'am."

"Oh, please don't call me ma'am, sugar. I don't wanna feel any older than I already am. Cash or credit, honey? Hey, Mr. and Mrs. Sutton, how are ya'll doing this afternoon?" She was temporarily distracted by an elderly couple passing through the lobby and heading toward the restaurant.

"Oh hey, Darlene ... doin' good. Hope you are."

"Doin' just great. Thanks for askin'. Sorry about that. They're regulars over at the restaurant."

"No problem at all ... I'm paying cash. Restaurant must be pretty good, I guess?"

"Oh, the food's just great. I love it. I bet I've gained twenty pounds working here!" She laughed. "Here's a menu. You can come in or order in, and they'll deliver to your room. Just give 'em a ring."

"Okay. Thank you very much."

"You're so welcome. Here's your key, and if you need anything else, just call me. I'll be here until eleven. Hope you enjoy your stay."

He took the key, politely smiled back at Darlene, and then went out and hopped back in the car. His room was in the first building behind the restaurant at the far end, with a black metal two on the door. He grabbed his travel bag from the seat and headed to the door. He found it to be a typical room with the bathroom just inside the door and a small closet space with an iron and ironing board positioned inside it. There was a queen-size bed and nightstand where the phone was located. In the corner there was a mini-fridge, and the heating unit was located by the room's only window. A four-legged table and chair served as a desk of sorts, and the television sat on top of a dresser directly across from the bed. The walls were decorated with old prints of the town and what the Hinson Scott farm looked like back when the Scotts had resided there.

He tossed his bag on top of the desk and flopped down on the bed. Because of his proximity to the restaurant, the pleasant smells had filled his nostrils, reminding him he had not eaten at all that day. He began leafing through the trifold paper menu Darlene had given him. After a few minutes, he decided he would give the place a try. He fumbled around his room, putting away the contents of his travel bag, and headed back over to the restaurant. He had not spent an hour in his room and came out to a parking lot full of cars and a line of people already waiting to be seated. He stopped at the front desk to see Darlene.

"Is it always like this?" he asked her.

"Sure is, sweetie, but like I said, if you want something sent to your room, you'll likely get it a lot sooner than if you wait around for a table. Sorry about that. I should have warned you. Hope you're not mad?"

"Oh no, not at all. I'm not a big fan of eating alone in restaurants, so eating in the room is fine."

"Well, I can understand that. Know what you want?"

"Yeah ... I mean, yes, ma'am."

She squinted, reminding him about not saying ma'am.

"Sorry, Darlene. Yes, I know what I would like."

"It's okay. I know you're just trying to be polite. Here ... take this, and write down what you want and how you want it, and I'll make sure they get it. You can pay for it when they deliver it to your room."

After writing down his order, he thanked Darlene and walked over just to take a quick peek inside. People had filled every seat at every table, though not that many tables were available, maybe twelve to fifteen Brad estimated. Voices drowned out other voices, creating a dull roar throughout the tables, while waitresses and busboys hustled from one group to another. A large black man went around shaking hands with the patrons and calling to those he knew by name. He looked vaguely familiar, Brad thought, but he was too tired to give it much thought.

Twenty minutes later, the knock at his door surprised him as he thumbed through the channels with his remote control. He glared through the peephole to see a busboy already there with his food.

"Wow, that was pretty quick. Just keep the rest."

"Oh, sir ... I almost forgot. Mr. Dub said to give this to you." He reached in his apron pocket and pulled out a folded piece of paper with *Brad Ford* scribbled in block letters on it.

"Thanks," Brad answered with a perplexed tone and retreated to his bed. He had been eager to eat, but now the note was his priority. He placed his tray at the end of his bed and sat down and unfolded the note.

Brad,

If you're the son of Frank Ford, I was a childhood friend of your father. Meet me at the Gas and Grill at 7:00 a.m. tomorrow if you have nothing else planned. If you can't make it, please let Darlene know. If you can, she can tell you where it is. Hope you enjoy your dinner.

Kindly,
Dub Barnes

He called Darlene to confirm he would be there and to arrange a wakeup call. Darlene promised to write down the directions and leave it under his door when she left work later that night. He hung up the phone and finally turned his attention to the food he had been ignoring.

Chapter 15

It was the loudest ring Brad had ever heard a phone make, and it startled him greatly from a deep sleep. He stood slowly, trying to focus his groggy eyes, and his feet were greeted by the soft fibers of the carpet. He yawned and stretched before his head turned enough to find the envelope lying by the front door just as Darlene had promised. He had fifty minutes to ready himself and did not want to be late. The coffeepot in the bathroom would have to wait for now. He turned on the shower and waited for the water to heat up.

He showered, shaved, and brushed his hair and teeth and threw back on his faded jeans and a college sweatshirt. He grabbed a jacket from the closet and slid his loosely tied sneakers on. He locked the door to his room and headed to the lobby to drop off a thank-you note for Darlene. He was only a block away, so he could slow down for a moment.

The Gas and Grill was just past the stoplight and was easily visible once at the intersection. The painted cinderblock building was surrounded by cars on all sides. People were flying all around, grabbing coffee, gas, cigarettes, and newspapers before trying to get to their jobs or school. Others with more time made their way into the café for a to-go order or a sit-down breakfast. It was organized chaos, but everyone seemed to know the routine, including the customers.

Brad had thought on and off the previous night, trying to recall a "Dub" Barnes but just simply could not do it. With everything else he had on his mind, he had trouble recalling much of anything. He stood just inside the door, and as much as he could without being in anyone's way, he looked around to see if there might be a familiar face, but no one caught his eye. A waitress approached as he scanned the room.

"You need something, honey?" she asked as her jaws pounded away at a piece of gum. She startled Brad with surprise to the point that he flinched.

"Oh, dear, you need to relax," she cackled. "Didn't mean to scare you." Her flaming red hair startled Brad as much as anything.

"I'm just looking for someone."

"Well, who you looking fer?"

"Dub Barnes."

"He ain't here yet, honey. He expectin' ya?"

"Yes, ma'am."

"Well, ain't you all nice and polite, and kinda cute for a city boy ... if you're a woman that likes her man all clean-cut." She laughed. "See that booth over thare? That's Mr. Dub's booth. Sit yerself over thare, but don't a sit facin' the door; that's his side of the booth, sugah."

"Thank you very much," Brad answered.

"You're welcome. Now git on over thare, and I'll be thare directly. Want coffee?" He nodded yes, and she winked at him. Then she shook her broad hips over to a booth full of older gentleman and proceeded to flirt shamelessly with them.

Brad had just made himself comfortable when the imposing figure of the same man he had seen the night before came from around the corner to his right and stopped at the counter next to the register.

"Mornin', ladies. How ya'll doin'? Everyone gettin' looked after?" His voice boomed a deep resonance over the noise of plates and ringing phone lines and conversations taking place at each of the crowded booths and round tables.

"Yessir, Mr. Dub, they sure are," the cashier gleefully and proudly answered the man.

"Well, good ... excellent!" His smile broadened with approval as he reached the booth. Brad stood up, and at once he recalled who he was there to meet as he extended his right hand to greet him.

"Sit back down, son. Damn, look at you all grown up! Makes me feel old as dirt," he said as he continued smiling.

"How are you, Mr. Barnes?" Brad responded.

"Doin' good, Brad. Doin' just fine. Any better, and I couldn't stand it." He laughed and began studying Brad. "What in the world are you doing in our little town?"

The truth was Brad had not spent a night in Kenly since his father passed away. He had driven through from time to time when he was in the area, just to check on the farm and house he leased to a young farmer and his family. It was just something else he received when his father passed away, and he avoided coming unless he was close because it was a reminder of how much he missed his father.

"I just needed to get away ... I needed a change, and this seemed to be as good a place as any to come for a change," he answered hesitantly.

"Still playin' golf?"

"No, sir."

"I was sorry to hear about all of that. I'm really at a loss, and that don't happen very often. I can't even imagine."

"Thank you. I miss them very much."

"How long are you staying? What are your plans?"

"Well, I was planning on staying here ... at least for a while. I need to find a place to live and a job, but I want to stay around here if I can work it out."

"Really? Hmm ..." Mr. Barnes leaned back and folded his arms across his wide chest. He let them rest on his protruding midsection as the gum-chomping waitress came over with their coffee.

"Thank you, Donna Jo."

"Yur welcome, Mr. Dub. Ya'll ready to order?"

"Usual for me. Brad, are you ready?"

She smiled at Brad. "Yeah, how 'bout you, cutie?"

"Could I get a BLT on whole wheat ... not toasted please?" he asked as he looked at the tabletop and then his host.

"Well, honey ..." she paused and stared until he looked at her, "you can git anything you want. I thought you would have figured that out by now." Her hand ran across the back of his head.

"Donna Jo, that's enough now! Leave the boy alone and try to behave yourself!" Mr. Barnes warned her sternly.

"Awright, awright ... sorry. I'll be back in a few," she said and then left to fulfill their order.

"Sorry about that. Don't pay her any mind. She flirts with everyone, and most of the men love it, but sometimes she tends to go a little too far, if you know what I mean." They both laughed, and whatever tension she caused was broken.

"So tell me, my young friend, what kinda job are you lookin' for?"

"I really don't know," Brad answered. "I hope you appreciate my honesty, because I know that this is going to sound odd or lazy or God knows what, but ..." Brad paused, trying to find a way to make what he was about to say sound better than it should, quickly realizing that he wouldn't be able to dress up what he was about to admit.

"With my father's blessing, I've always played golf. When I wasn't in school or helping him around the house, he let me play and practice as much as I wanted, and I loved every second of it. He never forced me, mind you; I wanted to play. I realize, thinking back on it now, he probably let me choose to do what I wanted to do because Mom was gone, and I think there was some guilt on his part—for what reason, I have no idea. Please don't get me wrong. I wasn't a bad kid. I never got in trouble, made good grades, was polite, no drugs, only a beer here and there to seem like the rest of the people I went to school with, but I never wanted to disappoint my dad.

"I know I'm rambling, and I'm sorry, and to answer your question, I just don't know. I've never had what would be considered a real job."

"Well, that's certainly honest, but your daddy did a fine job with you, and you just proved that."

"I know whatever I get will be a bottom-rung, entry-level start, and that's okay. I would expect that of someone I would hire, and I don't expect anything else. Golf is the only job I've ever had, and based on expectations and my results, I would say that my job performance to this point in my life would be considered mediocre at best."

"That's enough honesty for one day. Damn, Brad, we've gotta work on your self-esteem."

Donna Jo was back with their food. She smiled at Brad as she served them but managed to behave herself.

Mr. Barnes immediately began thrashing his over-easy eggs up and then thoroughly mixing them with his side order of grits. He took his knife and cut up the two fresh pieces of sausage into small bits and then added generous amounts of salt, pepper, and hot sauce and again mixed it all together.

Brad watched Mr. Barnes intently as he reached to yet another smaller dish next to his plate that had four slices of toast stacked on it. He grabbed the top slice and layered the mixture across the crunchy surface, and with the vigor of a man who had not eaten in days, he took a large bite.

"Mmm, mmm ... damn that's good! Almost as good as my grandma's. I've got a bunch of these places, but no one makes breakfast like Miss Mary. My grandmother is how I met your daddy. She watched over us during the summer while the rest of my family helped with the work on your grandfather's farm. Sorry, I'm running off at the mouth."

"You eat your breakfast just like my dad did."

"Ain't another way to eat a good breakfast, is there?" He grinned as wide as possible while devouring a mouthful of food. He finished his bite and said, "How's the sandwich?"

"Best BLT I've ever had," Brad replied once he had managed to choke down his first taste of his order, as the excess mayonnaise and part of the tomato fell onto the plate under his chin.

"Good. Miss Mary will be very pleased."

"You said you had a bunch of these places?" Brad asked.

"Yeah, twenty-five of them ... all about like this, more or less," he answered between bites. "This is the first, though. It was an old gas station I worked at when I got out of high school. I couldn't afford to go off to college, though your family offered, so I went to work for Henry Watson pumping gas and learning how to be a mechanic.

Ended up being his head mechanic, and when he was ready to retire, he offered me a chance to buy the place."

"So how did a gas station turn into this?"

"Good question, and it was nothing more than good fortune. Did you happen to notice any of the people around here before you sat down with me?"

"Well, I noticed how busy it was, but I'm not sure what you're asking me."

"Just think about it for a minute and take your best guess," Mr. Barnes said.

"Well ..." Brad paused and thought back to what he had witnessed as he arrived. "People were getting gas, food, some went inside the store and grabbed coffee and cigarettes, maybe a drink. Everybody was doing something or getting something."

"Not bad at all, but this was my thought. I would come to work every morning and stop for a bite of breakfast. The same folks I saw eating would then come get some gas from me. Then someone smarter than me opened up a convenience store that sold gas and drinks, cigarettes and nabs ... anyway ... Okay, why not have everything in one place so they don't have an excuse to stop somewhere else? That's what I asked myself, and then I hired Miss Mary. You gotta have someone that can cook, and that little woman can cook like no one else around here—and boom ... I was off to the races."

"That was pretty clever. And you decided to just start putting them everywhere?"

"Not clever at all. I thought it seemed pretty damned obvious, and no, not just everywhere or anywhere. I talked to people, bought a few places out, and got 'em running better, but I took my time deciding where to put each one. I'm sure I'm boring you, just wanted to brag a bit. Hope you didn't mind?"

"I'm not bored at all. I think it's great how well you've done. I admire self-made people. How's your family doing?"

"Oh hell, Brad, if you wanna hear me brag ..." He laughed and finally polished off the last of his food.

"Sure I do. Go ahead and brag. I would've loved to have made my dad proud."

"I'm sure you did. Well, let's see, my oldest is my daughter, a doctor in Charlotte. She's married and doing well. My son just made partner in some big, fancy law firm in Atlanta and is married as well. We got two grandchildren, one of each. Life's been really good, Brad, it really has." He finished his coffee and told Donna Jo to bring him a cup to take with him.

"What do you have planned the rest of the day? Are you busy?" he asked Brad as he waited for his coffee.

"Well, I need to grab a paper and go through the want ads and start looking for a place to stay, a job, and go by the farm and check things out."

"Well, why not spend the day with me?"

"Oh I couldn't. I would just be in the way."

"Nonsense. I'll be glad to have the company and show you around. It's my little world, and I promise we won't stray far. I like having all my businesses close by. Nothing I own is more than thirty or so minutes from right here. I've got all I need and then some. If you get bored, I'll bring you back." He swatted Brad across his shoulder with one of his massive hands.

"Sure, why not, but I need to grab a paper before I forget about it. Oh, and I guess I just pay at the counter for my sandwich?"

"Gimme that ticket!" he demanded as he snatched the thin piece of paper from Brad's hand. "I invited you, and I'm paying. It's my treat. Now go get your paper, and I'll pick you up at the hotel in a few minutes."

Brad agreed and looked around for a newspaper stand but found Donna Jo first. He reached in his pocket, grabbed a five-dollar bill from his money clip, and held it in his hand as he approached her.

"Where can I get a newspaper?" he asked her.

"You can find one in the store, sugah ... and you can have me anytime you want, and I mean that. If you're all friends with Mr.

Dub, I damn sure won't say a word to him, you pretty thang," she whispered in his ear.

"Miss Donna ... I appreciate it more than you know. I hope you have a great day. Thanks for being so nice," Brad said as he handed her the bill and then started heading to the store for a paper.

"You just remember where you can find me."

He smiled back and nodded to her. "It will be hard to forget where you're at, Donna Jo."

The large pickup truck was already waiting as he was unlocking his door and dropping the paper off. He quickly locked everything back and pulled his thin frame up into the cab where Mr. Barnes awaited. News talk radio blared from the speakers as the two of them pulled away.

"Damn, what the hell took you so long?" he demanded.

"Had trouble finding a paper, sir."

"Oh all right ... I was afraid Donna Jo might have had you treed. She has something of a reputation, I guess you would say."

"I'm sorry ... treed? I'm not sure what you're saying."

Mr. Barnes bellowed a deep laugh from his belly and turned to Brad and smiled.

"Well, it's a term used in hunting, Brad. When a hunting dog has cornered something or chases it up a tree, it's called treed, and seeing how Donna Jo was dogging you over breakfast, I thought she might have treed you." He laughed harder.

"Oh, I got you. No, sir, Donna Jo didn't have me treed, but I did thank her for the service. I bet she's a good employee."

"That she is, but you watch yourself."

"Yes, sir."

As he drove, he explained to Brad his daily routine. He visited all his businesses every day, Tuesday through Saturday. He would come by on a Monday just to keep everyone on their toes and never worked on Sunday. "That's God's day, and that's Momma's day. I make her put up with me all day on Sunday." They shared a laugh.

"Any of the vendors who call on us have to meet me at my office and schedule an appointment. Hell, I'm doing them a favor, and I'll see 'em when it suits me."

"Where's your office?"

"Back at the grill. I've got a little office down the hallway by the bathrooms. It's right across from the kitchen. I usually have my breakfast in there unless I'm meeting someone, like today. Miss Mary will bring it over as soon as she has it ready. To be perfectly honest, the ladies that run my places spoil me better than my wife ... but of course I'm paying them." His smile was greeted by Brad's laughter.

"The office ain't nothin' fancy, and I wouldn't want it to be. Fancy just ain't my style, if you know what I mean. The hardest thing about what I do is finding good people. With convenience stores and restaurants, it's a pain in the ass to find and keep good help, so I just have to make sure I don't give 'em a reason to wanna leave, and I've been mighty lucky ... very little turnover."

Mr. Barnes did most of the talking while he drove the two-lane back roads that made up most of rural Wayne, Wilson, Johnston counties. Each place they visited was much like the last one. The common element to each was the location. Mr. Barnes had picked crossroads for all of them and had either bought out existing businesses and then bought the adjoining corners at each one to eliminate potential competition and in some cases for additional parking. His busiest store was near a local high school, and there was not a single place for anyone associated with the school, students or teachers, to stop within five miles. People appreciated home-cooked meals for breakfast and lunch, and Dub Barnes had made a fortune giving them just that.

"Each place has gas, food, and sundries ... you know, the odds and ends sold at places like that. Hell, I sell enough gas at each place to pay all the bills—and I do mean *all* the bills! Every dollar spent on something other than gas is nothing but profit," Mr. Barnes told Brad.

"You've gotta be kidding me?" Brad said.

"I don't bullshit when it comes to money, son. Pardon the language. I take care of my people, and I mean *people*; they ain't employees. They're my people. You know what I'm saying? 'Cause there's a big difference." Brad nodded but wasn't sure what he was talking about for sure. "You see, Brad, my company gives health and dental insurance, bonuses, and a retirement deal. Grandma told me a long time ago that no one could out-give the Lord, and I've always believed her. You gotta look after people, and God will give you what you deserve."

Brad turned quickly and looked out the window. He wanted to know what he had done to deserve what he had been dealt. He tried to hold his tongue but couldn't.

"Yes, sir, but I think it's time to take me back ... sorry."

"Something wrong?" Mr. Barnes asked.

"With all due respect, and I truly mean that, it's probably not a good time to chat about the good Lord," Brad answered coolly. "The 'good Lord' may have been good to you, but he's forgotten about me. You really think I deserved no parents, the death of Susan and Will? I'm sorry. I couldn't help myself. That was wrong ... maybe you should just take me back."

"If that's what you want, I will, but I'm gonna give you some good advice from an old man, and I hope you listen to what I'm saying. God don't pick on anyone. Have you had some bad things happen? Hell yeah, you have, but God didn't want those things to happen no more than you did, and if he did, he had a reason."

"Well, all the same, I think I need to go back."

"You're right ... that's my fault. I won't say any more stuff about God but this, and I want you to look at me when I tell you." Brad turned, and Mr. Barnes slowed and pulled off the edge of the road.

"I don't expect you to believe me. I've been a lucky man, and I think God's the reason, and you haven't been so lucky, and I understand how you can think like that, and that's fine, Brad, it really is. I do think deep in my heart that God gives us only what he thinks we can handle. I know you're gonna think I'm full of shit, and that's fine too, but I think God thinks you're stronger than me. Have you ever looked at things like that? Have you ever thought maybe God has bigger plans for you than he ever did for me? Just spend a couple of more hours with me?" Mr. Barnes asked with a pleading tone.

"Okay, but no more of that ... I'm glad you feel the way you do; just don't be expecting the same from me."

"That's fair enough," Mr. Barnes answered calmly. "So, changing the subject, all that stuff I told you about—money and all—that stays between you and me. Right?"

"I'm not much of a talker to start with, and the only person I really know is Jimmy Kinslow, and he and his family ... well ... they're all the churchgoing types, so I have no one to tell your business stuff to."

"Oh yeah. Jimmy ... I know him. He's a good boy and has a nice family. Hard worker. Keeps your property looking good, doesn't he?"

"Yes, he does actually. I was thinking about giving him the house. I don't want it, and he needs it more than me. I need to talk to a couple of people, but I'm thinking that's what I'll do. That stays in here too, if you catch my drift?" By revealing that, Brad was struggling to apologize to his father's friend without saying he was sorry.

"Understood." Mr. Barnes reached for his coffee and took a long, deliberate sip and slowly placed it back into the cup holder on the dash. "What do you have planned tonight?"

"I guess getting started on the want ads and trying to find an apartment or something like that."

"Can I assume you have a resume?"

"Yes, sir, I do have a resume." Brad smiled, and some of the tension broke.

"Tell you what I'm thinking, if you don't mind my opinion. Let's stop at my next store, and then I'll drop you off. I want a copy of your resume, and you can start calling about apartments. Why don't you write down the addresses and rents, and I'll be able to tell you whether you're getting a good deal for the area. I'll make some calls and see what I can find out. How does that sound?"

"Sounds tempting but no thanks. I've got to do some things for myself. I've relied on people my entire life, and that was one of the reasons I came here. I have to start doing things on my own."

"Suit yourself. I was just trying to help. I like that you wanna do this on your own, but if you change your mind, I'd be more than happy to help. How about this then. Come over for dinner tonight. Momma's making pork chops and gravy, creamed potatoes, collards, and pan cornbread."

"I couldn't do that, but I appreciate your invitation."

"Don't you worry. If you don't want my help, I'm fine with that, but Momma makes plenty, and I wouldn't ask if I didn't want you there."

"Are you sure?"

"Absolutely, and be there at six, or I'll start without you." He pointed his right index finger at Brad and smiled.

"I'll be there, but if Mrs. Barnes doesn't want me there, I'll understand. Just call me, and I'll grab something."

"She'll be excited. I guarantee it, Brad."

Brad spent a couple of hours working his way through the paper. Not all of the time was used searching the want ads. He realized finding gainful employment in eastern North Carolina would be a job in and of itself. He decided that having Mr. Barnes help would be useful. Pride indeed was one of the deadly sins, and accepting help did not mean he was weak. He took a quick shower and put on some fresh clothes and readied himself for dinner with Mr. Barnes and his wife.

They had driven past the house earlier in the day while riding together. Brad had made a mental note of its location, and because of its vicinity to his farm, finding it again would not be a problem. His only concern was being late.

They lived in a spacious two-story house on a lot next to a pond that bordered on being call a lake. It sat nearly half a mile off Highway 581, which, along with Scott Farm Road, was the nearest paved road. The two met to form the apex, and the direction you were coming from determined the choice of roads, but the house could be seen from one direction and then only if you knew where to look.

Brad drove slowly down a path made of dirt and gravel that meandered through separate gatherings of pines, pulling up to a smaller, almost identical version of the larger and apparent main house. He looked around carefully as he stood from his car, surveying the pretty landscape and tranquil setting. Flower gardens dotted open areas of well-maintained sod, and a small, wooden deck sat at the edge of the water with what appeared to be a paddleboat roped to its side. He felt uneasy about the evening ahead and spending it with people he did not know. Brad was uncomfortable around those he did know and he was becoming nauseous with uncertainty. They were strangers, albeit friendly ones with a family history.

His moment was interrupted by the sound of laughter drawing his attention to a screen door inside a two-car garage adjacent to where he was standing. He walked toward the laughter, passing the truck and car housed inside. He climbed the brick steps leading him to the door and heard her humming something that reminded him of a song he had heard at his mother's funeral. He paused briefly and listened as she contently hummed away. He did not hear anyone else. He tapped the brass framing gently with the knuckles of his index and middle fingers, almost hoping no one would hear him, and the humming drew louder as she approached.

"You must be Brad," the small woman with graying hair said. Her face beamed with a sincere happiness he had not seen for a while.

"Yes, ma'am."

"I'm Rachel. Please, do come in. William, Brad's here. How would you like a glass of tea? Sweet tea, mind you ... very sweet," she said as she led him inside their home.

He followed her nervously. The stove was covered with different sized pots and a large cast-iron skillet. Steam rolled off each, drifting upward.

"Oh wow that smells so good!" Brad declared.

"Well, if you think it smells good, wait until you taste it," the now-familiar tone boomed from the room just past the kitchen. "Course she ain't always been able to cook like this, but I gotta say she's come a long ways in forty years." He and his wife shared a loving smile and a gentle laugh.

"Oh hush, William Barnes," she scolded him as he came to her and kissed her on the cheek. "But I'm afraid he speaks the truth, Brad. He'd left me a long time ago if his grandmother hadn't been around to teach me to cook."

"Let that be a lesson to you, Brad. Never marry a woman who needs to learn how to cook a decent meal."

"So you're telling me you would have traded her in for a lesser model that could cook? I find that hard to believe, knowing how smart a man you appear to be."

"Oh, William, I like him already," she said to her husband. Brad smiled at his father's friend.

"I think I better keep an eye on you, my young friend." His grin was wide and approving.

"I guess you found us okay. You take 581 or Scott Farm?"

"No problem. I took 581 like I was going to your store at Polly Houston's."

"Very good. Momma, how long before everything's ready?"

"It's ready now. Why do you ask? Are you hungry?"

"Always hungry, my dear, but I thought I'd show our young guest around if we had a few minutes?"

"Well, I reckon nothing will ruin as long as you don't go getting carried away."

"I'm too hungry for getting carried away. Come on, son, this is her little palace, and she deserves every bit of it and then some," he proudly stated as he looked at her with the same affection his father's eyes bestowed upon his mother when she was alive.

He spent ten minutes giving Brad a quick tour of their house, explaining that they had built it only after their children had left home, a reward to his patient wife who had devoted herself to raising their children and supporting his fledgling business ventures while they outgrew a smaller starter house in a neighborhood made up of the town's "good black folk."

"We better get to the dinner table before I get myself in trouble. We're coming right now, Momma," he bellowed heartily.

He and his wife sat down in their familiar places and instructed Brad to sit across from Rachel. They held hands, and Rachel blessed the food she had prepared, and in unison she and her husband said, "Amen." Brad followed with another a second later.

"You have a beautiful home, Miss Rachel," Brad complimented as he waited for the first dish to be passed his way.

"Why, thank you, Brad. I hope you're hungry. I've made pork chops and homemade gravy, creamed mashed potatoes, collards, and pan-fried cornbread."

"It smells incredible." He slowly started filling his plate, and it was quickly covered with small helpings. The three sat and talked and ate, and Mr. Barnes and Brad each had another helping of everything. By the time Brad had finished, he was bloated and embarrassed at the amount of food he had eaten. He could not help it though; it was something like his grandmother made when he was a small boy.

"Dear, did you ask him?" Rachel asked her husband coyly.

"Ask me what?" Brad said.

"Damn, Rachel ... no! When do you suppose I would've had the time to ask him?" She shot him a less than approving look for swearing at her dinner table.

"Sorry, dear." He turned to Brad. "Did you have any luck finding an apartment and all that?" he inquired.

"No, not really. I'm glad you asked, though. I know I told you I wanted to do this all on my own, but I don't really know the area very well yet, and I wrote some things down and was hoping maybe you would lead me in the right direction. I would really appreciate your help if you wouldn't mind."

"Well, that's what I ... uh ... well, we wanna talk to you about."

"Okay." Brad sat up straighter. Rachel brought them coffee.

"Pecan pie, anyone?"

"Oh no. Man, I'm so full," Brad answered.

"Oh yes, my dear, always. Oh, and how about warming it and a scoop of vanilla ice cream too. You don't know what you're missing, Brad."

"Maybe in a little bit. What did you want to talk to me about?"

"Okay, Brad. Rachel and I talked this evening before you got here. What do you think of my little business?" Rachel placed her husband's dessert in front of him and sat back down.

"What do you mean?" His face belied a puzzled look.

"I don't want you gettin' the wrong impression. I don't wanna get rid of it, but I'm ready to slow down some, and Momma's ready for me to slow down too. The only way I would ever consider doing that is if I knew I had someone I could trust. I know I can trust you. It's almost like fate, Brad. I want someone I can work with and rely on and slowly back myself out a little bit at a time."

"I can't do what you do. You smile and greet everyone. You know everyone. I can't do that. I'm looking for the opposite of what you do. I'm not good with crowds and never have been. You look like the local preacher working his way through a congregation on Sunday morning." Brad stared at the table, his hands nervously rubbing away at his thighs.

"We'll work that part out. Just let me tell you what I'm thinking."

Brad nodded his assent.

"You saw what I did today. I'll take as much time as we need to make sure you're comfortable. I'll make you the general manager or something. You get full benefits, 401(k), and all the normal things. My accountant and I will figure out a bonus structure based on profits. You know anything about computers?"

"A little but not much."

"Not a problem, but I want you to learn. I know I need to update things, and I'm sure that those contraptions will be more efficient, but that's gonna be one of your duties. Not a big fan of 'em myself, but I know times are changing, and we gotta change too. Brad, you can do this. What d'ya think?"

"I'm not sure. I'm afraid I'd let you down, and that's the last thing I want to do."

"If that's all you're worried about, then don't. Good. It's a done deal."

"But—"

"But what? You want a job, and I need some help. You ain't gonna let me down. I won't let you, and if that's your only concern, then this is a done deal." Mr. Barnes laughed with approval and smacked his heavy hands down across the table. "Well, good. Now that that's outta the way, come with me. I got something to show you." He slowly rose and then leaned down to kiss his wife on the cheek and thank her for another wonderful dinner. He motioned for Brad to follow him.

"We'll be back in a few minutes."

She smiled her approval.

He led them back through the garage past the cars again until they reached the smaller version of the main house that Brad had parked by when he first arrived. Mr. Barnes reached into his pocket and pulled out a keychain that must have weighed five pounds if it weighed an ounce. He fumbled through the collection, looking for one and only one key.

"I was meaning to ask you about this place. It looks just like your house."

"Momma and I built this place first. We had a couple of reasons for doing it, the first being our old neighborhood was getting bad—and bad fast. The builder had this thing up in no time, and it gave us the chance to get out. I wanted Momma to be here while they built the main house so it would be to her liking. Another reason was I wanted to move my grandmother out here so Rachel wouldn't have to drive over during the day to care for her. She would be here with us, and she deserved all the attention she needed. Since my grandmother passed, it's been sitting empty. The upstairs is nothing but storage, but let me show you around."

"I got to meet her once. I think I was thirteen or fourteen. I was fourteen actually, because it was after Mom died. She spent an hour telling me stories about my dad. It was awesome, and her recall was incredible. She was so feisty, and she was almost a hundred then." Brad laughed as he recalled his only meeting with Miss Mamie Barnes, and then his face, in an instant, became solemn as he thought of his father weeping when he heard of Miss Mamie's passing. He had only seen his father cry twice; the other time was when his mother died.

"Did you really? She was loved by everyone. It only took her a hundred years to be appreciated, but when she turned a hundred, she became the queen of our little town; that's for sure," Mr. Barnes recalled proudly.

They walked together, Brad following him closely and looking intently at every detail of the building. Mr. Barnes walked to an interior door just past the steps that led to the storage upstairs and opened it up. It was an open space measuring twenty by twenty-five feet. The carpet was generic light beige and covered all but two places, a kitchenette and bathroom, which had linoleum. The kitchen occupied the left corner of the room and the bathroom the right corner, just past a mirrored closet and vanity. The corner left of the door was a nook where a twin-size bed fit, and a small curtain could be drawn to hide it from guests.

"Washer and dryer are hooked up in the room we just came from. I'll get you either cable or a dish for a television. Come work for me, stay here, and I'll include it as part of your salary. We can dismiss two issues right now with a yes, and you'll make Momma mighty happy as well." He smiled at Brad.

"Why would you do all of this for me?" Brad asked.

"Because I know the people you come from, and they're damn fine people. They were good to my family when whites didn't have to be good to us. Your family was nice and decent people, Brad. They made not only me but my entire family feel like part of their family. Nobody gave a damn we were black, and I'm sure they heard plenty about it because I know how much your father did when we hung out together after school. He got called a nigger lover and all sorts of shit … pardon my language. Anyway, I know your father, and if my kids had ever needed something, they could have counted on him, so I'm just returning an unused favor." Brad couldn't maintain eye contact, thinking about the praise that was being told to him about his father.

Mr. Barnes tried a bit of humor. "Besides, if I don't start slowing down long enough to take Momma to see her children and grandchildren and a vacation now and again, she's gonna kill me. If you work for me and stay out here, I got nothing to worry about."

"Are you sure I can do this?"

"Damn skippy, my boy. Now let's go tell her." He swatted Brad on the back yet again. Brad's heart began racing with nervousness and fear, but he knew it had to be done. It had taken all of one day to find a job and a home. He would call Bill, Tom, and John tonight and let them know.

Part 2

Chapter 16

As had become routine, Brad woke precisely at 1:15 a.m. He had kept odd hours since arriving there. He opened his cell phone and pressed its red key, ending the constant beeping of the alarm, and let his eyes adjust to the darkness for a moment. His legs straightened, and his arms stretched over his head before he sat up. He finally stood once he was certain his blood flow was adequate and there was no chance of being dizzy from getting up too quickly. He walked over to an old armoire he had purchased along with a few other pieces of furniture at a used-furniture store that he passed on a regular basis. The third drawer down held gym shorts and old T-shirts. He grabbed one of each and a pair of athletic socks and sat down on a spindle-back wooden chair he used to change clothes. His arms crisscrossed his chest and pulled the shirt he had slept in over his head, revealing his broad, muscular shoulders that cut a distinctive V shape to his narrow waist. His stomach was taut and showed the rippled muscles of his torso. His forearms had grown thick, and their veins protruded. He pulled his shorts into place, grabbed his worn pair of running shoes, and sat back. He placed them on his feet carefully and pulled the laces tight and double tied them.

His workout was vigorous, regimented, and daily—save Sundays. Every part of his life was. His routine was spit-shined, polished, and left nothing wasted. His average body had been transformed into a trim and efficient unit. He hardly recognized himself, and no one who knew him would recognize him, and that gave him an odd sense of comfort. He had no desire to be recognized for his old life.

He walked outside, stretched for a moment, and started his run. He had carefully chosen his route. The paths he followed had been worn over the years near the trees that framed the fields of the various farms around where he lived. Tractors, plows, and harvesters had left their marks in the soil and had broken away leaves and branches that left a near perfect, upside-down L shape on the woods they passed.

When he first started his loop, it had taken Brad three months to finally complete it all and nearly an hour to run. Three and half years later, it took him just over thirty minutes on average. On a good day, he could finish in less than thirty minutes, but he never planned on it.

As he ran the paths, the powdery soil splashed from his shoes as they pounded down in rhythm, their impact leaving behind one small, dusty cloud after another. He sprinted for certain sections of his trail, sometimes just to make his lungs burn, force his body to its maximum, and enjoy the cleansing feeling that he was left with. It freed his mind from the things he could not stop thinking about, if only for a while, and the relief was welcome. Other times he would get a spooked feeling. Some parts of his run were lighted and left strange shadows along his way, or he would hear a creature of some kind stirring in the leaves beneath the trees. When he finished, he was drenched in sweat. The shirt clung to his rippled torso, and he pulled and shimmied his way out of it and grabbed a towel to wipe himself off. He maneuvered his way through a preset weight program on a multifunctional device he had ordered one night while he struggled sleeping. He worked his upper body one day and his lower the next. It sat next to a treadmill he had purchased to avoid running during the winter or when it rained. Sleeping had become much less of a chore since he started exercising.

He took a hand towel and wiped away a swath of steam that had formed on the mirror above his sink during the near-scalding shower he had just finished. He never looked directly at himself. He would look at his hair, which was cut so short he could be mistaken for someone who served with the military, or to see what part of his face he was shaving, but he would not look at his own eyes. His eyes told a story to everyone he met. Some saw them as cold, distant, blue dots on his face. Those who knew him saw the pain and loneliness he suffered. A day never passed that he did not think about them, miss them, and ache for her and her touch, her voice, her love.

He wiped a small dab of gel through his short locks until they settled into a place he considered acceptable. Then he grabbed the can of shaving cream. Hot water spewed its way down the drain as the can hissed and curdled, and he applied the foam and began working the razor across his face. Each stroke sounded like sandpaper against wood until his face was acceptably smooth.

His outfit was already laid out from the night before, and in a matter of minutes, he was on his way. He checked the digital clock on the console as he pulled away, pleased that he was already thirty minutes ahead of schedule. The short drive to his office was quiet. The early morning was still and dark, the only light coming from the full moon hanging against a near-black canopy that seemed to glitter. The cloudless sky revealed all its stars. He was alone on the road; the only sound was that of the engine as he made his way down the curling two-lane road. No radio, and he never gave it a thought. He had finally began reading the paper again, but that ended quickly the previous June while reading the sports section. A column by a nationally syndicated golf writer appeared just prior to the United States Open, wondering the whereabouts of the tragic one-round record setter from San Francisco, thus ending his reading. Susan loved reading books, and so Brad began reading. He despised reading in his youth but had grown fond of one author, and one by one he completed them. He scribbled a note to himself to stop by a bookstore and pick up the next one on his list as he arrived at work.

Like his workout, his job was scheduled, predictable, almost regimented. He demanded efficiency from those who worked for him and even more so from himself. Every detail he scrutinized until he had become confident that he had found the best way to handle his duties for Mr. Barnes. Every part of his life was now this way. His orderly ways helped him cope with a life he could not imagine living a few short years ago. His new life had taken shape. It was not the one he wanted, but it was better than the one he had left. He ate the same meals each day. He always had Sunday lunch with Mr. Barnes and Miss Rachel. Her fried chicken was too good to pass up.

It had taken time for him to adjust and learn, but he had done it with hard work, time, and the guidance of Dub Barnes, who had become another father to him. They were very much alike, Mr. Barnes and his father. The day-to-day business operations had all but been turned over to Brad, and at the age of twenty-eight, he was the vice president of Barnes Holdings, Incorporated. Mr. Barnes worked from home, much to the delight of Miss Rachel, thanks to a computer system that Brad, with the help of Miss Rachel, had convinced Mr. Barnes to buy. He reminded Mark, Bill, Tom, and John, when they could manage to get a conversation out of him, that his title made him sound more important than he really was. Their calls were always well intended but also intrusive. He appreciated their concern, but when they pleaded for information, he would cut them off and tell them he was content. Brad Ford was as content as he could be without his family.

He was greeted as always by Rose Grady, the night-shift manager of the convenience store. She had been with Mr. Barnes for ten years. As hard as she tried, Rose always appeared to be twenty years behind when it came to looks and hairstyle. Her hair was big and wide, consuming more than a can of hairspray a week. It thinned her face a bit but did nothing for her waist and hips that were thick from the birthing of three children. Rose and her husband, Lynwood, high school sweethearts, lived a comfortable small-town life. He had worked at the tire factory since he was eighteen, starting as a minimum-wage part-time employee, and was now a shift manager. Their schedules lacked for personal time with each other, but the children benefited from an adult presence at home. They recently upgraded from a double wide to a modular home on an acre of land they had bought a few years back, and they felt very proud of this accomplishment.

"Morning, Rose. How's everything?" Rose was chatting away with Michael Bryant, a deputy sheriff who stopped by for coffee now and again. Brad headed for the coffeemaker, his briefcase and mug in tow.

"Doin' good, been pretty steady." Her gleeful smile never wavered.

"Good. I'll be in my office. What's up, Barney?" Brad smiled as he swatted the young deputy on his back.

"Man, I'll be glad when you get tired of calling me that," the deputy said with some embarrassment while taking the ribbing well.

"Awright, Brad, if you need me to do anything, just give me a buzz," Rose said, referring to the intercom system.

He disappeared around the corner and down the hall to the office he had inherited from Mr. Barnes. The handle of his briefcase had a large keychain attached to it with a carabineer's straight gate used by rock climbers. He had keys for each of the twenty-five places and keys he had yet to figure out what they belonged to. He had begged Mr. Barnes to have one master key, but that idea was shot down, the only one he had not agreed with. Brad decided where there's a will there's a way, and with the help of the local locksmith, he purchased multicolor keys and had them stamped one through twenty-five, making his search for the proper key much easier.

His office, once the private domain of Mr. Barnes, was now his and his alone. The door was a heavy, thick metal door with two separate dead-bolt locks that when wrenched shut thrust solid bolts into a reinforced steel door frame, sealing the room much like a vault. He finally worked his way through the locks and tossed his briefcase on the edge of his neatly organized desk. A multiline phone and a stack of trays with various papers occupied the corners of his desk. The trays each had labels denoting what should be placed in them. A calendar lay across the center of the desk with to-do lists written down and the names and numbers of people who requested return phone calls. He sat his coffee on a stone coaster that he also used as a paperweight and then situated himself in his large leather chair that he had received as a gift from the Barneses. The firm leather had now softened and conformed nicely to Brad's frame as he alone used it. Once situated, he sipped his coffee as his thoughts moved to his daily tasks.

A slight motion on the monitor that displayed the outside cameras caught his eye. He was relieved to see it was nothing more than Barney pulling away. He smiled, amused with himself as he shrugged. He looked at his desk as his mind raced.

Why am I spooked? I've been doing the same thing for nearly four years, so why do I feel like something's not right? Brad thought.

Brad looked at each monitor one by one, but again the one displaying images from outside the building gained his full attention. A shadow moved at the rear of the building near the two smelly dumpsters Southeast Container Services provided. His hand slid slowly to his phone. His finger extended, clicking the speakerphone button, and the dial tone hummed as he readied to hit speed dial and ask the young deputy to return. The shadow slowly came around the side of the building to the lone door that was open at such an early hour. Brad clicked the speakerphone back off as the obscured figure came into the outside light and into focus with every step until finally in the store.

Darnell Watkins lived on the streets, a homeless drug addict. He had been arrested multiple times for drug possession and petty theft. His thievery allowed his drug habit. He came by the Gas and Grill during the night to refill a plastic coffee mug he kept stashed in an oversized pocket on his olive, drab army jacket he had lifted from a military surplus store. The mug was not there tonight, and Darnell was not the same. His constant drug use had left him rail thin. He wore the same clothes every day, and they were covered with dirt and had several worn spots. Through the security camera, Brad watched as Darnell eyed the store closely and twitched. He scratched his neck as he approached the counter where Rose stood. His right hand reached around to the back of his jeans and pulled a gun from the waistline.

"Oh God, please don't shoot me!" Rose said, trembling.

"Shut the fuck up and open it now, bitch!" he screamed at her.

Brad quickly got up, went quietly down the hallway, and calmly appeared out of nowhere. He held his hands in plain sight, slowly approaching. The last thing he wanted to do was startle Watkins and what had to be a nervous trigger finger. He kept the three aisles of merchandise between him and the counter where Rose and her assailant stood.

"Have we got a problem?" Brad asked calmly and then watched as the gun turned toward him.

"Who the fuck you be?" Darnell barked, his hand trembling as he tried to aim it at Brad.

"Well, I kinda run the place, and if you—"

"Are you crazy? I'll kill both of you right now!" Watkins wiped the beads of sweat dripping from his forehead and running down his face like water.

"You're right. I know you could. We both know that, and it would be for a lousy fifty bucks," Brad informed him, his voice and words slow and carefully chosen. He looked at Watkins, trying to connect on some level with him, if gaining nothing more than Rose's safety. Brad's mind was as calm and calculated as his speech. He breathed deeply, refused to show fear, and maintained all his focus on Watkins.

"Let Rose go, and I'll take you to the safe in my office. The safe is in there, and I haven't made yesterday's deposit." His eyes were fixated on the gun and Watkins's eyes. Watkins stared back at him. "You let her go, and it's all yours. Rose won't say a damn thing." Tears streamed from her eyes as she stood shaking. She nodded as Brad spoke, trying to reassure that Brad was telling the truth.

"You betta not be bullshitting me!" Watkins demanded. His arm extended as he took a couple of steps closer to Brad.

"I wouldn't do that, man; I just wanna work this out." Brad remained calm; his nerves were as close to being shattered as they had ever been. All he could think about was getting Rose safely out of the store.

Watkins waved her away with his gun, causing Rose to flinch and gasp. "Bitch, get out now before I change my mind and shoot your fat white ass anyway." She grabbed her pocketbook and raced for the door.

"Lock the doors and let's go," Watkins said.

Brad locked the door, knowing the gun was pointed at his back.

"Hurry up, we don't have all day! How much you got in there?"

"A couple of thousand at least ... sound a little better?" Brad answered, trying to keep his nerves steady. With each passing moment and his fear eating away at him, a rage began to build. The picture in his mind reversed backward like a movie being rewound. In a matter of seconds, he was back at the morgue. When he turned around, he no longer saw Darnell Watkins but the man that killed Susan and Will. He took a deep breath as he watched Watkins glancing about and then back to him.

"Damn right. Now hurry." The gun waved, and Brad led the way to his office.

Halfway down the hall, Brad glanced back to see how closely he was being followed. Watkins lagged behind, looking around, seemingly paranoid.

"Here's my office. The safe is in here." Brad realized it would be his only opening, his only chance. The rage returned as he left the door open halfway. It was a defining moment in time, and Brad knew it. *Seize this moment or regret it forever.*

Brad wedged himself quickly between two metal file cabinets behind his door next to his safe and draped his arms across the top of each. He hoisted his legs upward to his waist, drawing his knees close to his body. Watkins had lost sight of Brad and extended his right arm and hand with his grip wrapped tightly around the handle of the gun. His head leaned forward a bit, looking for Brad, hoping he was opening the safe and allowing for quick access to the cash. Brad saw the barrel of the gun and the hand that was on it and without hesitation reacted. His legs thrust forward, powered by fear, adrenaline, and anger. His feet landed perfectly square on the flat surface of the steel door, slamming it first into Watkins's head and onto the arm and hand holding the gun until it was pinned against the thick, hard corner of the metal door frame. A shot echoed out, its intensity magnified by the walls of the small room. The noise rang in Brad's ears, disorienting him momentarily. The bullet blasted through one of the monitors, shattering the glass and ripping through the guts of it before lodging into the wall. Wires hissed and sparked, and the smell of gunpowder hung in the stagnant air.

He screamed out. Watkins lay on the floor, clutching his shattered arm. The blow he had received to his head gashed open the skin between his temple and eyebrow, and the blood ran freely. Watkins clutched his arm as the pain spread. The screams drew Brad back, and he followed them. He stood over him with no remorse, staring down with hate. His breathing more and more rapid, his heartbeat pumping as if he was running, he used a foot to push Watkins flat on his back while his right arm lay limp. He saw Susan and Will lying dead, and he looked up, trying to calm himself. The gun was on the floor in his office, and he was about to pick it up and finish him off when something inside told him no. He locked the door and looked back at Watkins.

"Shooting you is too easy," he said as he stepped over Watkins. The dust broom leaning against a rack of potato chips caught his eye. Rose had been using it earlier while there were no customers. Brad placed his foot across the cover and began twisting the wooden handle loose from its base. His upper lip twitched as rage consumed him. The solid handle securely in hand, he turned back to him. Watkins had rolled back and with his good hand to his side tried to get to his feet. His blood was beginning to reach his shirt.

Brad raised the handle above his head and without thought began slamming it across Watkins, who instinctively shielded his arms from the blows his back and legs began to absorb. Brad was unrelenting, slamming his current weapon down again and again. Watkins pleaded for mercy and his life.

"Stop, please stop," Watkins begged.

"Don't think that's gonna happen." Brad sneered and then kicked Watkins's crotch. Watkins's eyes opened widely before they rolled back into his head. He groaned as his stomach weakened and then vomited first on himself and then the floor he lay on. Brad's eyes were red, almost aflame with hatred.

"You just puked on my floor, you piece of shit. Ha!" Brad's laugh was hardly one at all. He felt a sense of pleasure from the pain he was inflicting, but he was far from done with Darnell Watkins as he grabbed him by his waist and dragged his ragdoll body through the mess.

"You know something? You're beginning to be a pain in my ass. First you come in here pointing a gun at Rose and me, and then you shoot up my office, and to top it all off, you puked on my floor." Brad paced the floor while he glared at him lying on the ground. What did Watkins deserve next? Watkins's head was bobbling, and his eyes were closing as he struggled to open them back up. Brad placed an empty five-gallon bucket next to a cooler filled with bagged ice. The bag was solid and needed to be slammed against the floor to separate. Brad thought that would be a waste and placed the bag on the broken arm of Watkins and thrust his foot down on the bag. Watkins screamed again. Brad ripped the bag open and dumped half of it in the bucket and then filled it with water. He walked back to Watkins and dumped the icy mixture all over Watkins.

"Oh no … you're not gonna pass out on me! You'll feel all of this. You see, another excuse of a human being just like you killed my wife and son and then killed himself. Well, I'm gonna save you the trouble and do it myself." Watkins coughed and wheezed, unable to mutter a word while Brad watched him and then pulled him to his feet and held him upright by his throat with his left hand. His right hand curled into a tight ball, and his knuckles whitened as he drew his arm back and then fired it with every ounce of his being. His fist fit perfectly between the cheek and jawbones of Watkins, his arm extended fully and the sharp edges of his fist twisting and digging into the side of Watkins's face. The blow delivered enough force that when Watkins hit the floor and his mouth fell open, blood flowed, bringing with it two of his teeth. Brad's rage continued as he dragged him to the door he had been ordered to lock only moments earlier.

He slammed Watkins's face into the glass and then unlocked it and dragged the limp body outside.

Sirens blared off sequence in the background, but Brad was only barely aware of them as they became louder, approaching the store from different directions. His focus was Darnell Watkins and finishing what had been started. Brad turned Watkins over on his back and straddled his torso, his left knee grinding into the broken arm. He grabbed a handful of Watkins's hair, turned his head slightly, and landed another solid strike to his jaw.

"Tell me how you get to live and my wife and son are dead!" He lifted Watkins's head again, but this time he did not let go. He pounded away as blood began splattering, and Watkins's face swelled rapidly.

"Tell me, you sonofabitch! Answer me now!" Sweat dripped from Brad onto Watkins with each punch. Tires squealed to a stop, and sirens blared loudly, penetrating the quiet, still night. He noticed nothing, not even the flashing lights that lit up the darkness. Deputies emptied from both cars and raced toward Brad. He was about to deliver yet another solid strike to the side of Watkins's face when they reached him, grabbing his arm before the blow could be delivered and then pulling Brad off the motionless body.

"Get off of me!" Brad screamed. He sounded almost primal. He spit at Watkins as three deputies subdued him. Brad fought and struggled, using every ounce of energy he had to free himself and get back to Watkins, but it was no use. One deputy handcuffed him and placed him in the back of a patrol car, and the other called for an ambulance and then tended to Watkins.

"Brad, what in the hell just happened?" the deputy asked.

"Fuck off!" The rage was not relenting. It burned deep inside Brad. His face and clothes were splattered with blood. Brad shook his right hand as he seethed. It was swollen and bleeding from the barrage of punches he had landed.

"Handcuffs? You gotta be kidding me! I'm not saying a damned thing to you!"

"Brad, you haven't given me a choice. Damn, man, you could've killed that guy."

"Well, what would you do if he had pointed a gun at you and said he was gonna kill you? Tell me, smart-ass!" The deputy didn't say another word.

Another set of headlights flashed through the glass windows in the patrol car and glared briefly into Brad's eyes. He squinted, trying to ignore the glare and having no interest in who it might be. He still seethed; he wanted to hit Watkins more.

Mr. Barnes turned his lights away from the store and parked. He surveyed the chaotic scene. The ambulance had arrived, and the paramedics were working feverously over a body, but he could not make out who it was. The deputy walked over to Mr. Barnes before he could get any closer.

"Who is it? Who's that on the sidewalk?" he asked, praying it wasn't Brad or Rose.

"Darnell Watkins."

"Oh thank God. What happened? Where are Brad and Rose?"

"Brad's in the patrol car, and I guess Rose somehow got away and called 911."

"What's Brad doing in the patrol car? Boy, you better speak up and give me an answer." The voice carried a hostile cadence, almost accusatory.

"Mr. Barnes, it's not what you think, I swear. When we got here, Brad was—"

"I don't give a damn what Brad was doing, boy! Why's he in the back of your patrol car?" Barnes barked as he walked toward Brad.

"Mr. Barnes, please, when I got here, Brad was pounding that guy. I don't know if he killed him, but he's covered in blood and has cussed me up and down. I ain't gotta a choice."

"Bullshit! Don't expect me to believe that. Now you get the hell out of my way and let me talk to him. Go do what you gotta do."

"I think we should wait until we get to the courthouse."

"The courthouse! What the hell is he going to the courthouse for?"

"Mr. Barnes ... only for a second please. I'm begging you. I swear I'm just trying to do my job."

"Just let me tell him I'm here and right behind you guys."

"Okay, but please no more."

Mr. Barnes nodded his assent.

He found Brad a mess. He was sweating, and his head was rocking back and forth. Brad glared straight down, and his chest expanded and contracted as he breathed deeply. Mr. Barnes watched him, troubled. He tried speaking to Brad but could not get his attention.

"Brad ... Brad! Damnit, boy, I'm talking to you!" Mr. Barnes barked to get his attention. "I'm following ya'll down to the courthouse. Brad, I need you to pay attention to me please." Brad's eyes made their way to his eventually.

"I'm gonna call my attorney, and he'll meet us there. I don't know what happened, and right now I don't wanna know, but don't say another word. You hear me?"

"Yessir!" The one-word answer reeked of sarcasm and a lack of respect and remorse.

Chapter 17

The county's sheriff's department was part of the county courthouse and justice complex. The complex served as the home of the sheriff's department, the county jail, clerk of court, the entire court system, and other odds and ends as they pertained to the county legal system. Located on the corner of Green and Tarboro Streets, it was a massive, two-story, square building that occupied the better part of a city block. Brad was brought in, hands behind his back and tightly handcuffed while he stared at the floor. They led him to a small room across from a grouping of desks and cubicles. The room's walls were stark, with a long table positioned by the wall, opposite a wall that had a dry-erase board and cameras angled down from the top corners. The entire room was covered by them … nothing could go unnoticed.

There was one chair on the side of the table closest to the wall, and Brad was told to sit there. When suspects were questioned, they always sat in the chair against the wall to make sure it enhanced the feeling of being trapped, so that they would know they had but one way out. Two chairs sat across from him. If a fourth was needed, it could always be brought in. A loud click caught his eye … he was locked in, and they wanted him to know it. The click reminded Brad of the lock on his office door.

Mr. Barnes was waiting outside as the deputy returned. His eyes darted the opposite way. He could feel the hostility.

"Mr. Barnes, if I could—"

"Don't you dare try makin' excuses, boy. Did you handcuff him?" He was beyond furious. He stared the deputy down. The deputy's face turned bright red.

"You cuffed Brad like a common criminal, didn't you? That's fine ... don't ask him another question. His attorney is on his way, and I want the sheriff here too! Where's the sheriff? Tell me, boy!"

The deputy stared straight down. "Well, I guess he's at home, sir," he said, cringing.

Mr. Barnes reached into his pocket, pulled his phone out, and scrolled down the list of contacts he had. He had three numbers for the sheriff ... cell, work, and home, and when he got to the line that said home, he hit the send button and placed the phone to his ear. He turned away from the deputy and his panicked expression.

A groggy male voice answered after a couple of rings.

"Sheriff, Dub Barnes here. Sorry to be callin' at such an early hour, but I need you to come down here as soon as possible. Hell yeah, I got a problem. Have I ever called you before? Uh-huh, good, see you then." He closed the phone and turned his attention back to the deputy, glaring intensely until he had the good sense to walk away.

Stanton Williford walked through the double glass doors. He was an imposing figure; his six-foot-five frame announced his presence. He dripped confidence, and even at such an early hour, he looked impeccable. His thick brown hair was parted to perfection, and his dress was clean and crisp even now. A navy blazer, white oxford button-down shirt, gray slacks, and black loafers had been donned, and now he strode confidently toward Mr. Barnes. The only thing missing was his perfect smile, but he was pissed, and so was his firm's biggest client. The handshake was firm, and they were both all business.

"Walker's on his way," Stanton said immediately.

"Good ... you'll want this." Mr. Barnes handed him a briefcase.

"What is it?"

"Videotapes from the store. I grabbed 'em before I came down here. These idiots were so busy they never secured the store ... never even thought about it, so I grabbed them. Oh, and the sheriff's on his way too. Called him right before you got here."

"Good. Where's Brad?" Williford inquired.

"Not sure."

"Well, that's about to change. Follow me, but let me do the talking, okay?"

"That's what I'm paying you for."

Williford smiled, and they walked down the hallway, searching for Michael Bryant.

"Where in the hell is my client?" Williford bellowed.

The deputy, rattled from everything else that had taken place, spilled his fresh cup of coffee all over his desk.

"Where is Brad Ford?" Williford demanded.

"Uh, right here in this room, sir," he stammered and stood quickly. Williford and Barnes continued their approach. The deputy fumbled with his keys at the door, and Stanton stood in the doorway looking at Brad as he sat handcuffed.

"Why is he in handcuffs?" The deputy moved quickly toward Brad.

"I'm just trying to do my ..." The deputy paused. "I think I should just keep my mouth shut until the sheriff gets here. I got nothing to say." He removed the cuffs and slid them back into place on his belt.

"Probably a good idea on your part. Now leave us." Bryant left quickly and quietly.

"Brad, I'm Stanton Williford. I'm an attorney with the firm that handles Mr. Barnes's business affairs. I'm gonna have you out of here as soon as I can. Is there anything I can do for you?"

"A couple of things." Brad reached in his back pocket and pulled out a worn-out business card. The printing was barely legible anymore. "If you would call Bill McKnight, I would appreciate it."

"Okay, what else?"

"Leave Barney alone. He was just doing his job. I was out of my mind ... I'm not sure I'm in my right mind now, but he's done nothing to me. A cup of coffee would be nice too."

"All right, but I don't want you saying another word to anybody without me present. Deal?"

"Deal. I promise."

"Mr. Barnes wants to see you. Is that okay with you?"

"Yes."

"How is he?" Barnes asked as Stanton exited.

"Hard for me to say. I don't know him. He's remorseful, but I still don't know everything that happened. He wants some coffee and for me to call Bill McKnight. Do you know him?"

"Yes, a man he knows from Winston-Salem."

"Is Walker here?"

"Yes, he just pulled up. Sheriff Barrow just got here too. I'll grab some coffee if you can get me in to see him. I'll let you and Walker work things out with the sheriff. I hope we can get this settled quickly."

"Sounds good to me," Williford said as he made his way to Walker White. He shook hands with Walker and the sheriff, and after a brief interlude, he turned back to Mr. Barnes and gave him a slow nod, letting him know that it was okay to go in.

"Couldn't remember how you take it," Mr. Barnes said, trying to smile and not give Brad another reason to worry. He placed the cup on the table with packets of cream and sugar and a stir stick.

"Black is fine, thank you."

"Please tell me what happened." Mr. Barnes didn't want Brad to have to relive it, but he needed to know why Brad was there, and Brad agreed to tell him. He did his best to recall all of it, at least as he remembered. He told Mr. Barnes he noticed Watkins loitering around and then how he pulled the gun on Rose.

"All I could think about at first was getting Rose out of there. I had to do something. I wouldn't have been able to live with myself if I didn't try. I talked him into letting her go, and I saw an opening, and I guess I did what I thought I had to. I really don't remember much after that ... it's kind of a blur. I just reacted ... maybe overacted; I just don't know." Brad looked at the table while he spoke. He looked like he was in a trance. His eyes squinted, trying to recall things, but the harder he tried, the more difficult it seemed. He shook his head, certain that he had done the wrong thing, but as the fog lifted and he remembered more and more, the regret left him.

"Where did all the blood come from?" Mr. Barnes asked as Williford joined them, interrupting their conversation.

"Sorry about that, gentlemen," Williford said.

"No problem. I was asking—"

Williford held his hand up to stop him. "Let's talk at my office once you leave here." They agreed. "Brad, I'm gonna leave. I'm going to be talking with a few people and get you out of here. Just know I'm not going anywhere without you, okay?"

"Okay."

Stanton entered the sheriff's office while Walker and he carried on idle chitchat. They both sat up.

"How's our boy doing?" Walker asked.

"He's fine and has nothing to say. Why is he even here?" he asked as his head pivoted toward the sheriff, who sat in his monstrous chair that was set to sit up as high as possible.

"Good question. Let me round up the deputy who brought him in."

"Well, before you go get him, you might … never mind. Go get him. I'd rather ask him in front of you." Williford stopped himself and smiled at Sheriff Barrow. Barrow's look flashed concern.

"Stanton, do you know who Brad Ford is?" Walker White asked.

"You know, the more I think about it, his name sounded familiar, and when I saw him, he looked familiar, but I can't place him."

"US Open, 1998, San Francisco … Brad Ford shoots sixty-three in the opening round. Walks off the course and finds out his wife and son are murdered."

"You're kidding me? That's him?"

Walker nodded. "Did he tell you what happened this morning?"

"No, but Barnes knows. I'm sure of it. I told them not to talk about anything more until we get to the office. I can't wait to hear what that deputy has to say."

"Don't get ahead of yourself just yet, Stanton. His wife and son were killed by the same kind of guy. Druggie, robbing a place … just play it close to the vest for now," Walker reminded his aggressive partner. "Oh, and just to make your day a little better, Ed's on the way."

"Granville, our illustrious district attorney? What's that spineless twit coming down here for?"

"Not sure. I guess we'll find out soon enough." The senior partner's eyes shifted direction as the sheriff returned with his still-wet-behind-the-ears Deputy Michael Bryant and introduced him to Walker and Stanton.

"We've already met," Stanton said in a low-key voice that relayed his frustration.

"Michael, it's good to meet you. Sorry it's under these circumstances." Walker knew that they would get more from the deputy by being cordial.

"Nice to meet you as well, sir," Bryant said, nervously shaking his hand.

"Quite an eventful morning from what I hear, Michael?" Walker asked.

"Well, for me. Yes, sir."

"How long on the job?" Walker asked, smiling.

"Six months, sir."

"Good for you. I'm sure the sheriff is thrilled to have such a dedicated young man like you working for him."

"Thank you ... not so sure he agrees right this minute." The sheriff patted him on the back, and Bryant continued. "Just never had to deal with anything like what happened this morning."

"Baptism by fire, I take it?"

"I guess so, Mr. White." The sheriff told him to have a seat and pulled the chair to the side of his desk.

"Awright boy, tell us what happened," Sheriff Barrow instructed.

"I saw Brad when he arrived at work. I rotate through all the twenty-four/sevens ... uh, you know, the stores that are open twenty-four hours a day and seven days a week that have a single employee. Brad always gets there early, which is great 'cause it's one less place to worry about. Well, I grabbed some coffee and left. I headed down 301 toward the speedway to check on it when I got the call. I couldn't have been gone more than a few minutes. I turned around down there by the Jones farm offices. Maybe five or six minutes ... I'm not really sure. By the time I got back, Brad was straddling the guy on the sidewalk, just pounding him. Me and the other deputy who responded came up behind him and grabbed him and pulled him away from the guy. Man, that guy's face was pretty fucked up ... pardon my language."

Ed Granville had slinked his way there and joined the story halfway through and was now leaning smugly against the doorway. His short and unimpressive frame was covered with a cheap suit, a worse shirt, and a tie that did not match. The ceiling light from Sheriff Barrow's office gleamed off his bald head as he smiled.

"I just got an update on Darnell Watkins's condition. Serious, very serious." He continued to smile as he relayed the information. "Multiple facial fractures, skull fracture, ruptured testicle. How does a testicle rupture? Anyway, there's more, but I had trouble remembering the rest after they told me about the testicle."

"Well, that figures. Leave it to you to get distracted by a man's balls." Williford couldn't help himself, and the sheriff laughed so hard he had to cover his mouth. Granville, as always, walked right into a barb from Stanton Williford. "And since when did you give a damn about the well-being of armed robbers, Mr. Granville?" Williford's sarcasm continued.

"I won't have vigilantes in this county, Stanton!" Granville shot back.

Walker White stopped another comment that was obvious to everyone in the room and simply grabbed Stanton by the arm and shook his head, telling him to just hold tight a minute. "Stanton, it's okay. I know what he's doing, and that's fine. Patience, my friend." Walker smiled. Walker White knew there was a November election looming, and the primaries were only six weeks away.

"Are you charging Brad with anything?"

"Not yet, and he doesn't need to be going anywhere. We're certainly going to continue to investigate what happened." Granville's faced beamed with an almost orange color. Williford had embarrassed him, but he was confident too, at least for a moment.

Stanton Williford burst into laughter and had to pull a handkerchief from his coat pocket to dry his eyes. He had never lost an encounter with Granville, and he had no intention of this being the first. Williford had no respect for Ed Granville the person and even less, if possible, for him as an attorney. Granville was a politician first and foremost. His soul was for sale to whoever would keep him elected. As the county district attorney, conviction rates dwindled year after year, and the few good attorneys his office had left for private practice, disillusioned with public service due in large part to Granville's incompetence.

The people of Wilson County's confidence in Granville's abilities were sure to have him unemployed, and he saw Brad Ford as his saving grace. Granville would make a martyr out of Darnell Watkins and an example of Brad Ford. He would try to sell this bullshit to the minorities and win reelection. He was convinced of it, and that was fine with Williford, but not using Brad Ford. Williford could have cared less if the idiot won reelection ... it made his job a breeze, but Granville wasn't about to use one of his clients to pull it off ... ever.

Williford's toothy grin glistened as he rose from his chair. "Good luck with your investigation, Ed. My client and I will be excusing ourselves. If you want to talk with him again, call my office, and he'll come down here with me." Williford took a couple of more steps before he turned back. He just had to say one last thing to Granville, and he wanted them all to hear it. "Oh, Ed, just a piece of advice ... you might want to try and get past the testicle thing. I know a man's balls are distracting to you since you seem to lack your own, but you might wanna focus on the facts for a change." He turned and walked away, angry, motivated, and in disbelief that anyone, including Ed Granville, was this stupid and allowed to practice law. Williford was ashamed of the law but only for a moment before he burst into laughter again.

Williford opened the door and peeked his head in. "Brad, Mr. Barnes, we can leave." Brad remained quiet, and Mr. Barnes smiled. Stanton led them out while taking one last look at Granville, one last arrogant smile and then a wink. Granville turned to Walker White.

"That arrogant piss ant! You better reel him in, Walker!" Granville demanded.

"Ed, I'm going to give you some advice, and you take it however you choose to." Walker White's tone was the same as it always was ... calm. "Do not *ever* tell me how to deal with partners of my firm and don't *ever* make me feel threatened." Walker extended his hand, but Granville refused. "Fine, so be it, but you don't want me to consider you an enemy, Ed." Walker smiled and shook hands with Sheriff Barrow and Deputy Bryant and patted Bryant on the back. "Michael, thank you for your honesty and hard work ... keep it up." Walker White had just given Ed Granville a lesson in politics, but Granville was too dumb to have paid witness.

Walker caught up with them in the parking lot as Mr. Barnes was asking Stanton about his conversation in the sheriff's office.

"Let's talk about this at the office. It won't take long," Walker said.

"Did you get in touch with Bill McKnight?" Brad asked.

"I didn't speak to him yet, but my secretary should be available soon. I'll have her call as soon as we get there," Stanton replied.

Chapter 18

The office was a few minutes away, a block past the courthouse. The area had been partially rezoned after its construction, and Walker and his partners had bought a rundown, two-story Victorian home. After three years and more money than they wanted to spend, it was fully restored. It was breathtakingly elegant and the envy of every firm in town. It was white with black shutters, oak floors, and oriental rugs and reconfigured slightly for their use. The wives decorated, disagreed, and decorated more until the project was finally complete.

They parked behind what used to be a garage and was now used for the real-estate section of the firm, which only had one significant asset, Lauren Parker, the divorced daughter of Walker White and the firm's lone attorney who specialized in real estate. Lauren was stunning … striking and beyond modest. Tall, leggy, naturally blonde … every inch of her a perfect match. A paralegal by the name of Barbara Stinson was invited by Lauren to go to the club and spend the afternoon lying out by the pool. She was flattered that Lauren was a friend but made the point that every woman who knew Lauren was very clear about. "Lauren, you know I love you to death, but I'd rather be strapped to a bomb with Saddam Hussein than lying next to you at a pool in a bathing suit."

Doors rattled shut on each of the cars. Stanton followed Walker. Walker wanted the meeting to take place in his office. It was still very early. Lauren and the secretaries for Walker and Stanton were the only other ones there. Walker led them past Lauren's office. Her door was open, and he stopped.

"Morning, sweetheart."

"Good morning, Dad, and good morning to you, Stanton." Stanton smiled, and Lauren could only wonder how his wife put up with him.

Mr. Barnes walked past without a look, but Brad's eyes turned her way as he walked. It took a second or two for his eyes to process the picture they had taken of her. He stopped dead in his tracks.

She too had caught a glimpse of Brad before her attention turned back to the computer. *Something about him, who is he?* A quick shrug, and she made a note in her day planner and went back to work.

Walker White's office was a long and narrow converted sunroom. The back wall was almost all paned glass looking out on a small, well-maintained garden where clients who smoked could sit while waiting for appointments. His desk was nearly as wide as the room, and behind him on the wall was a place for books and a place for a television, much like a family room. He insisted that it stay this way. He was an avid reader, and the shelves were filled with books he had read. When he bought a new book, one was taken down and donated to the city library. He used the spot reserved for the television for just that. Working long hours was never an issue, unless his beloved Tar Heels had a game. Walker White did not miss Carolina basketball games, nor did anyone with the firm, save Lauren. She had finished her undergrad and law school at Wake Forest. At least her tennis paid for part of it, Walker constantly reminded himself. The rest of the firm were all graduates of the University of North Carolina, and they enjoyed themselves immensely in his office, watching the games and ordering takeout from an amazing Chinese place down the street and a beer or two.

Stanton was the last to join them after he checked in with his secretary. "This is your court, Stanton, please," Walker said, motioning Stanton to sit at his desk. Walker joined Brad and Mr. Barnes in chairs across from him.

"How are you doing, Brad?" Stanton wanted to see his client's eyes and hear his voice.

"Just sorry for making all of you go through this."

"So what's the story, Stanton?" Mr. Barnes asked.

"Long story, but the gist of it is this ... Ed Granville doesn't want to let this go, and I'm going to ruin his ass if he doesn't."

"Brad, just let Stanton deal with this. I feel certain all of this will work out," Walker added. The assurances weren't helping Brad feel any better.

"I guess I should have asked you earlier, but do you need any medical attention? Did the sheriff's office ask you if you needed any medical attention?"

"No I don't, and I don't think they asked me. I told you no trouble for Barney. He was just doing his job."

"Brad, please don't get defensive. I need you to trust me. You're covered in blood. Do you remember whether or not you were asked if you needed medical attention?" Williford asked again. Mr. Barnes nodded, and Brad knew he needed to answer. Williford had paper and pen ready.

"I don't think so. I don't really remember."

"Okay let's start with what you do remember, from the time you woke up this morning." Brad went through the story once again, growing tired of it quickly. Williford sat and listened and wrote.

"And now the blood. What about the blood? Do you have any idea how it happened?" Stanton asked.

"I guess it's his. I don't think any of it's mine," Brad answered.

"How do you think it ended up on you?" Stanton watched Brad as he sat thinking.

"I'm pretty sure I was trying to kill him." His answer was matter-of-fact.

"That can never be the answer. That cannot be a thought you ever had or admit."

"And why is that? He was trying to kill me!" Brad didn't need a lecture. His eyes moved away from Stanton and noticed a picture on the edge of Walker White's desk, a family portrait, and he reached for it. Walker sat up as Brad turned to him. "Your family?" Brad asked with a stunned look on his face.

"Yes, it is," Walker answered.

"And those are your sons?" Brad asked, staring at the picture. He gazed around the room and looked at the pictures. Family pictures were everywhere. The sons playing golf, the daughter playing tennis, college graduations—Walker was proud of his family. Brad's eyes continued on, and he suddenly stood up as if he had been looking at a ghost. A picture on the wall was one he had seen before. It was a picture he boxed up and gave to his in-laws when he left.

"Where did you get this picture?"

"My daughter, Lauren ... her and some sorority sisters at Wake Forest her freshman year. That's her right there. We passed her office on our way in," Walker responded.

"And that's my wife, Susan. I need to go." Brad handed the picture back to Walker White and left, passing Lauren on his way out. She smiled when she saw him.

"Excuse me, but haven't we met before? You look like someone I know ... I'm just sure of it," she said.

Brad didn't hear a word she said.

Not one word was spoken on the way back between Brad and Mr. Barnes. Brad remembered what Susan looked like; her image was something he saw every day. It was the first time since he had moved he had seen a picture of her. He was dumbfounded by the irony of all of it. *Here I am in the small town my father grew up in, and the attorney for my boss has a daughter that went to school with Susan. Un-fucking-believable,* he thought.

They stopped long enough for Brad to pick up his car, and when they arrived back, Miss Rachel was waiting. Brad went straight to his apartment, tearing off his bloody clothes, and then he turned on his shower. The room quickly filled with steam, and just as his mirror began to cloud, he caught a distorted view of himself and starting gagging. He almost threw up but managed to fight it back. He refused to give in.

He took his time in the shower, scrubbing and rescrubbing, making sure that nothing from Darnell Watkins was left on him. He wrapped the towel around his waist and walked to the kitchen.

He grabbed a freezer bag and filled it with ice and water. His right hand was swollen and sore, and he hoped that the ice would help.

He checked his cell phone to see a dozen missed calls and nearly as many messages. They would have to wait. He called Stanton Williford. He apologized for walking out and asked if they could just finish their conversation now.

"Sure we can. Are you up for it?"

"As much as I'll ever be, I suppose," Brad answered.

"Okay … the last thing we talked about … okay, yes. Do you understand about not telling anyone else what you told me?"

"I don't remember what I told you." Brad thought for a moment. "Oh, the blood, sorry, yes, I understand."

"What else should I know?"

"Nothing I can think of."

"So that's all?"

"Stanton, I appreciate your help, and if you need to know more, then I'll tell you, but I'm not talking to anyone about anything else unless I have to. It's a private matter, and I'm not going to rehash all of that again. It's taken a long time to get this far."

Brad put on a fresh set of clothes and walked over to see Mr. Barnes. He could hear them talking and knocked quietly on the door.

"I've got my phone if you need me," Brad said to Mr. Barnes.

"Where you going?"

"Back to work. I'm not sitting around here all day."

"I don't want you working. Wait until tomorrow, and I'll help you catch up," Mr. Barnes replied.

"I just want to get the deposits done and return some phone calls. The security company needs to come by, and it'll be all I think about unless I go do it. I know I won't get everything done, but the more I do today, the less I'll have to do tomorrow. I'm sorry for making things such a mess."

"It's gonna be all right. Don't you worry and don't you apologize to me again. You have nothing to be sorry about. You protected Rose, didn't let him take my money … you put yourself at risk, and I don't want that happening again, but I'd say what you did was damned heroic, and I'll bet Rose would agree with me." Brad nodded and walked back to his car.

He backed up and turned around so he was facing forward as he left and started making calls. The security company was first, then a cleaning crew and a list of employees, all very short calls relaying what they needed to know but not much else.

The cleaning crew met him at work. The crime scene had been released, and Brad showed them what needed to be done. Buddy Coles had a man start power washing the sidewalks and parking lot while the rest of them headed inside. They cleaned everything in sight—windows, shelves, floors—and they finished just as the security company arrived. A new monitor was set up and the wiring and camera checked while Brad listened to his messages. He swallowed five aspirins thanks to his still-aching right hand. He hadn't taken five aspirins in the last twelve months.

He raced to the bank and used the drive-through window. "I have some other things to get done. I'll come back for the deposit slips and bags this afternoon, or first thing tomorrow."

"That's fine, Brad," the teller answered, and he drove away. Working was much better than sitting at the house, but the day was taking its toll. He managed to make every stop, though each visit was much shorter than usual, and then he headed home. He was exhausted; he decided the bank would have to wait until tomorrow.

The long day was seemingly over as he finally crept down the long driveway. As he parked in his usual spot, he eyed a familiar vehicle parked by the Barneses' garage. The large, black SUV sat, the engine still making the small noises while cooling. It had not been there very long. Brad's head sank. *Not today. Hasn't it lasted long enough?*

He hadn't seen them since he left, and he rarely spoke with them, not because he disliked them or was bitter but because he wasn't. He still considered them his family, just like he did Mr. Barnes and Miss Rachel; he just wasn't ready to go there. Every time he did talk with them, he felt like he did just now. An uneasy feeling seized him, and he stared down to the gravel for a moment. He knew they meant well, they always would, and for this reason he would go see them. This, like everything else, would have to be dealt with at some point, and now seemed better than later.

He found them huddled around the kitchen table, all four of them, with Miss Rachel hustling around and being her always gracious self. When Brad entered the room, the Barneses looked at each other, quietly excused themselves, and disappeared, leaving Brad and his old friends, his old family, alone. Their shapes where unmistakable to Brad, and one by one they stood and turned his way. Brad found it difficult to look at them.

They came toward him one at a time, with manly hugs that did not linger.

Bill McKnight, Tom Rhodes, and John Hicks looked very much like they always had. A few more gray hairs, an extra pound here or there, but they had never worried much about those types of things.

"You guys didn't have to come down here." Brad was more ashamed than embarrassed.

"Well, why in the hell did you have Stanton call me?" Bill said with a smile.

"Because … well … I don't know." Brad fumbled around for an answer. He called because he still needed Bill. He needed them all when push came to shove. "Are you guys spending the night?"

"Yes, we are. Mr. Barnes already set everything up for us," Bill said. "The restaurant is amazing."

"That's good to know. Come on … sit down. Tell us what happened." They sat back down, and Brad began recalling his early-morning encounter. Brad noticed the Barneses walking nearby and asked them to join them. Brad realized two things while he told them the story: he was either out for revenge, or he was ready to die. His decision to confront Darnell Watkins had been a dangerous choice.

Brad was exhausted and was ready for some alone time. The guys needed to get checked in and eat, and they decided to meet the next morning for breakfast at the Gas and Grill.

Chapter 19

Brad had been hard at work for several hours when Bill, Tom, and John arrived. Mr. Barnes was doing his morning meets and greets with the breakfast patrons and directed the ladies to get another table so that they could all sit together. The guys were prepared to leave after breakfast unless Brad asked them to stay, although they knew a well-timed sit-down with Brad needed to take place soon. That had been their lone topic of discussion the previous night.

Mr. Barnes led them to Brad's office. Brad was diligently at work, scanning through printouts while his free hand banged away on an adding machine, verifying numbers and scribbling notes on each sheet for Mr. Barnes to review later. Brad looked up and saw the group watching him.

"What?" Brad asked, smiling.

"Just odd seeing you sitting behind a desk," John said.

"Ready to eat?" Mr. Barnes asked. Brad pushed away from his desk and followed them to the grill.

They had all ordered and were engaged in idle morning chitchat when two deputies entered the restaurant. They slowly approached the table and leaned down toward the group. The voice was low and cautious.

"Mr. Barnes, Brad … sorry to interrupt, but we need a word in private."

"Excuse us for moment, men," Mr. Barnes replied, and he and Brad led them to the office.

"Brad, I'm gonna need you to come with us."

Brad's head sank.

"What in the hell has he gotta do that for?" Mr. Barnes demanded.

"Questioning as it pertains to a possible assault." One deputy looked at the other.

"Assault, my ass! Who did he assault?" Mr. Barnes's voice hardened.

"There's a possibility that Brad will be charged with assault with intent to inflict bodily harm. Just doing our job, Mr. Barnes, and, Brad, we would appreciate your cooperation."

"It's okay. Let's go." Brad tilted his head and looked at Mr. Barnes. "Call Stanton for me?"

"On it right now ... right behind you—and not a word until Stanton gets there. You hear me, Brad?"

"Yes, sir." Brad followed the two young men.

Mr. Barnes had the food boxed into to-go plates, handed them to his guests, and explained what had happened.

"Ya'll eat in the car. I'll drive." He was on the phone as he cranked his truck, and Walker said that he and Stanton would meet them there. Bill McKnight was the next to make a phone call. In between bites of food, he completed a brief and informative call. It was a call that would soon have the full attention of District Attorney Ed Granville.

Ed Granville had become a desperate civil servant. He turned to public service after a very short and unsuccessful career in private practice. He learned quickly the art of being a kiss-ass politician and ingratiated himself to his predecessor before his retirement. Granville accepted and handled any heat or controversy for the last two years of Edwin Russell's tenure in exchange for his support. The support got him elected, but his ineptitude as a lawyer and a leader had him on the verge of unemployment, and Ed Granville knew it. He was reminded of this fact every day. He was ridiculed daily in the press, the center of gossip at the courthouse, and the butt of jokes at each firm practicing law in the county. Stanton Williford had made a career out of embarrassing Ed Granville, but Granville was certain he could turn his reputation around and salvage his job because of Brad Ford. Granville needed something good to happen if he was to turn away the challenge of Stephen West.

West was Granville's gravest concern. The one good attorney on Granville's staff, Stephen West, had given up a successful career with Walker White and Stanton Williford. He had it all and knew it. Stephen West wanted to be in politics, dreamed of it, and gave up a six-figure income to work for Ed Granville. He was young, handsome, and had old family money and the connections that came with it. His time had arrived. He worked with perfectly honed skill the art of making friends, friends with powerful connections. His charm, just another skill Granville couldn't think of having, worked wonders when he dealt with the everyday people, and they believed in Stephen West. Granville never saw it coming until it was too late. Granville clung to his one last chance.

Fred Moye was finishing his second term as the governor of North Carolina. His eighth and final year of office was soon to be over. He was now sixty-two years old but looked a bit younger. Governor Moye was a few inches past six feet and had a thick build not uncommon for a man his age. His dark brown hair had grayed considerably while in office and was coarse except for a little thinning on top. His handsome face that was framed with a strong, distinguished jawline. His voice was deep and commanding, and his smile made his constituents confident and loyal. His appeal made him the most popular leader in North Carolina history. Fred Moye preached the values of education, was tough on crime, and held himself and those who worked for him accountable, asking the citizens to hold themselves accountable as well. In his second year in office, an affair between two married staff members was uncovered by the "diligent" press, and true to his word, both were fired, and he asked his fellow North Carolinians to forgive his error in judgment for their employment, and they did. Nothing else under his eight years could ever be considered remotely scandalous.

When his old friend Bill McKnight called, he became appalled at what was relayed to him. He called his chief of staff and then the state attorney general. While his chief of staff compiled information on Ed Granville, the attorney general cleared his schedule for an unscheduled trip to Wilson and Wilson County. The driver pulled the governor's car up, and he and the attorney general took their respective places. Fred Moye was on his way, car phone in hand.

The two-tone beep from the intercom alerted him as always. His secretary's voice seemed shaky, but he didn't notice.

"Sir, Governor Moye is on the phone." The shock of speaking with him for just a moment had her heart pounding.

"The governor? Governor Moye? Are you sure?" Ed Granville asked with much more disbelief than that of his faithful secretary. He thought it odd the soon-to-be-retired governor would have any reason to call. He would have loved to collect his thoughts but knew better than to keep him waiting. He sat up quickly, pushing the flashing red button on his phone and placing the receiver to his ear.

"This is Ed Granville, sir. And what may I do for you, Mr. Governor?"

"Exactly this. I'm about thirty minutes away, and you need to make yourself available to me. I'll be picking you up."

"And to what do I owe such an honor?"

"There's nothing to discuss now. Just be ready when I arrive. I do not wait for anyone. Understood?"

Chapter 20

Stanton Williford's outrage was apparent to everyone present at the firm this morning. Brad had been picked up, and the phone call from Mr. Barnes came in before the deputies had left the parking lot with Brad. Williford was ranting while he paced back and forth. His secretary sat cringing as Walker White approached from his office. She peered over her glasses, and her eyebrows arched.

"You're an angel, my dear. I have no idea why you put up with him. I'm assuming he's alone?" Walker asked.

"I don't put up with him; that's why the door is shut." She smiled a motherly smile. "And yes, he's alone." The only times Stanton Williford kept his door closed was for a meeting with a client or when Marge shut it, and when she shut it, Stanton usually understood he was being an ass.

"Let's go," Walker ordered.

Walker White pulled his keys and headed for his old, half-rusted Suburban when Stanton stopped him.

"We're not going in that bucket. I have a client waiting, and while the courthouse is just down the street, Brad doesn't need that thing finally deciding to die now." Walker smiled and motioned for Stanton to lead the way. Stanton's car matched his personality. The pearl-colored Lexus was brand-new and top of the line. Stanton was flashy, loud, and damned good ... the car suited him. Walker could have cared less. The bucket was to go from work and home, to the club, and on occasional duck-hunting trips with friends. His wife drove the new car; God forbid the tennis gals see his wife driving something beneath *them*.

Bill rode upfront with Mr. Barnes while John and Tom sat in the back. Tom finished eating. John and Bill had left their food behind.

The three of them had discussed one thing on their way down there, and this was as good a time as any to broach the subject with Mr. Barnes. Bill volunteered to deal with it.

"Is Brad ...?" Bill looked at Mr. Barnes as he searched for a good way to phrase his inquiry.

"Happy? Is he happy? Hell no, he ain't happy. He's strong ... stronger than he gives himself credit for and stronger than any of us give him credit for, but he ain't happy," Mr. Barnes answered, staring straight ahead as he drove. "Brad's been like another son to me and the wife, and it tears us both up. You can see the sadness sometimes if you can get him to look at you long enough. His daddy and I grew up together, and it hurts my heart I can't help his boy any more than this." He told them about the first time they went riding together and how he had made the unfortunate mistake of bringing up the God subject and how Brad told him in very short order that he would not discuss it, and if that was what he wanted to talk about that he just needed to be dropped off.

"That's the last time I talked him about anything personal. I just figured if he ever wanted to talk about it, he'd come to me. Sometimes you gotta know when to just let things go."

"I agree, but I think all of us who care about him have let things go for far too long," Bill responded.

"I'll tell you fellas something else ... that boy's a damn hard worker. I'd trust him with my life and my family's life. I don't know a damned thing about that golf stuff he used to do, but if he worked as hard at that, well I suspect he was pretty damned good at that too. But he's missing something, and I ain't just talking about Susan and Will. What do you think?"

Bill stared ahead, knowing the answer, but didn't respond.

"You know I can set my watch by Brad. Same thing, same time, every single day. Never seen the boy vary, never seen him on a date, and I gotta tell you ... for this little town, there's a few single ladies who would love to get their hands on him, and a few married ones as well, but his only social life is Sunday lunch with me and Rachel.

She prays for him every night." The four of them knew it was time to force Brad to move forward, but no one was anxious to be the one who pushed the issue.

Brad was sitting alone in an interrogation room when Stanton and Walker arrived. Walker waited, and Stanton opened the door, finding Brad sitting there seemingly bored and not really surprised. His mind kept going back and forth. *Did I overreact? Hell no! Why doesn't someone understand why I did what I did? Hell, I don't understand why I did what I did!* He looked at Stanton and tried to muster a smile.

"Brad, I'm so sorry. You're here because of me right now."

"How is this your fault?"

"This is Granville's way of telling me I was out of line yesterday."

"Out of line how?"

"Before we left yesterday, I was ..." Stanton paused and fought back a smile. "Well, I guess you could say I was a bit of a smart-ass ... okay a first-class smart-ass. I poked fun at him. Granville's just such a shit sometimes. I just can't help myself."

"What did you say?" Brad smiled.

"Oh this and that. Sheriff Barrow found it pretty damned amusing, but I'm not so sure Walker thought it was so funny." Stanton smiled, and Brad let out a small chuckle of his own. Stanton Williford seemed to be an older version of Mark, and right now that was comforting to Brad.

"Mr. Barnes and your friends should be here any minute. Walker's waiting for them outside, but I wanted to come and apologize to you. Right now I need to find Stephen West. He should be in his office, but I'm not sure what he's up to for sure. I hope he can tell me what's going on."

"Who's he?"

"The assistant DA, but he's actually capable of thought. We play golf together; families are old friends, blah, blah ... anyway. He's challenging Granville in the primaries. I know he can tell me something—maybe he's heard something—but worst case, he can tell me what's going on in the pea-sized brain Granville carries around. I need you to sit tight here. I know this isn't ideal, but just bear with me and under no circumstances do you talk to anyone without me being present. Okay?

"Got it."

Stanton eased out the door and found the introductions already taking place.

"Stanton, I'd like you to meet Bill McKnight, Tom Rhodes, and John Hicks. Gentlemen, Stanton Williford, one of my partners," Walker announced.

"Very good to meet you, men," Stanton answered, shaking hands with each. He looked around for a moment. "Where's that little prick?"

"And who might that be?" Bill inquired.

"Granville," Walker replied. "But just hold on a minute before you start getting yourself worked into another frenzy, Stanton. You're going to love this. Bill, if you wouldn't mind telling Stanton about the phone call you made on your way over here?"

"I called a law school friend of mine." Bill smiled as he looked Stanton's way. It was more than obvious that Stanton had absolutely no regard for Ed Granville, and Bill was fine with that. Bill explained what he believed to be the facts of Brad's encounter, based on what he knew. "My friend made a couple of calls to see what he could find out and decided that it might be more productive if he and another man came to Wilson and had a little sit-down, you know, man-to-man, face-to-face, with your good friend Ed." Stanton smiled, and his face lost most of the redness that had been covering it due to the rise in his blood pressure.

"So who is this friend?" Stanton asked, hoping that Bill McKnight might have some kind of friend that was an attorney for an organized crime family somewhere.

"The governor," Bill replied calmly. Stanton smiled so wide his face began to ache.

"This is too good. Does anybody else know? West know?"

"I doubt it. He's got to be busy preparing or covering things in court," Walker stated.

"I'm calling West's office just in case he's in." Stanton reached for his cell phone and dialed while walking down the hall in a visible strut.

Granville stood rubbing his sweaty palms together on the concrete curbing at the base of the steps leading up to the courthouse as the governor's car slowed to a stop. The driver walked around the car and opened the door, and Granville entered and sat down, startled by the presence of both Governor Moye and State Attorney Simon Chadwick, now becoming convinced that there must be big plans ahead for him. He smiled and went to shake the governor's hand but was left shaking hands with the air. The governor turned his head toward Chadwick, who had yet to bother to look up from his laptop. There would be no pleasantries; neither offered a hello or a handshake as the car began to pull away.

As the car turned out of the parking lot, Granville faced an icy stare as he watched the governor fold his arms across his chest.

"Simon, if you would please, repeat the data we received and discussed while on our way here," Governor Moye said.

Simon Chadwick finally looked up; his nearly jet-black hair appeared lacquered in place, and his cold, dark eyes were boring through Ed Granville like a drill. Without hesitation, Chadwick began rattling off, one by one, every statistic available to his office concerning the Wilson County district attorney and his office and its rank among the one hundred counties across the state. He never looked down again, the numbers already memorized.

"But, Governor, if I may ..." Granville wanted to defend himself but was stopped when the governor leaned closer and wagged his right index finger in the face of Ed Granville.

As each number rolled off the tongue of Simon Chadwick, Ed Granville began to sink deeper and deeper into his seat. His chin dropped slowly as he continued listening, until finally coming to rest on the thick knot of his tie, which now felt like a noose around his thin neck. His faced flushed with embarrassment as Chadwick finally reached the end, and when he clicked his laptop shut, the sound was the only noise in the car. One of the governor's arms lifted, and he pinched the bridge of his nose before returning his focus to Granville.

"Thank you, Simon." Simon nodded but said nothing.

"Well, that was ... I was thinking unimpressive, but that wouldn't exactly be honest on my part, now would it? No, I don't think so. Appalling would be a much more apt evaluation. Yes, I think appalling sums it up. The only positive piece of information I recall hearing was the conviction rate of your right-hand man, Stephen West. Now, Ed, my sources tell me he's challenging you for your job. Is that true, Ed? Why on earth would Stephen West challenge his own boss? I would think that would be career ending, and if he has any political aspirations, I think you could have somehow managed to work out some kind of timetable and then taken credit for grooming him, but no, he's going to run. Any idea why?"

Granville, if he had an answer, did not offer it. His head never moved while the governor waited briefly for a response.

"Let me tell you why, Ed ... because you're done, and everyone knows it. The only career-ending decision Stephen West could make is to somehow seem aligned with you politically. There's only one question left to ask yourself now. Do you want to lose and while on your way out the door manage to get yourself disbarred, or just lose? I'm telling you right now, Ed, if you go after Brad Ford, you're gonna lose everything."

Granville wanted to speak, to defend himself and his office and to curse Stanton Williford and Walker White, convinced that this was their doing, but he couldn't. If he spoke one word, he knew it would be greeted with more venom, more needles, and he could not take another word. His time was up, and this was just a taste of the humiliation he would soon be consuming. The car stopped again in nearly the same place it had earlier to pick him up. The driver opened the door, and Granville crawled away without a word. He paused a moment on the curb and stared at the courthouse. He listened as the car drove away and then looked down toward his feet. He wore the look of a defeated man. He walked slowly, his shoes shuffling against the coarse surface, and made his way up the steps until finally back inside, only to be greeted by a group that included Stanton and Walker. It was another collection of unfriendly faces.

"Brad is free to go. We won't be pursuing charges of any kind against him." Granville walked away quickly, having no desire to be asked anything or hear anything from the men he was certain had put him through this. Stanton was just about to unleash another verbal assault. His mouth opened, but Walker's hand reached his chest first.

"Not now, Stanton ... it's not the time nor the place." Stanton knew Walker was right. "Get Brad and let's go to the office. I'll ride with Mr. Barnes and his guests, and Brad can ride with you."

Chapter 21

Walker White led Dub, Bill, Tom, and John to his office. They maneuvered chairs until they were all positioned in front of Walker's desk. As he sat down, John glanced at the wall of framed pictures to his right and became the first to notice. He tapped Bill on his shoulder without looking, his mouth hung open.

"What is it, John?" John Hicks just pointed. He was dumbfounded, and soon Bill was as well. The question was nearly the same as Brad's had been, and Walker's initial reply was the same. Tom Rhodes stood to see what had the two so mesmerized.

"Son-of-a-bitch, would you look at that?" Tom's voice echoed his disbelief.

"I had never really put two and two together until yesterday," Walker said. "To the right of Susan is my daughter, Lauren." Walker pointed as he spoke. "I knew my boys knew Brad. They played collegiately at Carolina, and Tyler and I followed Brad his last nine holes at the Open. Lauren was about to get married, and that was her and her mother's main focus. Lauren received a call from another friend that something had happened to Susan, but the friend didn't know any details at the time, and she missed the funeral. Tyler actually spoke with him for a moment after he finished, but it was before he heard the news."

"Did Brad see this?" Bill asked.

"Yes, he most certainly did, I'm afraid."

"Oh damn," John said. "How did he react?"

"Well ..." Walker waited a moment to collect his thoughts before answering. "He basically got up and just left. No tantrums ... nothing. He asked where I got the picture. Told me that was his wife. He said he needed to leave and didn't say another word."

"And he never said a word on his way home either," Mr. Barnes added.

"Well, enough is enough. All this time … not once have we made him confront any of this." John spoke with conviction. "Whatever happened with the thug or robber or whoever that guy was is as much our fault as Brad's for not helping him."

"That's bullshit. He didn't want our help," Bill said.

"That's where you're wrong, Bill. He needed our help. I'm not blaming you alone, Bill; we all knew and let him run away from it … all of it. That's all I'm saying."

"Agreed," Tom said.

"Well, damn it. Now I'm going to have to admit to Martha that she was right, and you guys know how much that pisses me off and how much it's gonna cost me." John laughed while Tom rolled his eyes and sighed. Both eventually smiled.

They discussed the one option that all of them knew needed to be addressed with Brad, but they wanted Dub's input. They needed his opinion because if anyone knew Brad now, he did, and if Brad could be convinced, they wanted to know what position that would leave Mr. Barnes and his business in. They all needed to be on the same page when they talked with Brad.

"So we're in agreement about this, right?" Bill asked, and Tom and John agreed. Bill then turned to Dub Barnes. "If we somehow can convince Brad to do this, what kind of position is that going to put you in?"

"My nephew Wayland is about to retire. Twenty years in the marines … he wants to come back here, and I'd love to help him, and I wanna help Brad too. He's a damn good boy who comes from good people that never cared what color my family's skin color happened to be, so let's get our boy right. I'll make things work. Say what you think you need to, and I'll back you fellas up. Just a bit of advice if I may though?" Mr. Barnes offered.

"Please do. Anything," Bill said, sitting upright.

"Don't tell him he's gotta move. I think he likes the anonymity of our little town. He feels comfortable here, and I'm not sure my wife could take him leaving. Brad's become another one of her children."

"Well, how would he work on things here?" Bill asked.

Bill's question was met with a quick answer from Walker White. "At Silver Lakes Country Club."

"Silver Lakes Country Club ... Walker, I'm assuming you still play?" John Hicks asked.

"You know each other?" Bill asked.

"Well, I thought he looked familiar. The years have changed us all, but when I saw the picture of him accepting the trophy for the Silver Lakes Amateur, I knew who he was."

Walker turned to look and then looked back at John Hicks. "Well, we do know each other, from the playoff, right?" John smiled and nodded yes. "Yes, I still play but not much, with the boys having moved away, and right now I'm finally doing my stint as the club president. I put it off for years, but there was no way to avoid it this time. I can guarantee Brad's acceptance, but I do have a couple of questions." Walker paused, leaned back in his chair, and propped his feet up on the corner of his desk. He had the full attention of everyone.

"When was the last time he played?"

"The last time you saw him play," John answered.

"Well, that would be one helluva comeback," Walker said. "What's it been ... five and a half, six years without playing at all? Add to that the challenge of finding his game and bringing it back to a level where he could compete professionally. That's a daunting task to say the least. So how are you gentlemen planning on getting him to change his mind?"

"I just want to apologize again for my behavior yesterday," Brad said as he sat with Stanton Williford in his office. Williford shrugged.

"Absolutely no need for that. I haven't exactly been exhibiting the greatest of behavior myself. It's been a long couple of days for all of us, and I can't imagine the shock of everything for you."

"I played golf against Walker's sons when I was at Wake."

Stanton sat up and pulled himself closer to his desk. "Walker mentioned that to me."

"When I saw the picture in Walker's office ..." Brad stopped and leaned away from the desk. He drew a deep breath and held it a moment before slowly letting it go. "It was the first picture I've seen of Susan since I moved here. I thought about that picture over and over riding back with Mr. Dub yesterday. I remember Susan telling me that someone she knew had a brother or brothers that played for Carolina ... something to that effect. Anyway, I guess I never connected things before. I mean, why would I, you know?" Brad's voice was exhausted. Stanton listened and nodded.

"Still play?" Stanton asked, already knowing the answer.

"No, not for a long time ..." His words trailed off as he gazed at something on the desk in front of him.

"Do you miss it?"

"Yeah ..." Brad stopped. "Yeah, I guess ... actually, yes I do sometimes. I don't miss all of it, but there are things about it I miss. Not much of an answer ... certainly not a very convincing one." Brad's smile lasted for just a moment. "Do you need me for anything else?"

"I can't think of anything," Stanton said as his phone beeped twice. "Just a second, Brad." Stanton pressed the intercom button. "Just take a message and tell them I'll call back."

"It's Stephen West, and he really wants to speak with you," Marge answered.

"Okay, I'll take it." Stanton pushed the speakerphone button and then the flashing red light that indicated what line Stephen West was holding on. He smiled at Brad, hoping to get the scoop about Ed Granville's encounter with Governor Moye.

"Stanton Williford," he answered.

"Stanton, Stephen West. I hope I haven't caught you at an inopportune time."

"Not at all. Just sitting here with Brad Ford, finishing things up with him. What can I do for you?" Brad tried to excuse himself, but Stanton waved a hand telling him to stay put.

"Am I on speaker?"

"Well, of course you are."

"Pick up the phone," West requested, and Stanton did.

"What do you know, good little buddy?"

"Granville resigned!"

"You're kidding me! Well, I'm not sure if that's good or bad." Williford laughed. "I'll meet you at the club for drinks later. Good-bye."

"Come on. I need to talk to Walker," Stanton said to Brad.

"Something wrong?" Brad asked

"Not a thing, Brad. Just some breaking news from the courthouse."

Stanton rapped his bare knuckles against the thick wooden door before he cracked it open.

"Ed Granville just turned in his resignation." Bill McKnight smiled.

"I guess your job just got a lot harder," Walker replied.

"Stephen and I can make things work; no need to worry about that." Stanton Williford smiled confidently and contently.

"Is Brad with you?" Walker asked.

"Yes."

"The two of you, join us please." White stood up.

Brad walked in behind Stanton.

"There he is. Doing better, Brad?" Mr. Barnes asked.

"Yes, sir. Thank you for everything ... thanks to all of you." Brad spoke barely above a whisper.

"Brad, Walker White and I know each other," John Hicks said as he pulled Brad closer to him. "Beat me in a playoff at the Silver Lakes Amateur. How long ago was it?"

"Too long," Walker answered, laughing. "I know my hair wasn't completely gray, and if I remember correctly, you still had some on the top of your head. Damn good times back then. Now I have to remember my game."

"Well, you guys have fun with your war stories; I'm ready to get going. I'm behind on work and need to get caught up." Brad turned and headed back to the door.

"No, sir, young man. Time for you to sit down, and I ain't interested in arguing about it. Work will be there." Mr. Barnes pulled another chair for Brad to join them.

Bill McKnight looked around the room and then said, "Brad, there's not a soul in this room that doesn't want what's truly best for you, and we hope you realize that. We wouldn't be here now if we didn't. Believe that because it's true. And before you remind us, nobody here has ever dealt with the things you've had to, but, son, I love you ... we love you, and this is it."

"This is it—what? I'm not following you. If this is about Darnell—"

Bill stopped him. "This doesn't have a thing to do with whoever the hell the guy was. It has everything to do with the truth, the hurt, the anger, the past ... it ends now. It ends right here, right now ... today, and we're all here to make that happen and help you. We're here to help you now. We should have done it a long time ago, and that's our fault."

"Forget it. I love you guys, but I'm not listening to this ... not ever." Brad glared at Bill and then turned his head away.

"Damn it, I'm talking to you!" Bill said. "And when I'm talking to you, look at me. I've earned that from you, and I expect you to show me some respect!"

Brad turned his eyes back to Bill. "Well, get on with it!" Brad said.

John Hicks stood but not fast enough. Bill walked over to Brad and with a heavy, open hand struck him across the side of his face. Tom grabbed Bill, and John stood between Brad and Bill.

"You were raised to be stronger than this, Brad Ford … to be better than this. You gave up. You quit, and it's breaking my heart." Bill's voice calmed and softened until he was near tears. "Just tell me what your father would think … What in the world would he think of you? I'm sorry, Brad." Bill collapsed back into his chair.

Brad rubbed his cheek. The room was silent except the sound of Bill McKnight trying to choke back his pain. Mr. Barnes pulled out his handkerchief and offered it to Bill.

"No … thank you, though. I'll be fine." Bill struggled to get the words out.

"I'm sorry … I was out of line, and I know it. Please finish what it is you all want to say," Brad said.

"It's time," John Hicks answered simply.

Brad's head lifted, and his eyes moved around the room from one face to the next, each one nodding in agreement with John.

"Time for what?" Brad responded with his head tilted to one side.

"Certain people are meant to do certain things in life, Brad. Look around this room, and you'll see this is true. Each of us has skills that, if we didn't know better, seemed born in us," John answered. "You have a skill … a gift, and with all due respect to Mr. Barnes, it's not running his business."

Brad shook his head and ran his sore hands through his short, thick hair and then over his face.

"Never in my life …" John continued. "Never in my life have I seen—"

Brad stopped him. "*Golf?* Are you talking about golf?"

"Hear them out, Brad," Mr. Barnes told him. Brad's mouth hung open as he stood. He paced slowly toward the far wall opposite Walker White's desk where he rested his hand against the mantelpiece that hung from the brick wall that housed a rarely used fireplace.

"Go ahead," Brad replied, staring at the mortar lines between the bricks.

"Brad, you have a gift, and you always have. I've never seen anyone look so natural or so at ease on the golf course. It's almost beautiful, and it kills me and the rest of us to see it go to waste."

"Do you … John, please …?" Brad's voice filled with a pleading tone. "John, for God's sake, please tell them it's impossible. Even if I wanted to …"

"You told me not fifteen minutes ago that you missed it. Did you not?" Stanton informed the group.

"Uh, attorney-client privilege?" Brad quickly responded.

"Doesn't apply to that information, Brad," Walker answered as he smiled, and his smile brought smiles to the others. Brad shook his head.

"Nobody said it would be easy, Brad, but my mother told me that nothing in life worth doing comes without work and sacrifice. You can do this. We all know you can. It's just a matter of making up your mind to go back to work," John said.

"I'd bet a hundred I'd top half a bucket before I could get one airborne," Brad insisted.

Bill stood up and walked over to Brad. His face racked with guilt, he could hardly look at Brad. Brad looked at his old friend and hugged him. "I'm sorry," Bill whispered.

"I know you are, and I know I deserved it," Brad whispered back. They broke before they both got emotional again. Bill laid the same hand he had struck Brad with on his shoulder.

"If you could find out … just figure out how to stay out of your own way, you can do this. We know it seems like climbing a mountain," Bill said softly. "All we're asking is that you give it a try. You don't wanna look back twenty years from now and regret not finding out. Money's not an issue … we're not asking you to move back home."

"This is my home," Brad stated frankly.

"We know that. We miss you, but we do understand that, I promise. Walker White is the president at Silver Lake Country Club. He says you'll be accepted immediately."

"What about Mr. Dub? I can't just leave him," Brad replied.

"Don't be using me as an excuse, boy. No, sir. We done talked about all that, and I'm prepared to fire you if you don't agree to try." Mr. Barnes smiled and looked at the others sitting with him.

"This is crazy. What about my clubs? They've gotta be ruined."

"Just another excuse, so stop making them. Ian Venters can have you set up in a matter of days, and you know that," John said.

"Not to mention I think you're on the verge of being fired. Right, Dub?" Walker White asked his client.

"That would be correct."

"You would really fire me? Miss Rachel will have your hide," Brad said, and Mr. Barnes smiled back at him.

"She might at first, until I explain everything to her. She knows how her biscuits get buttered, so don't go a thinking you got someone in your corner, my friend." His smile widened.

"So what's the plan? I'm assuming you guys have a plan?" Brad said as his voice relented.

Chapter 22

The sky was still dark and glittered brightly with stars as Brad left that morning. The forecast called for lots of sun, and a near ninety-degree temperature that would be enhanced with typical summer humidity. About halfway there, a yellow and orange glow began creeping its way up over the landscape. The morning sunlight was trying to awake, and soon bright rays would be working mightily to pierce through dense sections of pines along his way.

He followed Nash Street for a couple of miles until he reached a modest brick sign where he slowed and turned. The road meandered right and left, and he slowed even more as he reached the first of two speed bumps he would encounter. Two-story homes lined Country Club Drive and occupied the streets he passed. Sedgefield, Pinehurst, Carnoustie, and other famous golf courses had been used to name streets through Wilson's most affluent neighborhood, and with each house he passed, a vague memory seemed to come and go with them. He eased his window down and rested his left arm on the edge of the door as he came up to Silver Lake, the namesake of the club. The water was nearly still. A small breeze blew toward him, bringing with it the sounds of birds chirping away innocently to each other, faint sounds of mowers, and the smell of freshly cut grass. Silver Lake was beautiful and peaceful, but Brad Ford's stomach was not.

He stopped and stared at the serene beauty that made Silver Lake a gem; all the things that as a child would have made him awestruck now had him cringing as a knot began forming in his stomach. He took a deep breath, trying to ease the discomfort. His eyes panned the view again.

"What am I doing here?" he asked himself aloud as he eased his foot from the brake and slowly began rolling forward. The uneasy feeling would not relent as he made a left turn between the clay tennis courts and the massive practice area for golf that sat fifteen feet or so above and to the right of the tennis center. The main parking lot was positioned between the tennis courts and the clubhouse, which rested on a spot slightly higher than the practice area. An Olympic-size swimming pool sat behind the clubhouse near the eighteenth fairway. The front side of the clubhouse appeared as but one story then revealed itself and its girth as members made their way around the elegantly landscaped facade.

To his surprise, he would not be the first person there that morning to practice. A meager-framed boy, not more than ten or eleven, Brad guessed, pulled another practice ball from a pyramid-shaped stack and dutifully went through his routine. Brad watched him closely as he crept slowly past the young man. He smiled for the first time. *Don't let this game break your heart, little buddy ...* Brad shook his head, knowing his thought was true for most everyone who took up the game of golf.

Another parking lot was situated behind the ninth green and to the right of the first tee. The edges were lined with tall pines, and he found a spot he felt would provide the most shade when the afternoon arrived and the heat reached its peak, which in eastern North Carolina occurred daily from three to five in the afternoon.

He opened his door, walked around the back of his new GMC Yukon, and opened the bay doors, all the while eyeing the boy still hard at work. Without missing a beat, he sat on the bumper and pulled a brand-new pair of white saddle golf shoes from their respective bags. The leather was stiff as he worked the laces open and used his feet to slip his loosely tied sneakers off. He managed another smile. It had been a very long time, but it seemed like yesterday as he wedged a foot into one shoe, then the other, and then tied the wax strings tightly. He watched the boy swing again. The motion was graceful and fluid. He did not swing hard in an effort to hit it further. It was unhurried, and Brad closed his eyes again, hoping that his mind could capture that tempo and help his muscles remember it. His doubt was back as he opened his eyes, and the painful knot began its return when he noticed his legs and laughed at their pale appearance. *Nice look,* he thought, shaking his head. He had not noticed them in the darkness when he readied himself that morning, but now in the light, they looked almost sickly, and they would have been considered sickly by most if the pale skin had not been covering toned, muscle-laden legs Brad had developed running and working out these past few years. He knew the glare would be gone in a couple of days, replaced by some redness that would eventually turn brown and that he had no reason to feel any shame. His golf swing, he concluded, might be all together different. Yes, doubt and fear joined together.

The heat that had built up in the asphalt the day before had dissipated but would soon return. As Brad walked across the surface, he remembered when golf shoes had steel spikes and how the spikes would sink into the pavement during the summer. The shoes now had plastic spikes shaped like spider legs. *Dreadful things,* he thought. He followed the curbing until he reached a concrete cart path that ran beside the Silver Lake clubhouse. Golf carts were staged in a neat row near the golf shop, which was located on the bottom right corner of the building and seventy-five feet from the first hole. The large putting green came into view as Brad rounded the corner. He peered through one of many long and narrow windows at the small space. From side to side and front to back, it was crammed full of all the latest golf merchandise. Clothes, hats, clubs, balls, gloves, and more were neatly arranged for the members to purchase. This early in the morning, only one person would be roaming around, Brad had been informed.

Jerry Beaman was the head golf professional at Silver Lake Country Club. The son of a golf professional, Jerry was born to be one as well. Now forty years old, he had been serving as the club's head professional for nearly a decade. Few professionals were afforded the opportunity at such a young age at a club like Silver Lake, but Walker White had been the chairman of the search committee at the time, and Jerry Beaman's background had been hard to ignore.

As Brad opened the door, and the bell jingled, Jerry was folding shirts and straightening the merchandise as needed. His hair was beginning to gray slightly around his ears, and his hairline was receding, but for the most part, it was still thick. Neatly attired, as was his reputation, his pants were pressed perfectly, and his shoes were shiny.

"Good morning." Jerry smiled. His voice carried a soft southern pitch. His face showed the sincere look of someone who loved what he did for a living.

"Good morning. I'm Brad Ford. Jerry Beaman?"

"That would be me, Brad. It's good to see you. Walker called and said you might be out here today." Jerry shook Brad's hand firmly. "I think he has a match lined up for the two of you ... whenever it is that you'll be ready."

"Well ..." Brad shook his head. "I'm glad he's got that much faith in his game, because I'm not really sure how long it's gonna take me to figure this out ... or if it's even possible."

"Anything's possible, Brad. Anything," Jerry responded.

"I sure hope so. Who does he have in mind?"

"Oh, it's gotta be Stanton Williford and Stephen West. Those two have won the last six club championships but still have a long way to catch Walker."

"Really? How many?"

"Fifteen."

"That's a lot of them for sure. Who's the kid banging all those balls out there?"

"Carson, my son ... he loves it." A look of pride came over Jerry.

"He's got a great swing. Are you his instructor?"

"I've shown him a few things, just basic fundamental stuff, but I only help him if he asks, which isn't very often. He's got a lot of hard work ahead of him if he chooses to continue, to be as good a junior as you were." Jerry smiled. "We've met before. I'm not sure you remember it, but I was an assistant at the Hawks Club when you won our junior golf tournament. I think it was right before you left for Wake Forest. Do you know you still hold the tournament record?

Three straight rounds of sixty-six, and somebody said you shot sixty-five in your practice round?"

"Oh wow ... that was a long time ago." Brad paused. "It seems like a lifetime ago or another life ... sorry." Brad shook his head. "One of Bob's boys, I take it?" Brad asked, referring to legendary professional Bob Wainright.

"Yes, I was very fortunate. He and my father taught me everything I know about being a professional. You saw where Carson was hitting balls, right?"

Brad nodded.

"At the opposite end of the practice area, there's another tee. It's not as big, but it'll give you some privacy. I give all my lessons there unless it's a short-game lesson. Grab a cart and follow the path back there. No distractions, a lot more privacy."

"I think I might do that because getting one airborne is goal number one." Brad tried to laugh, but reality would soon be sinking in, and he knew that no matter how positive he tried to be, the task he had in front of him would be difficult if not impossible. He knew what they wanted of him, and with little over a year before the 2005 United States Open in his home state looming, his mind felt like it wanted to seize up.

"How long has it been?" Jerry asked.

"Well ..." Brad hesitated. "Did you see the 1998 Open?"

Jerry raised his brows. "Really?"

"I'm afraid so. Daunting task, would you not agree?" Brad laughed at the reality he was facing.

"Make yourself at home, Brad. It's good to have you with us. If there's anything I can do, please ask."

"That's very kind. I guess it's time to start. Thanks for everything." They shook hands again, and Brad made his way out the door.

He grabbed the last cart in the line and headed back to his truck to get his clubs. Each passing moment brought another wave of nerves. The anxiety poured through him because he had no idea what to expect. Making a fool of himself at something he once was considered pretty good at doing was the thought that dominated his mind.

He pulled the large, white golf bag out and strapped it into place on the back of the cart. It was filled with the latest version of the clubs he had been playing with before. Their perfect appearance would soon be gone. With everything he needed in its proper place, Brad drove off, heading for the back practice area Jerry had mentioned to him, but not before stopping to watch young Carson Beaman take a couple more swings. He parked behind the small cedar-sided building where restrooms and water coolers were located. Brad watched Carson and his resolve, admiring the young man. At the end of Carson's next swing, he drove off. He sat quietly, staring at the pristine tee and what lay in wait for him.

Brad spent a few minutes stretching, but it was really more of a way of delaying what he felt was going to be a certain debacle. He grabbed an iron from his bag, unzipped one of two long side pockets, and pulled out a plastic sleeve that resembled a clear envelope containing one of a half-dozen leather golf gloves that he stored together. The flap sounded as though cloth was being torn as the Velcro separated. The supple leather opened, and he began gently working his fingers into their proper places with the help of his other hand, using his thumb and index finger to tug the glove toward his wrist. The leather smelled good and hugged his hand and skin like a long-lost friend. His chin raised, and his shoulders straightened. In this benign, seemingly insignificant moment, Brad Ford became excited for the first time in years.

His focused shifted to the middle of the tee where a large, gray plastic trash can was positioned, filled to its brim with new practice balls. A large, metal ice scoop lay perched atop of them, awaiting its first use of the day. He stared at it. *How many of these trash cans is this gonna take?* He shook his head, knowing that he didn't need to think that way. He looked at the glove again and back at his golf bag. *I can do this. I want to do this!* That last thought triggered something inside him, and he strode toward the balls. He grabbed the scoop and dug into the pile and hoisted the balls. He walked over to the right side of the tee and poured them into a neat, little pile and then went and snatched a club from his bag.

He, like Carson, pulled a ball over and then stood behind it. He placed the club first in his left hand and knew that something didn't feel right. Holding a club is like riding a bicycle; it's something you do not forget, so he adjusted its position but again decided that could not be right.

Brad closed his eyes and began to think back. Images formed, and he tried to hold them, but they came and went quickly, as another would flash before vanishing. The mental slideshow clicked again and again until his mind went blank. He opened his eyes, greeted by the bright morning sunlight that illuminated the sky, and felt disoriented. He backed away and shook his head as he sat down in the golf cart. Brad looked around for a moment before his eyes fixated on a bottle of water as his mind drifted away.

He saw his father, as his eyes closed, standing with another man. They stood behind an eight-year-old Brad Ford, watching him bent over, placing a bright yellow practice ball on a white peg he had already placed in the ground. He backed up after awkwardly getting the ball to stay put and tugged the bill of his cap to straighten it back up. He placed his left arm to the side of his chest, eyeing its exact location, and when satisfied, he turned his attention to the small iron head attached to the metal shaft. His right hand gripped the short, bare steel, being careful the head wasn't tilted one way or the other. He placed his left hand on the black and green rubber grip at the end of his club. He paid no attention to the two men huddled together behind him, as there were too many details that needed his undivided attention. Everything had to be just so before he could do anything else. He watched his right arm repeat the same routine as his left, adjusting things until he was ready. His small hands melted together, and he approached the ball. His head tilted back toward the men, but his eyes never left the only important thing in his world.

"I've never seen anyone so natural before," Bob James whispered as he stood with Frank Ford. James pushed his glasses up and took a draw from the cigarette hanging from the mouth of his leathered-skinned face. Brad's father smiled.

"That's kind of why I asked you here, Bob," Frank whispered back. "I'm not a good player, and he begged me to bring him out so he could hit some balls with me. He keeps getting better and better, but I have no desire to be one of those parents who thinks their kid is better than they really are. I know I can trust you and your opinion."

"Brad, your father and I are gonna step away and talk for a bit. Okay with you?" Bob asked.

"Yes, sir," the little boy answered and then went back to his club and basket of balls.

Bob kept watching in silence. Brad swatted another ball, and again the result was perfect. He flicked the glowing ember from his half-burnt cigarette until it fell to the ground. He stepped on it until it was completely out and put what was left in his back pocket. Smoke slowly drifted from the corner of his mouth as he studied Brad.

"Never seen anyone his age hold a club and have it look so natural. It's like his little hands were made for no other purpose," Bob said. Frank Ford smiled again, but it was reserved like his personality.

"What happens when he hits a bad one? How does he react?" Bob had just asked the most important question, and on Brad's very next swing, he got his answer. It was by far the worst ball Brad had hit.

Brad backed away and frowned. He looked down at his little club, his hands, and his arms and made a slow practice swing. He never looked their way, never spoke. He grabbed another ball on the tee and started over.

"That's what he does," Frank responded.

"You're kidding?" Bob asked, lighting another cigarette. Frank shook his head no.

Brad smiled as his daydream ended. He remembered Bob James watching him that day with his father. He loved golf much like

Carson, but now the only thing on his mind was getting started. He had been out there for fifteen minutes without making one swing.

Carson had noticed the man just standing there and thought it was kind of weird. He leaned his club against his golf bag sitting behind a stack of balls and began jogging his way over to the back tee. He wasn't certain if the man was waiting for his father to give him a lesson or if something else was wrong, but he thought he would check just in case.

"Excuse me, sir?" Carson asked. He waited for a moment after getting no response. "Hey, mister, are you okay?"

The man turned toward Carson slowly, as if he had been asleep.

"I'm sorry ... yeah everything's fine." The man smiled and seemed to be moved by Carson's concern.

"I can get my dad if you need him ..."

"You're Carson, right? I'm Brad. It's nice to meet you."

"Same here ... how'd you know my name?" Carson asked.

"I met your dad earlier. I'm just having a little trouble getting started. It's been a long time since I hit a golf ball."

Carson's hands rested at each side of his narrow waist. "Getting started how? I'm confused," he said.

"Just trying to remember everything ... there's a lot to remember."

"Well, there's nothing to it. I can show you if you want me to," Carson said.

"I hate to interrupt your practice."

"No problem!" Carson confidently exclaimed, striding purposefully toward Brad. "I like to help, but I have rules when I help."

"Okay, let's hear them."

"Rule number one is no getting mad. Golf is the greatest game ever, and getting mad won't make it easier. Rule number two is doing your best to do what I ask you to do. Rule number three is if it helps, you owe me a Gatorade. Is it a deal?" Carson asked.

"It's a deal." Brad smiled.

Carson led Brad back over to his practice area and asked him for his club. Brad handed it to Carson.

"Okay, first things first ... take a deep breath and relax. That's really important," Carson said. He meticulously placed Brad's left hand on the club. With the same amount of care, he then took his right hand and placed it on the club as well.

"Sir, you're just gonna have to relax. I promise I know what I'm doing." Carson's voice, young as it was, was filled with confidence.

"Sorry," Brad replied.

"It's okay. Okay, now look at your hands and feel how the club rests in them." Carson backed away to have a better look for himself. His left hand rubbed his chin and then tugged his visor as he scrutinized the adjustments. "Okay, that's good, but your arms ..." He walked back over, moved Brad's arms, and backed away again.

"Looks good from here. How does that feel?" Carson asked.

"Weird, but at least it feels familiar," Brad answered.

Carson bent over, picked up a ball, and positioned it for Brad. "All right, the blue flag ..." Carson pointed in its direction. "When you're ready, hit it there."

Brad stood there looking frozen and then backed away.

"What's wrong?" Carson asked.

"I'm not really sure I wanna do this," Brad said.

"Just make a couple of practice swings and brush the top of the grass." Carson leaned down and brushed the damp, tight green grass with his right hand. "Just like this, except you do it with the club. Let me see you do it." Carson wiped his hand on his shorts.

"Okay." Brad made a few tentative practice swings and then started all over. The final attempt brought a smile to his face as the club started back down. "I'm ready," he said, looking at Carson.

Brad aligned himself once again to the blue flag Carson had chosen for him and finally made a swing. The club and ball clicked, and the dimpled orb took flight. Brad and Carson both watched its short flight as it landed a few feet short, bounced forward, and nicked the right edge of the white metal stick holding the flag in place, finally stopping a foot from the hole.

Carson's mouth dropped open.

"Kinda like that?" Brad asked Carson.

"Yes, sir, exactly like that!" Carson smiled and removed his visor, wiping the sweat from his face before returning it to where it had been resting. "You owe me a Gatorade. Don't forget, okay?"

"No problem. It's well worth it. I'll come and pick you up when I take a break. Will that work for you?"

"Yes, sir. Hit 'em good." Carson smiled and then hustled back to his own clubs, excited he could help whoever that guy was.

Chapter 23

Jerry and Carson, along with twenty or so small children ranging from ages five to ten, were gathered around Brad as he showed them how he began playing golf. His father would take Brad around with him and let Brad hit chip shots and putts, and he told them the same things his father had taught him. He was beginning his downswing when a high-pitched voice traveled straight into his ear.

"Mommy!" one of the small ones screeched. Brad was unable to stop his swing, and the ball ricocheted off his club, sailing off in a direction he certainly had not planned, leaving him a little embarrassed and the kids laughing.

While Jerry tried to settle the children down, Brad panned the parking lot. He saw her waving back. Her blonde hair bounced up and down against her shoulders with each graceful stride she took. Brad held up his hand, attempting to deflect the glare, leaning to his right and then to his left, trying to see her better, but from this distance it was impossible to tell.

"Should we give it another try, Brad? I wouldn't think that's the shot you wanna finish up with," Jerry said.

"Sir?" Brad replied.

"One more for the kids?" Jerry repeated politely.

"Sure. Sorry." Brad looked at the children watching and waiting.

"Last one, kids ... let's try one from the sand. How does that sound?" The children approved with glee, and Brad asked the little boy to come over.

"What's your name?" Brad asked.

"Um, Trot!"

"Trot, it's nice to meet you." Brad shook his small hand.

"Kay ... me too." Trot looked up at Brad, squinting his eyes.

"That's an interesting name you have," Brad said.

"Is not my real name, named after my Paw-Paw."

"Well, I think that's great, Trot. I want you to pick the hole that I'm gonna hit the ball to."

"That one ... the white one." Trot pointed as the flag fluttered around.

"Okay, Trot, go stand with Mr. Jerry and Carson and let's see how I do."

"Kay." Trot galloped back over, and Brad realized how appropriate the nickname was as he looked at Jerry, who smiled back.

Brad dug his feet in and then turned away and back through. The club thumped against the ground just before the ball floated into the air, engulfed by grains of sand that began falling back to the ground. In a moment, Brad knew his shot was a good one as it landed close to Trot's choice and finally found its way into the hole.

The children went crazy, bouncing up and down while Brad pumped his fist a couple of times as he and Jerry exchanged a laugh.

"Do it again! Do it again?" a little girl pleaded.

"My father always said to finish on a good shot, and I think that one qualifies. Kids, please thank Mr. Brad," Jerry requested.

"Thank you, Mr. Brad," the children responded in unison, and they followed Jerry and Carson toward the pro shop to their awaiting parents. Walker White passed the children as he headed toward Brad, stopping for a moment to speak with Trot.

"You made quite an impression on my grandson." Walker said as he reached Brad.

"Glad to hear that. I take it Trot is Lauren's?"

Walker smiled and nodded. "Rumor has it that you shot sixty-seven with Carson yesterday as well."

"I guess news travels as fast here as anywhere else," Brad replied.

"I have my sources," Walker said. "How much longer are you going to be out here?"

"Almost done. Why?"

"Let's have a beer. Lynn's playing tennis, some kind of women's night thing. Hell, I don't know," Walker said, smiling.

"A beer sounds great, but I need to clean up before I meet you."

"Great. I'll see you in a bit."

After a quick shower, Brad changed into some fresh clothes he kept hanging neatly in his locker, standard attire that would cover the club's various dress codes. The navy blazer covered a starched button-down, and his slacks were a lightweight blend with immaculate creases. His thick hair was short and required little attention, and with a spray of cologne, he walked swiftly to the bar where he found Walker enjoying a beer with Stanton Williford and Stephen West.

"There he is. Brad, I'm sure you remember Stanton," Walker said as the three of them stood.

"I do. Good to see you again," Brad responded as he shook hands with his former attorney.

"Likewise, Brad. Much better circumstances, I might add." Brad smiled in agreement.

"And this young man is Stephen West, our newly elected district attorney." Walker smiled as he finished the introduction.

"Brad, I'm very glad to meet you." West offered his hand, and Brad accepted, all the while eyeing the young man. Stephen West certainly came across as a young man born for politics. His handshake was crisp, his eye contact was constant, and he had handsome looks and polished speech with just a trace of the South.

"I bet you say that to everyone now that you're in politics. I'm just kidding … nice to meet you as well. I've heard nothing but good things about you from Stanton and Walker." Brad smiled.

"That's very kind of them, and no, I don't say that to everyone, but it *is* good to finally meet you," West reassured Brad as they all sat down.

A waitress approached them and asked if anyone needed anything.

"Ice water and a beer for me. I feel a little dehydrated," Brad answered.

"How long did you practice today?" West asked.

"It depends on what you consider practice. I walked nine holes, which took a couple of hours, spent an hour helping with the kids' clinic, and five or so hours working on my short game and irons."

"In that heat?" Williford asked with a stunned expression.

"It's not that bad. I exercise a lot and am pretty used to it. Cold weather bothers me much more than hot weather does," Brad replied.

"When do you have time for that?" Walker asked. He motioned to the bartender in such a manner as to relay he was ready for something a bit stronger.

"I'm up at four thirty every day. It takes about an hour ... thirty minutes of cardio and thirty minutes of weights. I clean up, grab a protein bar, and head out here. Six days a week. Miss Rachel won't tolerate me missing Sunday lunch, and after I eat with them, I'm in no condition to play."

"How's it coming? And don't lie, because we already heard about your round with Carson," Stanton said.

"It's hard to say. A casual round of golf on your home course is nothing like tournament golf," Brad answered quickly as he entertained the chat he would soon be having with his diminutive friend Carson.

"Think you're ready for a little match?" Walker asked, smiling. Williford and West smiled as well.

"What's the match?" Brad asked.

"Us against them," Walker replied.

"And the bet?" Brad asked.

"A dollar. It's our standard bet," Williford said, smiling.

"A dollar? You're kidding, right? You play for a dollar?" Brad asked as the waitress approached again.

"A dollar a yard ... you know, the first hole is 470 yards, so the hole is worth 470 dollars," Walker answered.

"Wow ..." It was the only word Brad could muster before finally asking the waitress to bring him what Walker was having.

"Didn't know you liked scotch," Walker said.

"I don't. It tastes awful, but I can sip it." Brad waited for his drink, and the table was quiet. Brad thanked the young lady while Williford gazed lustfully at the woman's backside. Brad took a long sip, which made his face grimace, and sat the tumbler down.

"We'll take the bet," Brad finally answered, and the rest of them smiled. Their conversation was abruptly interrupted as they heard Trot's voice.

"That's him, Mommy! Sitting with Papa … Papa!" Trot raced over and leapt into his grandfather's lap. "He hit it right in the hole I pointed to, Mommy. Didn't you, Mr. Brad?" Brad stood up and smiled at Lauren. It was his first encounter with her since seeing her at the law firm.

"He hasn't stopped talking about it," Lauren said, smiling.

"Just … just a lucky shot," he answered.

"Well, Dad and my brothers have told me enough to know it wasn't all luck."

"Thank you … that's very kind of you to say," Brad replied, fumbling so awkwardly Stanton and Stephen West were having trouble keeping straight faces.

"Trot, it's time to go. Say good-bye," Lauren said.

"Kay." Trot hugged Walker. "Bye-bye. Love you, Papa." Trot hopped down.

"I love you too, Trot. Be good for your mother."

Trot nodded. He tugged on Brad's hand, and Brad looked down at him.

"High five, Mr. Brad?" Trot asked him. Brad smiled and bent down, holding up his hand, and Trot smacked the palm of Brad's hand.

Lauren leaned forward and kissed her father good-bye and waved to the others.

"Lauren?" Brad managed after mustering up the courage.

"Yes?" she said as she turned toward him.

"I'm sorry I was so rude to you that day in the office. It was ..." Lauren put her free hand on Brad's hand. He stopped speaking the second her skin touched his.

"Please forget about that. I promise *I* have. It was wonderful to see you again," Lauren said.

"It was great to see you again as well ... and thank you." Brad turned to see the three sets of eyes staring at him.

"What is it?" Brad asked after Lauren left.

"Nothing at all, nothing at all." Walker shook his head and smiled.

Brad finished his drink quicker than he normally would as he tried to calm his nerves. He then made his leave.

Brad and Walker blistered the first nine holes. Williford and West were outmatched, but they knew that before they arrived. The match had moved along at a decent pace. The four had eyes watching them. Brad was the only one that did not know of their presence. They rode in separate golf carts, positioned strategically so Brad would not notice them. Armed with binoculars and walkie-talkies to communicate with one another, they watched anxiously. They would compare notes later, they had decided, and they were all taking notes, jotting golf shorthand on blank scorecards found on the carts. John Hicks knew his game the best. He knew his habits, his swings, and its flaws. Things had certainly changed; a lot had changed with his game, his body, and his mind-set. John Hicks quickly decided these were all very positive signs.

The match continued, and so did the onslaught. Brad and Walker won four of the first five holes on the back. There was no mercy rule, and they continued on. Williford and West watched in disbelief. Walker White hadn't played this well in years, and to finish the round, they watched Walker finish with birdies on seventeen and eighteen.

"Thank God that's over with," Stanton Williford said as he shook hands with Walker, who stood there smiling. The total damage totaled nearly three thousand dollars. After the handshakes and congratulations, they agreed to meet at the men's grill.

Brad drove to the parking and put away his equipment and then meticulously cleaned his shoes. He finally made his way to the grill and as always was the last one to arrive. He smiled as he spotted the extra guests waiting for him.

"I should've known. I really should have ... you guys took a dive, didn't you?" he asked his opponents.

"You shot sixty-four, and you're asking that? Are you shitting me?" Stanton Williford said.

"I don't recall you being that long." John Hicks smiled.

"Weights. Who knew?" Brad said, smiling. "New equipment, new balls, lots of things changed."

"So I see. Changes for the good, I think," John said.

"We've been keeping tabs on you with the help of some new friends down here. We just wanted to see for ourselves, let you know we care. And we're here to help if you want it, but that's up to you," Bill McKnight said.

Chapter 24

Lauren had barely sat down at her desk that Friday morning when the calls started. They always did when there was an upcoming social event.

"Hello, Caroline," she said after finally answering the phone. "Yes, I'm planning to attend. Why do you ask?" Lauren knew the answer as she forced herself to listen to Caroline. "I'm going alone." Silence again on Lauren's end as she listened to her friend ramble on and on.

"Caroline, I know you mean well, and I know all of you do—including my mother—but please let this go. I've met both of them, and my answer is no. I have a man, and yes he's my son, and between him and work, it's really all I have time to deal with. If you really want to help me, tell everyone so I don't have to waste half my day answering calls about this. My mind isn't going to change. Just tell them we've already spoken, that I'm going, but that's it—please? I'm begging you. Please?" Caroline sighed.

"Thank you, Caroline." Lauren hung up the phone and placed her head in both her hands.

"Ugh … will it ever end?" she asked herself.

"Will what end?" Walker asked his daughter as he leaned against the door frame.

"Oh nothing. The girls … you know, trying …"

"And Mother, I presume? I understand," Walker said as he walked over to her desk and sat down. "You could just find someone to go with you. You know, someone like you that doesn't have the time for a relationship. Someone that you could show off to your friends and that needed someone to show off to their friends as well." Lauren sat and thought about her father's idea. "I have to warn you though, if you do, you'll give them something else to chat about. It's a damned if you do, damned if you don't situation, princess. They'll always find something to talk about. I love your mother with all my heart, but we both know how she can be." Walker stood as his daughter smiled.

"It's an idea. I'll take that under advisement," she said, smiling as the face of such a man came to her.

Brad was beginning to regret his decision after his first two tournaments. He realized having any expectations at this point would do him more harm than good. He hadn't played poorly; he just couldn't take advantage of his good shots or make the putts he knew he needed to make. Missing cuts was still a familiar feeling, and it nauseated him as much now as it had when he quit playing. The third and final tournament he would play in was two weeks away, and he was on his way home to rest and work.

As he waited for his car to cool down, he grabbed his cell phone and checked his missed calls and voice mails. He didn't recognize the number as he listened to his voice mail, but soon her pleasant voice began speaking. He was surprised and decided to replay the message again.

"Brad, hey, ah … this is Lauren. I was hoping you could give me a call when you have some time. It's not an emergency, just a question. My number should have appeared when I called. It's my cell. Thanks so much."

Brad continued listening to the rest of his messages. So many people calling to encourage him, and what he felt was one of two things … kindness should have been what he was feeling, but it felt more like pity.

He called all of them back, talking to some, leaving messages for others. He called Lauren back last. He was nearly home, but she said it was just a question, so he felt the conversation would be short.

"Lauren, Brad Ford. I got your message. Sorry it took so long," he said after she answered. He could hear Trot rambling away and another woman's voice.

"Hey, Brad … could you hang on just a second?" she asked.

"If it's a bad time, you can call me back."

"No, now is fine. Just a second ... Trot, go with Nana. Trot, please, I'll be right there."

"Who is that?" Brad heard a woman say.

"Mother, please!"

"Well?" the woman said.

"Brad Ford. Now, please!"

Brad covered his mouth, afraid she would hear his snickering.

"Who's Brad Ford?" the woman asked.

"He's a golfer, Nana," Brad heard Trot answer, and he smiled.

"Is he coming to dinner?" the woman asked.

"No! He's probably already hung up."

"Does your father know him? Let me see that thing."

After some commotion, Brad heard the woman on the phone, saying, "Brad, I'm Lynn White. How are you?"

"Just fine, ma'am. How are you?" Brad's stress level raced past anything he had encountered the past couple of weeks playing golf.

"I'm just wonderful. Lauren's busy with Trot. Where are you at, dear?"

"Well ... on I-95 about to pass Wilson. Why?"

"Oh good! Walker's grilling steaks. Come eat with us. I insist!"

"Oh no, ma'am, I couldn't. I really need to—"

"I will *not* accept no for an answer," Lynn said.

"Is Brad coming, Nana?" Brad heard Trot ask.

"I feel like I would be intruding," Brad said.

"Oh please ... that's not at all the case. I've heard so much about you. Surely a home-cooked meal is in order?"

Brad clinched his teeth. "May I bring something?" he answered with dread.

"Nothing at all. Next time a bottle of wine! I'll let Walker and Lauren know you're on your way. We're at 1627 Country Drive. See you in a little while."

Lynn handed Lauren her phone. She was immediately greeted with a disapproving stare from her only daughter.

"Trot, please go out back with Papa." She kissed him on his cheek.

"All right," Trot replied as he scampered through the house while his mother returned her eyes to Lynn.

"What on earth are you doing?" Lauren demanded.

"I've heard your father speak about him and found it very curious that he would be calling you. That's all," Lynn answered as innocently as she could while sipping her wine and preparing the salad.

"With all due respect, Mother, that's utter bull! My God, you're worse than my friends. He was returning my call."

"So what did you call him about?"

"Well, wouldn't you like to know!" Lauren said as she marched outside to see her father and son.

"Is he coming? Is he?" Trot asked as soon as he saw his mother.

"But of course. Who can turn down Mother?" she replied, looking at Walker.

"Is who coming?" Walker asked.

"Mr. Brad the golfer. I can't wait to show him. I've been practicing hard." Trot's face beamed.

"Brad? Why is Brad coming?" Walker asked.

"Well, I took your advice from this morning ... and the first and only person I could think of was Brad." Lauren fidgeted and kicked at some bricks that lined a flowerbed adjacent to the patio. "Bad idea?" she asked.

"I wouldn't begin to have an opinion. Sorry, sweetheart, but I'll tell you this ... you might want to wait inside and head your mother off," Walker advised.

"Oh no ... good thinking, Dad." Lauren bolted back inside to see she was already too late.

"You must be Brad." Lynn greeted Brad with a pretty smile. Lynn White was shorter than her daughter, with blonde hair as well but cut closer to her face. She looked much younger than her age. She was dressed casually in a shirt, shorts, and sandals. "Come in, come in. Well, aren't you the cutest thing. Oh my goodness, your arms are so strong." Lynn slid her arm around Brad. "Everyone's out back. It's this way," she said, leading him.

"Hi," Lauren said as they made their way to the kitchen, feeling mortified.

"Oh, there you are, dear." Lynn winked at her daughter and mouthed a silent, "He's cute," while nodding her approval.

"Hello," Brad replied. "I feel like I'm interfering with family time."

"Oh don't be silly. Right, Lauren?" Lynn said, patting Brad's chest.

"Mother wouldn't have it any other way, Brad. Dad's outside. Care for a drink?" Lauren asked.

"Beer is good, thank you." Brad walked outside and tried to say hello to Walker, but Trot was ready for him.

"Mr. Brad, hey, come here, come here." Trot grabbed Brad by the hand and led him to his little pile of balls.

"Trot, just a couple of more, okay? Brad's had a long day."

"Yes, sir. Mr. Brad, I've been practicing hard."

Lauren approached them and gave Brad his beer. "I'm sorry. Overwhelming for you, I'm sure."

"No, it's good ... I needed to clear my head. I guess we can talk after dinner?" Brad asked.

"If that's okay?" Lauren replied, and Brad nodded in agreement.

Dinner went well in spite of Lynn's steady interrogation of Brad. He avoided some questions with Walker's help. Trot was enthralled with him, and Brad spent most of his dinner talking to the little one while Lauren and Walker eyed Lynn, trying their best to hold her at bay.

Brad sat with Trot as he bombarded him with questions and told him all about his favorite toys while Lauren, Lynn, and Walker cleared the table. Lauren was incredulous at her mother's behavior and constant questioning.

"Time for Trot to take a bath and time for you to spend some time with that handsome young man, my dear," Lynn whispered to Lauren. Then she smiled and scooped up Trot. "Let's go, my little man," she said. "Good night, Brad. It was wonderful meeting you."

"Pleasure was mine. Good night, Trot," Brad said.

"Are you leaving, Mr. Brad?" Trot asked.

"Pretty soon, but I'll see you at the golf course, okay?"

"Kay. Bye." Trot waved, and Lauren kissed her son.

"Do as Nana asks. Promise?" she said to her son.

"I promise, Mommy."

"Love you."

"Love you too." Lynn and Trot disappeared.

"Let's sit outside," Lauren suggested.

"Okay," Brad answered. He followed her back outside, and they sat in a pair of wrought-iron chairs that faced each other.

"I need a favor, Brad, and it's sort of a big favor." She then began explaining her situation, her friends, and that she was not looking for a relationship. She told him about the demands of her job and trying to spend time with Trot.

Trot's father lived in Georgia and really had nothing to do with his son; her brothers did not live close by, so Walker and Lynn and Lauren were all the family Trot knew. She explained what her friends put her through every time something came up.

"I guess you probably know the feeling," she said.

"Well, actually, my friends know better." Brad laughed. "My personal life is mine, but I do know what you're saying."

"Well ..." She smiled. "My dad had an interesting idea. I mean ... he didn't say you ... oh God this is coming out all wrong." She stood, frustrated at her inability to converse.

"It's okay, Lauren. Sit back down and relax. What's on your mind?" She explained in detail her father's idea. Brad smiled and listened quietly.

"What's the event?" he asked.

"Local art auction for a children's charity, and it's black tie. I can't believe I'm asking you to do this. This is a bad idea. I'm sorry." Lauren's embarrassment was now complete.

"Art auction? Black tie, tuxedo black tie?" he asked.

"It's okay … I understand. Like I said, it's a bad idea."

"Sounds great … well not really, but sure. I'll do it, and I promise not to embarrass you. I had just been thinking I needed a new tuxedo. No problem at all. When is it?" Brad smiled.

"Next Friday," she replied nervously.

"Just call me with the details, but I do need to go. It's been a long couple of weeks, and I need to run, but count me in."

"Are you sure?" she asked.

"Yes … positive. I'm gonna say good night to your dad. Go be with Trot, and we'll talk next week, okay?"

"Okay, Brad … thank you."

"You're welcome." Brad smiled again, and Lauren smiled back.

Chapter 25

The faster Friday approached, the more apprehensive Brad became thinking of his agreement. Far too many people had befriended him, and the least he could do was be a friend to Lauren. He did indeed understand her circumstance but an art auction? Brad had very few interests, and art was not one of them. It didn't matter. He reminded himself again, although with a frown.

On Monday he had driven to Raleigh and had a tuxedo fitted, and as he posed in front of his standing mirror, he thought it looked adequate, which for Brad was a compliment to himself. He spent nearly four hours playing a practice round at a golf course that was on his schedule later that year. The alterations were completed when he got back, and after he picked out all the other accessories, his Visa took a hit for $1500. He shook his head.

He took the jacket back off, placed it on the hanger, and walked outside, hanging it up carefully. He placed a bottle of wine and a long-stem yellow rose in the front seat and headed off. The wine and rose were for Lynn White in hopes of catching her off guard and stunning her tenacity long enough for Lauren and him to leave.

The evenings were much shorter, and by the time he arrived, it was dark. They had agreed on eight so she could be fashionably late and watch her friends huddle and gossip at the sight of her with a man they did not know. Brad was amused by all of it, but he knew where Lauren was coming from, and the thought of making her friends wonder what was up actually sounded fun. Men and women were very different beings. He grabbed his gifts and strolled slowly up the walkway. He had taken no more than three or four steps when the lights by the front door came on and Lauren opened the door. She smiled at him, and her black dress draped her long curves. The light from the front door caught her at just the perfect angle, illuminating her. She was stunning.

"Your jacket?" she asked.

"Hanging up in the car. You look ... wow," he said as she looked down and tucked her blonde hair behind her ear.

"Thank you. You look quite handsome yourself," she replied.

"Well, this is as good as it gets for me," he said, laughing. "I feel like I'm going to the prom."

"Now that you mention it, I think you're right. After all these years, thank God I didn't have to stress over acne," she said, almost giggling.

"These are for your mom. I thought maybe a good distraction so we can leave," Brad told her.

"I wasn't going to give her the opportunity, but she'll enjoy them," Lauren responded. Brad watched her leave the wine and rose and return to him. He simply offered his elbow to Lauren and walked her to the car. He stopped short of the door and opened it. They he offered his hand to her as she climbed inside, and she accepted. Her skin was warm and soft, and Brad looked away as he felt his face flush. He shut the door and made his way around to the driver's side and sat down. She gave him directions as they went.

"I hope you realize I'm not the most outgoing person in the world," he said.

"I know, and I want you to be yourself. I think it's great." She paused. "The less my friends know the better. Caroline will be persistent, but when you feel she's crossed the line ... wink at me, and I'll handle it," she told Brad.

"You'll handle it how?" Brad asked, giving her a sidelong look.

"Pay attention to the road ... Brad, just follow my lead. This is going to be fun. If you find me hanging on you, don't be alarmed. I'll look at you and explain. Sound okay?" Lauren asked.

"The way you explain it, it sounds great."

"If things go the way they should, it will be. I really do appreciate this," she said as they pulled into the parking area of the community arts center that was playing host to the event.

As many years as it had been, Brad continued to remember his manners ... opening her door, offering his hand again, and walking at her side. Lauren was easy to walk beside. When the door opened, the dull roar of conversations taking place between the couple hundred patrons who had already arrived greeted them. While they checked in, Caroline and Sallie Beth spotted her and excused themselves. They whispered back and forth and walked as quickly as they could. Lauren looked up just in time.

"Here they come. Could you get me a glass of white wine, and I'll meet you in a minute?" Lauren asked.

"Sure thing." Brad walked toward the bar, and Caroline and Sallie Beth tried to stop him, but he smiled and continued walking. They stared at each other for a moment before refocusing their attention on Lauren. Brad had to contain the chuckle that he was feeling.

"Lauren, you look fabulous," Caroline said as they all spent a few moments inspecting each other's dresses before they could wait no longer.

"I thought you were coming alone, Lauren. Who's your friend?" Caroline asked.

"A family friend," she answered. "And he's being a dear, so let me catch up with you later." She leaned in, touched cheeks with them, and made her way over to Brad. She walked away from them, smiling at Brad.

"Your wine." He handed her the glass, and she put her mouth to his ear.

"Are they watching?" she whispered. Her warm breath grazed his ear, causing him to blush again. He smiled at the two women.

"Yes," he whispered back.

"Just smile back. Let's go walk around and let them stew for a while." She led him around the arts center that was filled from one end to the other with every conceivable type of art.

"So what did you tell them?"

"I said you're a friend of the family. I'm sure that at some point they or their husbands will corner you. If that happens, I'll come get you and tell you something like 'you have to see this piece.' How does that sound?"

"Good, but I can handle myself, I think." Brad laughed.

Walker sat in his large, brown leather chair with his feet resting on the ottoman, reading a book, when Lynn entered the room. She had finally managed to get Trot to sleep and was ready for a talk with her husband. She bantered on about Brad, hoping Walker would provide some insight, but he was of no use to her. Lynn wanted details.

"Honey, I don't know any more than you do, and I'm willing to bet you'll know more by lunch tomorrow than I care to know." At least part of his statement was true. Lynn turned her head away from her husband and then stood.

"Well, the other night, I overheard Lauren say she decided to follow your advice. What advice did you give her?" Walker ignored her and kept reading.

"I'm going to bed," she announced, thundering off to their bedroom.

"I'll be there shortly."

They had managed to avoid her friends for most of the night. The auction had helped greatly, occupying everyone's attention for over two hours. Lauren and Brad had each bid and won. Brad planned to give his winning to the Barneses. It was the only art piece he had seen that night that he thought they would like. Lauren had found something that needed a bit more interpretation than he was capable of doing.

"I'm ready to go. I just need to go to the ladies' room," Lauren said.

"Okay, I'll be right here," Brad said.

Lauren was barely out of sight when Hart Brownlee and Scott Novac made their way quickly to him, introducing themselves, and when their wives saw the three shaking hands, they quickly closed in as well. Brad met Caroline and Sallie Beth and husbands Hart and Scott.

"I take it you're here with Lauren," Hart started as the rest listened.

"Yes." Brad smiled.

"Quite a gal. We've been friends since grad school," Scott chirped in. "Ya'll seem quite cozy."

"Did we?" Brad asked in return, looking past them in the direction of where Lauren had gone.

"Why, yes you did. Didn't you think so, Sallie Beth?" Caroline asked.

"Oh my, yes. I haven't seen Lauren glow like that in years," she replied.

Brad smiled as he saw Lauren and flashed his hand. She tilted her head and raced over to him.

Brad looked over at Sallie Beth and smiled. "I think she glows like that all the time. Maybe you don't know her as well as you think you do." His statement was greeted with a frown as Lauren finally arrived.

"Would you like to come over to the house for a nightcap?" Caroline asked almost desperately.

"I'm afraid we can't. Mom and Dad have Trot, and we haven't truly had any alone time yet, so if you'll excuse us," Lauren answered. She smiled and snuggled up affectionately on Brad's arm.

"Sorry, I'm with her," Brad said. Lauren grabbed him by the hand, wrapped his arm around her waist, and led him away.

"I don't believe I caught your name," Hart said, watching them leave.

"Good night," Brad said.

"You didn't even get his name?" Brad and Lauren heard Caroline ask in a tone that let Hart know he had failed his wife.

Brad and Lauren had just reached the curb outside when Lauren burst into laughter.

"You were brilliant," she said. "And believe me, they'll have your name in the morning when they meet my mother for tennis."

Brad drove her home. The ride was quiet, and when they reached her parents' house, the lights were off except for a lamp in the living room. He walked her to the front door where he stood awkwardly as she fumbled through her clutch looking for the house key. The clear night sky allowed the moonlight to shine enough for him to see her face. Lauren's features were breathtaking.

"Got 'em. Sorry … I should have done that in the car," she said. "Thank you so much. I really appreciate you tagging along."

"Not a problem. Now get inside and lock the door." She nodded back to him and opened the door. Brad started walking away, and she grabbed his arm and placed her hand on his cheek.

"You're a dear man." She kissed him on his other cheek. Her warm lips nearly caused him to break out into a sweat.

"Good night." It was all Brad Ford could muster.

Chapter 26

There was no easy explanation for it, Brad thought, driving from his home. His mind tried to make sense of what had happened that week. Brad's mind had been free of the clutter he had learned to live with for the first time since he lost them. But what was the reason? He kept asking himself that question over and over as he drove his normal route to the club. His mind wandered, as it always did, but not to memories of Susan and Will. In the end, he forced his mind to think about the day ahead. Any thoughts of last night made him feel guilty.

Brad had been hitting balls for nearly two when he saw Lynn White arrive. He could only hope Caroline and Sallie Beth had hangovers ... as much for Lauren's sake as his own.

Lynn waited impatiently for Caroline and Sallie Beth to arrive Saturday for their standing doubles match. Lauren was still asleep when she left, or she would have given her only daughter the third degree. She had to wait, and Lynn hated to wait.

"Where are they?" she asked. Caroline's mother, Cathleen, shrugged and took another sip of her bottled water.

They slowly approached from the parking lot, both showing the signs of a long previous night where it was obvious they had reached their points of no return.

"Well, it's about time," Cathleen announced.

"It was a long night, Mother," Caroline replied. "I can't believe we agreed to this, knowing we had a party to attend." Sallie Beth nodded slowly in agreement.

"Well, you did, and now it's time to take your lumps. Besides, I need details, girls," Lynn told them.

"Wouldn't you just rather hear about last night?" Sallie Beth offered.

"Yes, but another hour or so isn't going to kill me. Besides, look at these legs! Three kids, almost sixty, and they're still perfect. Now let's go." It took less than an hour, barely thirty minutes, for them to discard Caroline and Sallie Beth, who felt no better.

Several tables were positioned on a patio that was attached to the tennis shop. They settled into the one that provided the most shade. It was quiet for a moment, and then another group entered the vacant court. The sounds of bouncing balls throbbed through a pair of temples. Caroline rubbed away.

"Who was with Lauren?" Caroline asked.

"Brad Ford," Lynn said.

"Who?" Sallie Beth chirped.

"Brad Ford. Apparently he's some sort of golfer. I have no idea ..." Lynn paused. "I tried to talk to Walker last night, but he just ignored me." She pulled her cell phone out and laid it on the table. "I called my sons, and of course they were no help. Men ..." She sighed.

"Is he famous? Should we know him?" Sallie Beth asked.

"Well, after getting nowhere with Walker or the boys, I did a search for him on the Internet. What I found out was awful. He led the US Open once. Our boys played against him when he was at Wake Forest. Lauren knew his wife."

"He's married?" Caroline barked.

"Oh heaven's no. His wife and son were murdered," Lynn said, and the trio of women collectively gasped. Lynn had done her homework. Thanks to her trusty computer, she passed along the details. She recounted their efforts to get back home so Lauren could attend her friend's funeral but with no luck. Circumstances that she did not know about had Brad Ford living in Wilson.

"Sounds like he has a lot of baggage," Caroline said.

"Lauren was all over him last night," Sallie Beth reminded.

"Well, she scammed you both, with his help," Lynn replied.

"What do you mean?" Caroline demanded.

"It was a setup. He came over to the house for dinner. I was insistent, and of course Lauren threw a little hissy at me doing so, but anyway ... I overheard a couple of things and put two and two together. She's tired of everyone meddling. What better way to stop it than to present someone to those she thinks are meddling, and maybe everyone we will back off. I think he's a handsome thing. You should feel his body ... mmm," Lynn added.

"You're awful, Lynn," Cathleen told her while Lynn laughed.

"Well, Trot worships him. Apparently he helped with a clinic of some sort. I like him, but I liked that loser she married, so what do I know," she said, shrugging.

Brad carried on with his practice. He had watched as they all showed up and now were just sitting there. He reached inside his golf bag for his phone and called Lauren. It went to voice mail, and he left her a message, hoping she would get it before her mother got back.

Chapter 27

It wasn't Brad's favorite course, but he played it like it was. He won back-to-back Atlantic Coast Conference individual titles and now his first Carolina Tour title. A perfectly struck three wood left himself fifteen feet for eagle. He made his putt, but he still needed help. The eagle left him a shot behind, and the leader would have to make a six for Brad to even get into a playoff. He felt bad for the guy who had lost. He played the last hole the way one should with the lead. He had played safely, leaving nothing but a sand wedge to the green only to have it finish in a sand-filled divot. His next shot was heavy and pulled and found the slope short of the green that carried into the lake. The leader had just made a seven, and somehow Brad had won.

Brad felt phone drunk after speaking with Bill, Tom, and John. He got the round of "atta-boy" and "see, we knew you could do it." He finally called the Barneses, who were elated for him. Her fried chicken, mashed potatoes, and collards would be his victory dinner. He was starving ... he could smell the kitchen at their house when the phone rang.

"Congratulations." Walker's voice boomed with excitement while he waved Lauren into his office. "Damned fine playing ... I just got off the phone with Dub."

"Is that Brad?" Lauren whispered to her father. He nodded back with a frustrated look.

"Did he win?" she asked. Her father nodded again, his glare intensified. "Oh my God!" She pushed his speaker button. "I'm so proud of you. Trot's going to be so excited."

"You're acting like your mother. Say good-bye, Lauren."

"It's okay. Today was a good day. I have one of those big checks in the backseat. I'll have to show it to him," Brad replied.

"We'll call you later," Lauren said.

"Well, the Barneses are expecting me for dinner, so how about tomorrow?"

"Oh, okay, sure." Her disappointment was apparent to her father as she left.

"How did it play out?" Walker asked.

"Backed into one, but a win is a win," Brad said.

"Yes, it is. I'll call you tomorrow, and we'll have a beer to celebrate," Walker offered.

"Sounds great. Just call me," Brad said and clicked his phone off. With their call over, Walker used the intercom system to call his daughter.

"My office now!" he demanded. She made her way to her father's office, looking like a teenager who had broken curfew. She sat down in front of his desk.

"Two things ..." he said. Her mouth opened, and he calmly held his hand up.

"The first thing ..." he paused. "Do not let Trot's affection for someone affect your decisions. If you're happy, that's what will be best for Trot."

"And?" Lauren asked.

"I like Brad. I'm pulling for him, but I'm afraid he still carries things with him from his past. I'm not sure if or when he'll get through what happened." Walker stopped. He wanted to choose his words carefully. "He's been through a lot. Be careful."

"It's not what you think, Dad," Lauren retorted.

"You can bullshit your mother, your friends, and maybe even yourself, but you cannot and will not bullshit me. I know my daughter. I see the way you look at him, how excited you get. When was the last time you ever gave a damn about who I was on the phone with?" Walker said. She stood and said not one more word.

Dub Barnes greeted Brad before he reached the garage with a massive, proud hug. "You know I don't know much about that golf stuff, but

Walker said what you did was damn near impossible," he said as they walked inside. Miss Rachel stood proudly over the stove, cooking the dinner she had promised. She checked everything carefully and then walked over to Brad, greeting him with a smile filled with pure joy. She placed her hands on his shoulders.

"Come give Miss Rachel a hug, darlin'." Her hand rubbed up and down his. "We're so proud. Are you proud, baby? You should be."

"Grateful … very grateful. I feel bad for the guy that lost," he answered.

"And that's what makes you such a fine young man. William, watch the food for me." She led him into the den where they sat on the sofa. "I want you to always be grateful for the good fortune you receive, but I want you to know it's all right to be proud of yourself on the inside. You've been working so hard. It's okay to feel joy, baby. No matter what you go through in life, don't feel guilty for feeling joy for something." She held and patted his hand. "Now it's time for dinner. Go wash up." She smiled and stood.

"Yes, ma'am." Brad smiled, and he did feel proud. He was feeling a lot of things.

Brad struggled to fall asleep that night, so he made a list of the things he needed to do the following day. Bills, laundry, cleaning, and any chores Miss Rachel might need help with. He still could not sleep, though he felt thoroughly exhausted. It was ten o'clock, and he wanted to call. He tried to think of a good reason … an excuse to call that late, but he couldn't think of one. It was still early on the West Coast, so he called Mark.

"Hello," Mark said.

"Busy?" Brad asked.

"Roomie! What's up! No, just watching game film from last year. What are you doing?" Mark said.

"Not much. Was having trouble sleeping, so I thought I'd call and see how you've been. So … how've you been?" Brad asked, laughing.

"Oh, so that's how I get a call ... nothing better to do, huh? And why do you sound so chipper?" Mark shot back.

"No, and I know, I know. I should be better about calling and returning calls, but I've been busy ... so what kind of game film?" he asked.

"My new coaching gig, bud."

"What new gig?" Brad asked.

"Well, I've been working on my master's, and when I got it, I was offered an assistant coaching job at San Jose State," Mark said proudly.

"Bob Knight had been a head coach for a while at your age," Brad said smartly.

"Yeah, well Tiger Woods has won ... never mind."

"Never mind what?" Brad asked.

"You don't play golf anymore. Bowling? Do you bowl?"

"I started back," Brad calmly replied while smiling. "And yes, he's won more events than I've played in. But I have beaten him before ... Are you there?"

"You're playing? When? How's it going?" Mark asked. "Why haven't you called before now to tell me? God damn those old farts! I can't believe ... do they know?"

"Yes."

"Well, son of a bitch! The old farts and you never call to tell me anything."

"Well, I've been busy, and I've only played in three tournaments, and you're right. I have no excuse why I didn't call and tell you," Brad answered.

"After all we've been through ..." Mark paused. "Well, give me the details. Wait—why did you start playing again?" Mark asked.

Brad spent nearly an hour explaining the events that led him back. His job, the robbery, the Barneses and Walker White, and how Bill McKnight confronted him.

Brad finally got to the golf. He admitted how nervous he had been and downplayed winning.

"You won? Already?" Mark exclaimed.

"That's enough about me. What's that thing ... quid pro quo, I think," Brad said.

"What's that?"

"I think it's Latin for your turn. I can't believe you got your master's! Mail order?" Brad smiled.

"No, I went to class. It's legit, smart-ass."

"So what made you go back?" Brad asked.

"I really like coaching, but I want to coach something other than middle school, JV, and high school, and it keeps Dad off my case."

"How are they?"

"Doing great, they really are."

"You still chasing as bad as ever?" Brad asked, referring to Mark's playboy demeanor.

"Not a lot of time for that right now, but when I get settled into the job, I'll be good to go. How about you?" Mark asked.

"No. I'll never find another Susan," Brad answered quickly. If he told him about Lauren, the conversation would continue on for another hour.

"I understand," Mark replied.

"You guys ever on the tube?" Brad asked.

"Not where you are. Maybe if you get ESPN or something. Check into it. That would be nice knowing you got a chance to see us."

"Will do," Brad said and added that to his list of things to do. "Okay, I guess I'll hit the sack."

"Brad ... I miss you, bud," Mark said.

"Me too. Night."

"Night."

Brad worked the next morning. He worked hard, and before he knew it, most of the day had passed. Miss Rachel had no pressing things for him to do. The banking and the cleaning could wait one more day. When his phone beeped, it was Walker White. He had already promised to meet him, so he answered the phone. He needed to make some lists.

"You sound exhausted. We can get together another time," Walker said after hearing Brad's weary voice.

"No, I'm good. A beer will do me some good. I need to relax for a little while," Brad replied.

A short while later, Walker rounded the corner to where Brad was waiting.

A small blur appeared, and when it had slowed enough, the small boy hurled himself into his grandfather's lap but only long enough to hug Walker. Just as quickly, he left Walker and held his arms out to Brad. Walker eyed Lauren while Brad was distracted by Trot. Their private chat would have to wait. Brad glanced up for a second and caught the look being exchanged between the two of them. Maybe there was more to this meeting than just a celebratory beer.

"Hey, Lauren, how are you?" Brad asked.

"I'm doing well, and I hope you are?" Lauren replied.

"I'm a little tired but well." Brad finished his beer and stood. "Walker, I should get going. I need to grab a bite to eat and get cleaned up. Call me tonight and we can catch up then?" Brad asked.

"Sounds good," Walker answered.

Brad walked off, and Lauren stared her father down with a look he wasn't sure even his wife could muster. She grabbed Trot off her father's lap and left without saying another word. Walker knew talking to Brad was the right thing to do, but this was a battle that would end ugly if he did, so he drank his scotch and decided to keep his mouth shut and tell Lauren he had no intention of speaking to Brad.

Chapter 28

The last few weeks had seemed weird, awkward; something wasn't sitting well with him. Brad continued to immerse himself in his practice. He diligently continued his routine. There had been a few phone calls from Lauren, but they were just for coordinating dates for him to accompany her to some upcoming Christmas parties, and he wasn't sure what to think about that. He missed her from time to time, which made him feel even worse. There was something about her, but it made him very cautious. Getting out of town for Thanksgiving seemed like a good idea.

Brad owed them all a visit and a lot more. He would always admit that. He had been absent from their group holiday celebrations since he had moved to Kenly. Their families always shared Thanksgiving dinner together. The wives had insisted on it years ago, and now with grandchildren waddling around the house, it made things just right. Martha, Nancy Jo, and Mary Nell agreed that the tradition would continue, and Brad knew exactly where to find them. He hoped they would still consider him welcome and not an unannounced intrusion.

Bill, Tom, and John did what they did best—hiding and peacefully watching football downstairs until the doorbell chimed and Bill's border collie began barking. Upstairs, their wives looked at one another with puzzled faces.

"Everyone's here. Who on earth could that be?" Martha asked. They shrugged as Anna appeared.

"Would you like me to get the door?" Anna asked.

"Oh would you, dear? Thank you," Martha replied and went back to finishing her present task.

Anna pulled the door open, and when she saw Brad standing there smiling, her mouth dropped open, but nothing came out … not the slightest sound. Anna raised her hand to cover her mouth.

"Who is it, dear?" her mother asked as she turned the corner.

"Oh my God." Mary Nell was barely able to say even those words. Anna began to cry as she opened the door wider, and her mother joined her. They were soon joined by the others, all of them equally shocked.

"Hope I'm not interrupting too much," Brad said. Mary Nell grabbed his arm and pulled him inside.

"You better hold on to me because I might faint if you don't," she said.

"Well, don't do that, please!" Brad said while holding her. "Just thought I might surprise everyone." And he had. Mary Nell sent Anna after the men.

"We have company!" she announced at the top of the stairs that led to their cave.

"Who the hell visits someone on Thanksgiving?" Tom barked as he climbed the stairs.

The mob had made their way into the kitchen when the trio of old men finally emerged and turned around the corner of an open doorway, still unable to see who it was.

"Well, who the hell is it?" Bill asked, his tone less than patient. The crowd around Brad parted and exposed him. Brad smiled.

"Surprised?" he asked them. He looked happy. It was the first thing everyone noticed. The next thing they wanted to know was why.

"Darlin', your timing is perfect. We were just about to eat," Martha told him. "Go on with them. I'll make you a plate."

"Please don't. I'm nothing to fuss about. When I leave here, I have to go somewhere else and eat, and they actually know I'm coming," Brad answered.

"Don't be silly, dear. Now go."

"Somebody's grinning like a Cheshire cat, don't you think, John?" Bill asked. John turned around and winked at Brad.

"Yeah, but how's that a problem?" John asked. They made their way down the carpeted steps where a television echoed the sounds of one of the traditional Thanksgiving Day football games.

In a matter of minutes, the smell of food worked its way to them on trays, so they continued to watch. Martha led the parade, and like men do, they continued barking at the game. Brad managed to say thank you to Anna.

"Grab a beer, son. Fridge's still in the same place," Bill told him.

"I think he met someone," Anna whispered in her mother's ear as they walked upstairs.

"So the son-in-laws aren't invited down here? Brad asked, smiling as he sat back down.

"Huh … no, collective group of pussies," Bill responded while Tom and John nodded. "Our daughters have short leashes."

Brad laughed. *They'd be even more pissed if they ever had a notion that their little girls were not in charge*, he thought quietly.

"Tell us about the off-season plans," John said.

"Lots of practice. The win was great but lucky," Brad answered.

"Very few wins do not involve some degree of luck," John answered.

"True. I'm planning to play the Carolina Tour again. I'll do a few Monday qualifiers if I have an off week and it's reasonably close."

"And the Open?" Bill asked.

"I haven't decided yet," Brad said calmly as his head shifted downward.

"Why?" Tom asked.

"It's just too early. I want to see how I'm playing … how I feel." John stared at Tom and shook his head, telling him to let go; it didn't go unnoticed by Brad.

"You'll know if you're ready, Brad," John said, patting Brad on the back. "How long are you staying?"

"I gotta head back in a couple of hours. I haven't spent much time with the Barneses, and I promised a friend I'd do something Saturday evening, so I've got to cram a lot of things in a short amount of time without getting out of my routine."

"Who's the friend?" Bill asked.

"I'm not saying. You guys will think something's going on, and it's not. Just doing a friend a favor … a *friend*, mind you," Brad answered defensively.

"Anyone we know?" Bill asked.

"If you did, I'm sure that my golf game would have come up after a thorough cross-examination, Counselor," Brad replied while laughing.

"It's been a long time, Brad. No one—" John started.

"I know … and thanks. Coming here is still a big deal for me, so that should say enough. It brings back a lot of memories, mostly good and some bad. I do the best I can."

Brad wasn't about to reveal that he had agreed to be Lauren White's companion to four other parties, including the New Year's Eve party at the Silver Lake Country Club.

After a couple of hours, Brad started saying his good-byes. Before he could get them all in, Mary Nell pulled him aside, the dining room now cleaned and free of the others.

"We all miss you so much." Her graceful southern cadence flowed. "You look happy, and we hope that you are."

"I am. I miss you all as well. I'm sorry that I haven't been very good about staying in touch. I was weak and defeated for a long, long time. I wanted to see you all very much, and I wanted to see how far I had come. I'm glad I came," Brad answered.

"Are you seeing someone, darlin'?" Mary Nell asked. "Oh dear, that was blunt, wasn't it?"

"Yes, ma'am, a bit blunt, but to answer your question, no. Why do you ask?"

"It's just been so long since we've seen you smile like this. We were just curious. You know how mothers can be."

"No, ma'am. I have a friend I do things with, but we're friends and nothing more," Brad answered, wondering what on earth had given him the urge to admit even that. The second he finished, he heard something akin to giggling. He stood up and walked to the door that opened to the dining room and listened.

"I knew it!" Anna said proudly as Brad opened the door. Martha, Nancy, and Anna's faces went pale at being caught eavesdropping.

"Ya'll get in here. It's not like I don't know she's gonna tell you anyway." Brad waved them in.

Brad wanted to admit to them that for the first time since Susan, Lauren White had his attention, but he was still having trouble admitting it to his own heart.

Chapter 29

Caroline and Sallie Beth had already informed Lauren of her mother's betrayal, which she had anticipated. She didn't care either. Brad also knew that Lauren's friends had knowledge of their original deviousness, but it strengthened their collective resolve to continue to make them wonder if the only person truly snowed by all of this was indeed Lynn. What if Lynn was wrong? they had wondered. It would make Caroline, Sallie Beth, and Lynn consumed with madness, not knowing the truth. The three previous parties had made Lauren realize she had missed Brad during the month prior to the holidays. She reminded herself of her father's words of caution. Brad had yet to give her any signs that his feelings were moving in the same direction as hers. Lauren had given her feelings a lot of thought.

Brad was easy to be around, and she knew she could count on him after all of their outings together. She enjoyed looking at him and talking to him. She certainly wasn't going to be told by her friends with whom she needed to socialize. Pedigree hadn't worked out for her in the past, and there didn't seem to be anything wrong with Brad's upbringing—what little she knew about it. Decency, honesty, and kindness topped her list of important attributes, and Brad seemed to have them all. Susan would have never even gone on a first date with Brad if he didn't have those qualities. Had he changed because of what happened to Susan and Will? The only evidence to the contrary was the incident with Darnell Watkins, and that could be easily explained away in her mind. She also had Trot. She would be a package deal, and in a way it helped her understand Brad. His past made him a package deal as well.

She always told her mother, Caroline, and Sallie Beth that when she found him, she would know, and there was a part of her feeling that way ... when she was alone in bed at night, having trouble sleeping and wanting to hear Brad's voice because it would calm her. On the chilly winter nights, she thought about having the warm body of a lover next to her, getting out of bed only to have him pull her back to him because he had to hold her just a moment longer because of what they had shared the night before. She thought of him looking into her eyes and making her feel like she was amazing and beautiful at six in the morning without saying a word, just his smile and touch letting her know. Those thoughts were always of Brad. When she touched his arm or shoulder and felt his muscles, she yearned to feel his bare skin. She thought about those feeling more and more. Then her father's words would echo in her mind.

New Year's Eve would be their biggest challenge. It would be the only holiday party in which Lauren's parents attended as well. The party was the event of the year that no one missed without his or her social status taking a tumble. Other than in the case of the death of an immediate family member, you simply needed to be there.

Brad secured a stretch limo for the evening. In order to play his part properly, a few drinks would be required, and a few more to tolerate Caroline, Sallie Beth, and their tiresome husbands. There was no need to take any chances. He had decided to be a little more social tonight, and a little was a lot for him, but it might help sell their story. Brad was nervous, though, as he donned his tuxedo. He paid very close attention to every last detail and then stopped and looked at his reflection, asking why—only to realize it was for Lauren, not for the others. He forced himself to pay attention and rid his mind of that thought altogether; one last look in the mirror, and he felt ready.

Brad felt his tuxedo purchase was now paying for itself. The night was bitter cold, a gusty north wind making it seem even colder. It forced Brad to don a silk-lined, black, camelhair overcoat and scarf. Part of him felt rather silly as he had eyed himself in the mirror. Maybe the scarf was too much, he thought. He looked like a character in *The Great Gatsby*. *Let her decide*, he finally determined.

He grabbed her corsage and a couple of beers from the refrigerator when the lights from the limo appeared. As Brad approached the car, a tall, slender, rather nondescript gentleman emerged from the driver's door in uniform, including a dapper hat. Brad shook hands with him and introduced himself. His door was opened, and as he entered, he handed the address to the driver.

"Very good, sir," the driver replied. Brad smiled at the formality, but then again, it was going to be a formal night.

Brad pulled out a beer and twisted the cap off and inspected the ride. It was warm, the heater on to take the chill off the leather seats, whose scent permeated the riding area. As the car began moving, a one-way window lowered. The driver apologized for his intrusion and told Brad which buttons and switches did what. He said if there were any changes in plans to let him know, and the bottle of champagne he had requested was already chilled in an ice bucket positioned opposite of where he was sitting.

Lauren's secretary had graciously agreed to let Trot spend the night, and Trot was thrilled. His best friend since beginning preschool had been Ellen's son, Rob. She stood in front of the mirror, checking her makeup, hair, and dress one last time. The black formal gown covered her shoulders and worked downward toward her chest. She thought the dress seemed to accentuate her natural attributes, and her cleavage was covered, which was a priority to her. Nothing made her cringe more than speaking with men only to have them stare at her chest. A diamond pendent dangled from her neck, and matching earrings glistened from each ear. She found herself anxious. She had tried to stop having certain thoughts about Brad Ford but couldn't.

Sleeping the previous night had been nearly impossible. Her body ached each time she closed her eyes and imagined feeling his touch, his lips touching her skin, staring into his eyes, and then having him whisper in her ear how beautiful she was. She found herself on the edge of pleasing her own urges before getting out of bed and watching television until finally falling asleep. The next morning, Lauren tried to argue away the thoughts and desires she had been thinking.

He might be a dreadful lover. What if he was clumsy and heavy handed and had no idea what it took to please a woman? She kept those thoughts to fight off her physical desires, and when that didn't work, her father's words rang in her ear.

But tonight as she waited for him, nothing could calm her. The clock ticked, and as each second passed, with each tick of the second hand, that sound became his kisses—kisses embracing her neck, her cheek, her lips, his hands caressing her. She knew Brad would not be a heavy-handed lover. His hands were strong but gentle every time he had ever helped into his car. She stood up and left the room. She felt herself on the verge of breaking into a sweat when she opened the door so the cold breeze would calm her. It lasted for only a moment. He was there. The doorbell rang, and she quickly gathered herself. When she opened the door and saw him standing there, her initial thought was to grab him by the arm and simply thrust herself upon him. But what if he rejected her? she thought. Brad stood silently looking at her. Lauren was breathtaking, and he struggled to say hello.

"This is for you," he said, handing her the corsage made of white roses and baby's breath. "I'm not sure whether it's appropriate, but I thought just in case."

"It's beautiful but not necessary. I do want to save it, though. A keepsake. I hope that doesn't offend you?" she asked.

"Not at all. Lauren, you look amazing," Brad said with his head turned.

"You aren't even looking at me, silly man." She smiled.

"It's hard to do without staring, and my mother taught me not to stare," he replied humbly.

"Well, if it makes you feel better, I'm struggling not to stare at you. Let's stare away. It'll help us get through the evening."

"Sounds great." He helped her with her wrap. "Is the scarf too much? I think it's too much."

"I love it. Are you ready?" she asked.

"Absolutely." He opened the door and waited as she secured the dead bolt. He held her hand as she walked down the trio of brick steps. He led her to the limo.

"A limo? What on earth?" she asked.

"Good evening, ma'am," the driver said as he opened the door for her.

"Well, I thought it might be wise. Dealing with social events has never been a strong suit, and it being New Year's Eve, I decided to have a little fun too and didn't want to take the chance of being pulled over," Brad replied.

"We could have just taken a cab back to my house and worried about your car in the morning," she said, smiling.

"I would never impose on you, and I wouldn't want your neighbors to get the wrong impression of you," he answered, looking away from her and seeing the champagne.

"You would never be an imposition, and as for my neighbors, well … they'll think what they want to think." She clutched his hand. Her skin was warm and soft, and now she had him on the verge of perspiration.

"I almost forgot the champagne," he said.

"We'll save that for later. We're almost there." She smiled, her hand still in his.

The car pulled into the half-circle drive leading to the main entrance of the club.

"Follow my lead tonight. Promise?" she asked.

"I promise," Brad replied as the door opened. He stood and waited, offering his hand to her as she exited the door and stood with grace and elegance.

They made their way to the door. Muffled sounds of music and conversation were audible as Brad grabbed the polished brass handle and opened the door. A young man approached them after they signed in. Brad helped Lauren with her wrap, handing it to him and then removing his own coat.

"Would you like a drink?" Lauren asked.

"Scotch and water."

"You drink scotch?"

"I sip scotch, so I'll do that." He detested scotch, but it would be a long night, and he needed to pace himself. She smiled back. "Let me check our coats, and I'll be right there."

Brad tipped the young man who gushed over the twenty-dollar bill. Brad then tugged the cufflink-bearing sleeves of his shirt, adjusted his posture, and made his way to the bar. He stopped at the doorway and pawned the room, starting with the bar. His eyes began to move when an arm slid around his.

"I thought that was you." Sallie Beth smiled. "Don't you look scrumptious … hmm!" Her eyes appeared glazed. "Maybe you could give my husband some exercise advice. The thought of his sweaty, out-of-shape ass climbing on—"

Brad stopped her. "Whoa, Sallie Beth … too much information, way too soon," Brad said with as polite a tone as he could muster. He managed to give her a smile.

"Sorry." She giggled. "Lauren's over here." Sallie Beth led him to a round table in a back corner that seated six.

Six. Great, he thought. *They're trying to trap us.*

Lauren reached for Brad's hand, and he leaned down and kissed her cheek.

"Thank you for getting my drink. Sallie Beth is hammered," he whispered.

"You're very welcome," she said, holding his jacket. She kissed him on the cheek. Their little interaction was not lost on the others who stared.

"Good to see you again," Hart Brownlee and Scott Novak greeted Brad.

"Likewise," Brad offered, a bit unenthused before catching himself and smiling back, shaking hands with them.

"How's the golf?" Scott asked.

"Fine. Just getting ready for the season."

"How does one go about that in this kind of weather?" Hart asked.

"It's not easy, but there's always something to do." The last thing Brad wanted to do was talk about golf.

"Where there's a will, there's a way, isn't there, Brad?" Lauren said, beaming at him.

"Would you like to dance?" he asked with a smile he had not made in many years.

"I'd love to," she replied, and he emptied his glass before she led him away.

"I thought you *sipped* scotch," she said, smiling as the band and its singer did a remarkably good rendition of Frank Sinatra's "Under My Skin."

"I do, honestly. I guess I need to get to my comfort zone for lack of a better explanation," he said as Lauren's eyes fixated on him before she laid her head on his shoulder. No sooner had they grown comfortable in each other's arms than Lynn White tapped her daughter's shoulder.

"May I cut in?" she asked.

"Mother! No, you may not!" Lauren replied under her breath.

"It's okay. I'll be able to say I danced with the second prettiest woman here as well." Lauren smiled and kissed his cheek again.

"Second?" Lynn asked as they started moving.

"Nothing personal, Mrs. White, but no one here can hold a candle to your daughter." And with that, Lynn smiled.

"Are you having a good time, Brad?" she asked.

"But of course."

"And your intentions with regard to my one and only daughter?" Lynn inquired as the song ended and the crowd politely applauded the group's effort.

"Thank you for the dance, Mrs. White. You look beautiful." Brad smiled and walked back to Lauren.

Eventually, the night settled down. Instead of being concerned with the status, if any, of Lauren and Brad's relationship, everyone managed to enjoy the party, and as the clock neared midnight, the crowd gathered in and around the bar to watch the ball drop in Time's Square.

"Ten, nine, eight ..." they counted down. When they reached one, Lauren gently turned Brad, her hand on his cheek.

"Happy New Year, Brad Ford." Her lips touched his cautiously at first. Sounds of noisemakers and paper horns surrounded them, and finally their lips melted into each other. Their arms wrapped around each other. They were lost in each other.

Chapter 30

She sat very close to him on the ride home last night, which was what Brad wanted. He had draped his arm around her, letting her know that was how he felt. She invited him in and made some coffee, and as they waited for it to finish, she wanted to speak. The kiss had answered many questions, but she needed to hear how he felt. She needed to open up and share her feelings. She would have to break the ice and hope that the kiss was telling her the truth; it certainly told her that if they ever shared a bed, Brad knew what he was doing. She rubbed her hands nervously across the kitchen counter and gathered her strength. She poured the coffee and began to speak.

"I lay in my bed at night wanting you to be with me," she said as she stared at her hands, afraid to look at him. "I can't believe I just said that to you." Tears welled up in her eyes.

That honesty and those words, he repeated over and over again in his mind. Seeing her crying and vulnerable was hard. He wasn't sure what to say as he walked over to her. She turned and buried her face into his chest and sobbed.

"Let's go sit," he said. He was about to open up to her about Susan and Will—it would be the first time he opened up to anyone, even Mark. Lauren needed to know everything; she deserved to know everything before anything else happened between them. He hesitated and remembered the limo.

"This is gonna take a while. I need to send the limo away. I can get a cab later," he said.

"You don't need to call ..."

"Don't say that yet." He cautioned her. "I want you to know what I've been like the last six years. How far I plunged, how much hate, how lost I was. I want you to know the truth, all of it."

"You don't have to," she said.

"Yes I do. I have to," Brad told her. "I'll be right back."

"Why?" Lauren asked. Brad just held up his hand and walked out to the limo. The driver rolled down his window, and Brad told the driver that he could leave. He thanked him for his service, remembered the champagne, and finally tipped him. He came back inside to find Lauren waiting.

"When I won that golf tournament ... even before your father called me and you came on to congratulate me too ... well, when I won, my mind drifted away, which it does far too often, and Susan and Will weren't what came to my mind." Her head lifted as she heard his words.

"It wasn't a bad thing, and I wasn't upset, but when I was driving home that day, Susan wasn't what I was thinking about, and that made me feel guilty. I mean guilty like I was having an affair when your father called." Brad paused.

"What do you mean?" Lauren was confused.

"I know it sounds crazy, but you're the first woman other than Susan I've thought about since our freshman year of college. As much as I want to comprehend that, I'm having a hard time understanding it." He held her hands and forced himself to look up at her. Lauren's eyes were fixated on him.

"And then I heard your voice. I knew it was you, and in hindsight, I was hoping you would be around your father when I called. I wanted to drive straight there. I wanted to see you. I wanted to see you more than anyone, but I couldn't do that. I'm afraid."

"Afraid of what?" she asked.

"After Susan and Will died, I lost it. Are you sure you want to hear this?" Brad asked her again.

"Yes, and if I want you to stop, I'll tell you." She squeezed his hands.

He told her how he attacked Joe Erickson at the morgue after identifying the bodies. He wouldn't leave the house except for necessities. For six months he slept on the couch, hoping he wouldn't wake up the next morning so he could be with them again.

"The phone would ring, but I never answered it. I turned the ringers off, threw away the answering machine. I hid when friends came to check on me. Pretty pathetic, huh?" She shook her head, telling him she understood how he felt.

"So what changed? Something—right?" Lauren asked.

"I saw myself in the mirror one morning and didn't recognize myself anymore. I grew up in that house. My mother passed away in the house that I was living in, and my dad and I took care of each other in that house. Susan and I moved in and were raising Will. The memories never stopped, and the nightmares didn't either." Brad paused.

"I didn't know what to do, but I had to get out of the house. I didn't know where to go, but I had to go somewhere and start over. I started boxing up everything. I still have all of it in a mini-storage place, but I've never been back to it."

"Never?" Lauren asked.

"No."

"Why?"

"That's the problem, Lauren. I haven't made friends with the past. I am now because of you, but it isn't your responsibility to help me do that. It's easy to do because of you, but shouldn't that be taken care of before anything happens between us?" Brad asked.

"So how did you meet Mr. Barnes?" Lauren changed subjects.

"When I left, I went to Kenly. My father grew up there, and I thought it was a perfect place to hide from the past. No one knew me, and my past would be just that. I had no idea what I would do for a living. I just hoped things would somehow work out. In my mind, I knew it couldn't get any worse."

He told her about staying at the Kenly Inn and Mr. Barnes inviting him to breakfast.

"His name sounded familiar, but I couldn't remember why." Brad told her about their meeting and how Dub offered him a job. Mr. Barnes promised he could work whatever hours he wanted, that Brad could stay behind the scenes. Brad admitted to Lauren that even while working for Mr. Barnes he still wasn't happy.

"I worked. I went home. I started working out. I was making the time go by. I still live in their mother-in-law suite next to their house. My social calendar consisted of one weekly event ... Sunday lunch with Mr. Dub and Miss Rachel. For five years, I guess, nothing changed until Darnell Watkins showed up one morning." He stopped.

"Lauren, I almost killed him," Brad admitted. "I couldn't stop, and no one was there to stop me. I'm afraid of myself still.

"Mr. Dub called your father, and I was an ass about that." He continued on, giving her a little detail about Bill, Tom, and John.

"I guess it was like an intervention. I relented. I was certain that playing golf again was the last thing I wanted to do, but I was wrong. I was afraid of family again. I had my share of it. I was wrong I think. I hope I was wrong, but I'm still afraid.

"It's hard, Lauren. I know that I'll be thinking about you when I'm not here. I already do. Unfortunately, I'm all of what I've told you, maybe more. I just don't know. I think you deserve more, and you're half of that equation."

"Trot adores you," Lauren said.

"I adore him as well, but there's too much to—"

Lauren stopped him. "Okay, I've listened to you, and now I want you to listen to me." Brad nodded his consent.

"I'm willing to try. I want to try. You're a good and decent man, Brad Ford. I know why Susan loved you. You failed to give yourself credit for saving a woman's life that night, somebody's wife and a mother to small children. Your heart is kind." She took her hand and lifted his eyes back to hers.

"How ... how will we know?" Brad asked her.

"Tomorrow's a new day. We'll take tomorrow and work our way through it. We'll talk and commit to being open with each other."

"I want you to think about what I've told you. I'm leaving tomorrow for three days."

"I remember," Lauren replied softly. "Is it okay to call you?" she asked.

"Of course. There's still a lot more to talk about." Brad smiled.

"I know."

"I need the phonebook so I can call a cab."

"I want you to stay."

"I don't think that's a good idea."

"Sleep here. I promise not to bite. Besides, we're not arguing on our first night, are we?"

"No."

"No, we're not," Lauren said and kissed Brad. They agreed to, Brad the reluctant one. The bed would be okay. Nothing happened, but when Brad woke in the morning, he realized he hadn't slept that well in years. *Over six years,* he thought.

After a light breakfast, Lauren drove Brad home. Her car came to a rest in the Barneses' driveway, and he reminded her again to think about everything while he was gone. He told her if she had a change of heart he would understand. They kissed one last time.

Brad walked inside his little abode and tried to organize his thoughts, but last night played over and over again. One thought led to another, and questions came with each, three of which he could not answer. Susan, Lauren, and Lauren's family ... Brad's attention left the distractions behind. He would only be gone a few days. He would deal with them in time. He began packing.

He was deep in thought as he drove. In spite of everything else that was going on, he regained a little focus on his plans for the upcoming season and what his intentions were for the next three days. There was a lot of golf to be played on courses he had never played and lots of notes to be taken. "Mental note, stay focused ..." No more had he said that than he thought of another question. "Does Lauren understand how much I'm gone?" he asked. Today would be his hardest day of the three, and it was meant to be. He needed to do this if he was to ever move forward.

Chapter 31

Rita heard the phone ring and looked at her husband, Victor, as she stood. Like every morning since Victor's retirement, they shared a pot of coffee and the newspaper on the patio of what once what been a vacation home in Atlantic Beach. It was a chilly morning, and the coffee more than offset any discomfort. The phone rang on and on until she finally reached it and said hello. She knew his voice in an instant, even though she hadn't heard it in years.

"Hi, it's Brad. How are you?"

"It's been a long time, but I know who you are, and we're fine. How are you doing?" she answered.

"I'm sorry … I guess I feel strange just calling out of the blue like this."

"Please don't be sorry. How have you been?" Rita asked.

"Well, I'm headed your way and was hoping to stop by if you have time to spare."

"Victor and I play bridge with a group of friends until the middle of the afternoon. What time are you thinking of?"

"I can be there whenever you tell me to be there," Brad answered.

"How does four sound?"

"I'll see you then … and thank you for taking the time."

"It'll be good to see you," Rita replied. She walked back outside and told Victor. Victor never looked up and never uttered a word.

Brad left the golf course and headed straight to the hotel he had booked. He unloaded everything and quickly arranged the items the way he liked them and in the places he liked them to be. He showered quickly and changed into a pair of jeans, a mock turtleneck shirt, and wool socks before he slipped his gumboots on. The chill hadn't left his bones as he climbed into his SUV. His heart rate increased the closer he got to their cottage.

Victor sat silently as Rita finished preparing herself. He wasn't happy, and she knew that, but there was no turning back. In her mind, Brad had suffered as much if not more than they had. They still had two children to love, and Brad had been left alone. If he finally wanted to see them, she was happy to see him, no matter the reason. Victor was not ready to see Brad again and wasn't sure he ever would be.

The doorbell rang as Rita finished. She warned Victor that he should still think of Susan and Will and what they would want and how she would expect her father to treat Brad.

When Rita opened the door, she barely recognized him. She managed a smile and invited Brad into their home. Victor was outside, his mind racing, his mind angry that after all this time Brad was in his home.

Rita led him out back to the patio that she and Victor used every morning. Victor took his time and finished the article he was reading, not knowing what Brad was there for after all this and not really giving a damn either.

"What do you want?" Victor asked bluntly. Rita eyed her husband with disapproval.

"I understand why you're angry with me," Brad responded. "I can't begin to tell you how selfish I've been, shutting out everyone for so long. I know that was wrong, but … I'll never be able to convey in words what or how I felt. Today will seem no different to you, because I'm here in a selfish capacity."

"What do you mean?" Rita asked.

"For almost all of the last six years, I've mourned Susan and Will. I never went out. I worked, I ate, I slept. I never thought I would ever meet someone that would compare to Susan," Brad said with his head down. Rita reached her hand over to Brad's.

"But you have?" she asked.

"I think so, yes ... and I didn't want you to hear about it from someone else." Rita squeezed his hand. Victor's face flushed red with anger.

"Get out of my home!" Victor slammed his clinched hand down on the glass tabletop, which cracked but didn't shatter. "Get him out of my home, Rita!"

Brad stood up immediately and walked back into the house. Rita hurried after him.

"Wait ..." He stopped at the front door. She grabbed his hand again. "Victor's angry, and I'm sorry, but I'm not. Susan wouldn't be angry either. It's been a long time, Brad. If you've found someone you think makes you happy, then I'll be happy for you." Brad hugged Rita for what she knew would be the last time. Then he stepped through the doorway and left.

Lauren hadn't seen her mother since the New Year's Eve party at the club. She knew if her father wasn't home, her mother would be all over her, and he wasn't home. She walked inside, and Troy immediately clutched onto her. He was happy to see his mother even if Lauren wasn't excited about seeing hers. He quickly started telling her all about his day as Lynn walked over to the two of them. Lauren held up a finger as her mother's mouth began to open.

"Not in front of Trot and not a word to Dad. I mean it, Mom; you betray my trust, and I'll never tell you what's going on. We can talk tonight after he goes to bed." Lynn reluctantly agreed.

Chapter 32

Brad sat at her desk, neatly and carefully filling out the application for the Open. Lauren sat on the sofa with a book and read but could not help glancing at him when she turned another page. His diligence captivated her, and she found his attention to detail sexy, hoping that attention would soon be placed upon her in a more intimate environment. Over the past three and a half months, Brad had been everything she thought him to be. When he was gone playing, he called thoughtfully, and when he wasn't playing as well as he had hoped, he never let it affect their phone calls. When he was in town, she felt she was the most important thing in the world to him. He had been perfect, but they had yet to be intimate.

Lauren stopped reading when he finished.

Seven years had passed since the last time he had filled out his official United States Open Championship application. He carefully folded it and placed it in the envelope he had already addressed. He had promised one and all that he would try, and he had told Lauren he was comforted by how well he had performed through his first seven tournaments. Two wins and no worse than a tenth-place finish in the other five had Brad leading the Carolina Tour money list. He closed the envelope, looked at Lauren, and shrugged his shoulders.

"What would you like to do tonight?" Lauren asked.

"I've been gone three weeks, so you decide. Anything you want's okay with me. I want to thank you for understanding the travel. I miss not seeing you every day." Brad smiled.

"Anything I want? Anything?"

"Of course," he replied.

"Okay, I guess we'll see about that," Lauren answered, smiling. "How about dinner and a movie at home tonight?"

"You cook?" Brad asked jokingly.

"Funny man … I was thinking you would cook for me."

"Oh really? Well, it's been a while, but I might surprise you. I'll do it. I can nail this—pick up a movie and swing by the store. What would you like for dinner and a movie?"

"Something funny, and I love pasta."

"I can do that. Enjoy your book, and I'll take care of everything."

A while later, Brad returned with the necessary ingredients for lasagna, salad, and some bread and handed her a romantic comedy.

"Have you seen this?" Brad asked.

"No I haven't, but it looks good."

Lauren would read a little and then walk in the kitchen and tease Brad, repeating this over and over, hoping to set a mood that Brad would not be able to resist.

Dinner was surprisingly good. After, they curled up on the sofa, the lights turned down, and began to watch the movie. Thirty minutes later, Brad was asleep, and Lauren was hurting. *There has to be something wrong with me*, she thought to herself.

Lauren's mother immediately greeted her the next morning when she arrived to pick up Trot, who spent the night so that Lauren and Brad could have a night alone. Lynn saw a disappointed look etched across her daughter's face, and when their eyes met, Lauren shook her head, letting her mother know the answer was no.

"Are you serious, honey? Did you do exactly what I told you?" Lynn asked.

"I really have no desire to talk about this, Mom," Lauren answered with a tone soured in disappointment that vanished as quickly as Trot appeared, excited to see his mother.

"Did you see Mr. Brad yesterday?" he asked as he clung to his mother.

"Yes and he said to tell you hello," Lauren said. "I'll call you later, Mom." Lauren gathered up Trot and his bag and headed back to her car while her mother stormed back inside.

When the tires screamed to a stop, it startled Brad. He looked up, waiting for the crunching metal of a wreck that usually accompanied such a sound. Instead he found Lynn White striding purposely toward him with a look upon her face that was anything but friendly.

"Brad Ford, we need to talk," Lynn demanded.

"Yes, ma'am, if you think so," Brad answered politely but obviously put off by the intrusion.

"The first question I have for you is ..." Lynn paced, looking around to see who might be within earshot of her pending conversation. "Is something wrong with my daughter? Because if there is, I would like to know what it is."

"No, ma'am. Why would you think that?" Brad asked.

"Are you gay? I mean, I'm not judging you, but be honest about it."

"Gay? With all due respect, ma'am, I'm certainly not gay. I've been married before, and as nosy as you've been, I feel quite certain you already know that ... again, with all due respect. What's this all about?" Brad asked defensively.

"Well, if you're not, and there's nothing wrong with Lauren, I'd like to know why it is that ..." Lynn paused and then stomped back and forth more. "Lauren planned ..." Lynn stopped again, and Brad finally realized what she was there about.

"Not that this is any of your business, Mrs. White, but—"

"When it deals with my children and their happiness, it damn sure is my business, mister!"

"I didn't mean it like that, but that's a part of our relationship I just don't think it's appropriate to talk to you about. It's complicated for me, and if Lauren's that unhappy, then maybe I should stop seeing her," Brad said.

"Don't be ridiculous. I think disappointed is the better term than unhappy. She says you're holding back, and I think you're going to lose her if you don't talk to her about this."

"Lauren and I discussed all of this before we started seeing each other. I care about her a lot ... a lot more than I ever thought I could, but I'm not ready and don't know when I will be," Brad answered calmly.

"Let me talk to her, honey. I'm sorry I interrupted. I just needed to know, and now I do. It's a momma thing." Lynn patted his arm, smiled, and walked away.

Chapter 33

"Brad, this is Wallace Fay. We received your application, and if you would be so kind as to call me as soon as possible, I would really appreciate it."

The message was the only one on his phone. He checked it, hoping Lauren had called. After talking with her mother, Brad had gone back over to talk with Lauren. She had asked him for a little time, and he understood. He jotted down the number Wallace Fay had left. He loaded his clubs up, sat on the bumper, and dialed the number. He was placed on hold and began removing his golf shoes, meticulously brushing off dust and grass before sliding the cedar shoetrees into place.

"Brad, thank you for calling me back," Wallace said. "How have you been?"

"Better than when we met. How are things with you?" Brad asked.

"Good—busy but good," Wallace answered.

"Glad to hear it. You mentioned something about my application. Is something wrong?" Brad asked.

"No, not at all," Wallace said.

"Well, I thought it a bit odd that you would call about it," Brad said, joking but nervous.

"When your application was received, I was contacted by a member of our staff that processes them. They remembered your name, but I didn't recall you living in Wilson."

"Actually, it's Kenly," Brad corrected him.

"Yes, right, Kenly."

"I moved after I got back. My dad grew up there," Brad said.

"Understandable. I checked with Michael Nance who's the executive director of the Carolina Golf Association, and he's friends with John Hicks, and John said that it was indeed you."

"Okay …" Brad said, wanting Wallace to get to whatever point he was trying to reach.

"I met with the executive committee last night, and we were in agreement that you're exempt from qualifying. You'll be receiving your invitation by certified mail," Wallace said.

Brad's mouth dropped open. He regained his composure before answering.

"I'm sure someone deserves an exemption more than I do. If I don't make it, then I don't deserve to be there. I need to earn my spot, Mr. Fay."

"You did. You earned it seven years ago and didn't have the opportunity to use it. We reviewed a lot of things, Brad. We know you're playing well, which we're thrilled to see. If we thought this was a reach, we wouldn't do it, but we don't. I look forward to seeing you in June."

"Thank you." Brad wasn't sure what else to say.

"You're welcome, and like I said, there's a lot of stuff going on, so I need to get going. I just wanted to let you know personally, and again, I'll see you in June."

Brad looked at the screen of his cell phone, watching it flash that the call had ended. He shook his head in disbelief. He wanted to call Lauren but didn't. He walked inside the pro shop instead and asked Jerry if he could use his computer for a moment.

"Sure you can. Is everything all right?" Jerry asked.

"Oh yes. I just got off the phone with the USGA. They gave me an exemption," Brad told him.

"Congratulations," Jerry answered.

"Thanks. Do you think Carson would like to caddy for me?" Brad asked.

"I'm sure he would, but I would hate for him to get in the way. I think he might get too excited," Jerry said.

"I can't think of a better caddy for me. I'd really like you and your wife to think it over. I'll pay him just like I would another caddy," Brad said.

"If you really want me to, I will," Jerry said.

"I do. I wouldn't ask if I didn't," Brad said, sitting down at the computer. He pulled up his e-mail account. He sent out a group e-mail to everyone except Lauren. He clicked on her address.

> *Dear Lauren,*
>
> *I'm sorry to bother you. I just wanted to let you know I received an exemption for the Open and don't have to qualify. I hope you are well.*
>
> *Miss you,*
> *Brad*

"Thanks a lot and call me when you guys decide," Brad said.

"I'll do that," Jerry answered.

While making his way back home, his phone began ringing. He ignored one call after another and just drove. He was tired, and none of them were Lauren.

He pulled up the drive. Mr. Barnes was talking to Lauren. Brad was glad to see her and nervous as well. He hoped she hadn't been put off by the e-mail. She said she needed some time, and he felt like maybe in hindsight he had violated her wishes.

Although she smiled, her body language was sending a different message. Her arms were folded against her chest, and most of her weight shifted to her right leg. The breeze blew her hair a bit. Mr. Barnes excused himself.

"Hi," Brad said. "Sorry about the e-mail, but I thought you would wanna know."

"What e-mail?" Lauren asked.

"I sent you an e-mail. It's nothing really, if that's not why you're here," he said.

"I just wanted us to talk, Brad."

"Okay. Come on in. I don't think it's too bad in here." It wasn't a disaster, but it could have used a cleaning.

It was Lauren's first visit to where Brad lived. It was simple and uncluttered except for a pile of dirty clothes at the bottom of his closet. Brad quickly shut the door.

"Sorry," he said.

They sat at a small table near his kitchenette. Lauren finally uncrossed her arms.

"I don't know what to think, Brad. I'm not sure I can handle all of this."

"I understand," Brad replied. It was the response he had been afraid of, but he refused to show any emotion about it.

"That's it?" Lauren asked.

"What do you want me to tell you?" Brad asked.

"Something other than you understand. I need to know you care."

"I do. I told your mother that," Brad said.

"My *mother*? How does that help me, Brad?"

"I care about you more than I thought I could. I think about you … I've missed you, but …"

"But what?" she asked.

"Actually …" Brad looked around and then finally back at Lauren. "You—and if I'm wrong, just tell me—but you want me to tell you my feelings, and when have you told me how you feel?"

"I'm in love with you," Lauren said.

"I'm in love with you too, and now that we have that out of the way, here's the rest of how I feel. I want our relationship to be strong enough to withstand anything. I want it right, completely and wholly, before we take the next step. I know this will sound strange, but Susan was the only woman I ever slept with. I think there's going to be a perfect time for us to take that step, and I think it'll be soon, but until then, know that I'm really in love with you."

She kissed him and smiled.

"Are we okay?" he asked.

"Yes, we are. What did the e-mail say?"

Brad walked over to his computer and logged in.

"Oh my God, you're playing the United States Open," she uttered.

"I know ... pretty cool."

Lauren did a little celebratory dance while Brad smiled. What a great day it had become.

Chapter 34

Brad had played three more Carolina Tour events since the call from Wallace Fay. He finished seventh and third in the first two and won six shots in the last one. He spent his last week at home making arrangements more than practicing. He knew that would be the case, but he wanted all of the details done when he left. The week had flown by. Jerry and Cindy had agreed to let Carson caddy, and his mom would stay in a condo that Bill McKnight owned while Brad stayed at one owned by John Hicks.

Mark would be flying into town to be a backup caddy or, in Mark's case, the guy that carried his bag. He hardly thought Mark would be needed as excited as Carson was about his job.

Brad and Lauren worked through things before he left, and he was glad. That was not the kind of distraction he wanted to have before he left. Her admission had caught him off guard, but he was content with life for the first time in years. His admission to her was a tremendous step for Brad, and Lauren knew that and was content in knowing Brad loved her.

He hoped to spend two full weeks at Sandhill Village Resort, the site of this year's United States Open, only because he lived two hours away. In order to do so, he would have to make the cut. Making the cut was his ultimate goal and would eliminate making a fool out of himself, which was his second goal. It was a career ago since he had played his first and only Open, and all he could do was hope that he remembered what it was like. Brad knew that until the crowds that came for the practice rounds arrived, it would be tough to know how he felt.

He left a week prior to the tournament. He drove down Sunday afternoon, arriving before darkness settled in. He stopped at the grocery store and bought some things to tide him over and partially stock the condo. By nine that night, he was completely settled. He called Lauren when Trot was sound asleep, and they chatted like love-struck teenagers for thirty minutes before saying good night.

Wallace Fay found Brad hitting balls and stopped by for a courtesy hello and to warn Brad that the media had already contacted him. All the major media groups covering the event had interviewed him for a piece about Brad Ford.

"And they want to talk to you, Brad." Wallace held his hand over his eyes to shield them from the glare.

"There's nothing I have to say," Brad said.

"Understandable, but in my opinion, and it's just my opinion, when you finish your practice round Monday, have one press conference and get it over with," Wallace advised.

"Thank you, but it's not going to happen. I'm not going anywhere near the media center if I can help it."

"It's your choice. Play well, good luck, and I'm truly glad you're here."

"Thank you again for the exemption." Wallace drove away, and Brad shook his head, thinking this might have been a bad idea regardless of how he played.

"This better be the place. Brad, where are you?" Mark Lewallen said as he burst through the front door.

"Back here." Brad was changing after a much-needed shower, still bare-chested.

"Damn, Brad, when did you get so ripped?" Mark asked, and Brad laughed. "This place is in the middle of fucking nowhere. What's so special it gets to host the Open?" Mark asked.

"I could tell you, but you wouldn't understand."

"I'm good, man, just tired. Where is she?" Mark eyed the condo intensely. "You know damn well who I'm talking about. My best friend in the world, and I've gotta find out about Laura ... no, Lauren from the geezers?" Mark smiled.

"She's working, and unless I make the cut, you won't be meeting her. Unlike us, she has a life."

"What? I've got a life. What does she do and why isn't she here?"

"She's an attorney, and she's not here because I'm going home if I don't make the cut. I've already been here a week," Brad said.

"She's an attorney. Nice … and?"

"Not going there, Mark. Don't even start," Brad warned.

"Okay. So when's the kid getting here? How many times do I have to lug that bag?"

"His name is Carson. He'll be here Tuesday night. Don't mess with him. He's a good kid."

"I won't. I promise. I'll be good. Where's the beer?"

Brad pointed at the refrigerator.

Mark grabbed a beer while Brad took his bags down the hall to his room. They piled down in the den and watched television, catching up and deciding what to do for dinner. Brad suggested a place that those familiar with the Sandhill always made time for.

Hillcrest looked like an old Irish pub that had been brought from Ireland and placed at its location a hundred years ago. The dim lighting did nothing to quiet a nearly overflowing crowd.

"Oh yeah, this is my kind of place," Mark said, observing several pretty women moving from table to table. "I'll be here if you can't find me."

"What a surprise," Brad responded.

Once they were seated, the waitress came over and took their order.

"In town for the tournament?" she asked, and they nodded.

"Rooting for anyone?"

"An old college friend," Mark answered.

"Really? Who?" she asked.

"Nobody you would know unfortunately," Brad answered.

"If I tell you to tell a guy to take a hike, do it," Brad said as he and Mark made their way to the practice area. Brad had found a dozen requests for interviews in his locker. He tore them up and threw them in a trash can. He told Mark about them.

Brad had not hit a ball that day when he was approached.

"Thanks for your time. I'm—"

Brad cut him off. "I don't care who you are or who you're with. I'm here to play golf and nothing else. I know you don't think this, but I'm trying to be nice. I have nothing to say," Brad said calmly. The reporter glared at Brad, and Mark walked over, towering over the reporter.

"Did you misunderstand him, or should we get security?" Mark asked. The reporter held hands up and backed away.

"Only a couple more days, Mark."

Chapter 35

Carson had been perfect. Quiet and attentive. Carson set down Brad's bag, reached into the pocket of his caddie's apron, pulled out a few tees, and placed them back in a jar on the scoring table. He was clearly exhausted. His twelfth birthday was next week, and he had made it obvious to Brad that after three days of the hard work he had performed, he wouldn't have traded the experience for anything he had ever done in his young life.

Brad's nod let him know it was okay to grab a bottle of water, which he quickly consumed. All they could do now was sit and wait.

Brad was six over par after two rounds, and since it would take seven more hours for the rest of the field to finish, they had no idea where the cut would fall. It would move up and down all day, and Brad told Carson there was no need to hang out and wait. Brad did not want to practice anymore, so they headed back to the condos.

"Carson, I want you to take a shower, eat, and rest. I'll call you later, and we'll see how things look, okay?"

"Yes, sir," Carson said timidly as his mother came out.

"How did it go?" Cindy asked.

"If I was as good as my caddy, I'd be leading. We're close, but it'll be a while before we know. Whether we make the cut or not, the condo is free to use until Monday. Oh, and before I forget ..." Brad reached into his console and pulled out an envelope. "Carson's weekly pay and two tickets for Saturday and Sunday, just in case."

Mark had just finished his shower when Brad got back. Mark smiled, and Brad shook his head, indicating no, and Mark's smile disappeared.

"That bad?" Mark asked.

"No, but I don't think I'll make it. You going out?"

"Yeah. Hillcrest has a lot of talent. How close do you think it's going to be?" Mark replied.

"One or two shots. Just be quiet when you come in. I'm gonna get cleaned up, eat, and take a nap."

"Sure. Are you still leaving tonight if you don't make it?"

"No. I'll go back tomorrow. It'll be late before I know, and if I miss, then I'm going to get drunk," Brad answered, smiling.

"Well, don't wait up; it might be a long night," Mark said as he walked out the door.

When Mark left, Brad finally called Lauren, only to catch her with a client. By the time she called him back, he had fallen asleep. The ringing phone startled him from his slumber. "I just got off the phone with Dad. He said you made it!" she exclaimed. Brad was still a little woozy from his nap.

"What? How does he know? I don't even know yet."

"He watched you play both days. We didn't tell you because you didn't need distractions. Anyway, he's still out there, and of course he knows somebody that's in the know. He's been trying to educate me about the cut, but I still don't understand it, and he said the cut's at eight or nine and that there's no chance of it going to five. That means you made it, right?" she asked, her voice still giddy with excitement.

"And he's sure?" Brad asked.

"Can you hear this?" Lauren asked. He heard the sound of a car alerting the need for a seat belt to be clicked.

"Yes."

"I'm on the way. I just have to swing by the house and pack. I'm so very proud of you. I can't wait to see you. I've missed you." Lauren's voice turned almost sultry.

"I miss you too, but I wish you would wait until it's official," Brad told her.

"Brad Ford, you will have happy thoughts and be positive. I didn't pack last night because I didn't want to jinx you. Having said that, do I ask for a lot?" Lauren asked.

"No, not usually."

Lauren laughed. "That's right. I'm coming, you're making the cut, and we will enjoy this. It's another battle won, and besides, who knows what could happen? You have to be in the tournament to have a chance," she reasoned.

"You're right. Just don't get your hopes too high and please be careful and call me when you're close. I love you," Brad said.

"And I love you. Bye."

Brad's phone rang again quickly.

"You did it. You did it!" Carson's high-pitched voice blared in his ear.

"No, *we* did it, and I thought I told you to get some rest," Brad said while smiling at Carson's exuberance.

"I just couldn't. I had to know," Carson answered.

"Are you up for two more rounds?"

"Yes, sir."

"Okay. I'll call you later about the tee time and when we'll leave." Brad hung up and lay back down. He watched the end of the second round while waiting for Lauren.

Lauren never reached for her bags when she arrived. She was too excited and went straight to the door. Brad quickly answered, and she wrapped her arms around him. He smiled, and they kissed.

"Where are your things?" he asked.

"In the car." Lauren smiled.

"Okay, I'll get them," Brad offered.

"Thank you. Do you mind if I clean up a bit?"

"Of course not. It's the last door on the right down the hallway. I'll leave your things in there." Lauren nodded as she felt a tinge of disappointment until she opened the door and realized it was Brad's room. She quickly disrobed and headed for the bathroom, turning the shower on. As soon as she realized the water was hot, she entered and let the water splash and soak her.

Brad waited in the hallway until he heard water splashing, and then he stepped in the room just far enough to place her things on the edge of the bed. He walked into the kitchen and grabbed a beer from the refrigerator and waited. He clicked off the television. Unlike Mark, he sipped his beer slowly. He was grateful for making the cut, grateful Mark was there, and most grateful that Lauren was there. He heard the water shut off. He wanted another kiss, but he sat and waited.

"Brad, can you come here?" he heard her ask.

He gently tapped his knuckles against the door.

"Are you decent?" he asked as she opened the door.

Lauren was wearing a silk robe that barely covered her. She looked at Brad and smiled. He kissed her softly and walked to the edge of the bed. His hands moved slowly down her arms to her waist where they found the belt in a bow holding her robe closed like she was a present. He tugged on the end of it until he felt it release, and the kiss stopped as Lauren gasped. Brad moved his hands back up her arms until he reached her shoulders. His hands worked toward her neck gently, then up the sides of her face, cupping her beauty, and then as he kissed her again, his hands slid back to the collar of her robe and helped it to the edge of her shoulders where it fell like a feather behind her. She pulled him into bed and on top of her. She wrapped her legs around him. It had been a long time for both of them, and they savored each other slowly, exploring one another. Brad kissed her cheek and then neck, and Lauren smiled blissfully and squeezed her legs tighter around him.

Mark came stumbling in. As usual, he simply spoke his mind.

"Hey, Sparky, where are you?" he asked just as he saw Brad sitting on the sofa. "Man, I just got what can only be described as a masterpiece of a blow—" Mark stopped as he saw Lauren walking up the hallway in one of Brad's golf shirts and smiling.

"And so did Brad," Lauren said as she walked up to Brad and straddled him. Brad smiled at her. "I take it that's Mark?" She kissed

Brad again. "You're an amazing man, Brad Ford," she whispered in Brad's ear.

"I gotta hand it to you, Brad. You wait a long time, but when you pick one, you know how to pick them," Mark said.

"Mark, this is Lauren. Lauren, this is Mark," Brad said, struggling to get those few words out.

"Let's go to bed," Lauren whispered.

"Okay," Brad replied, smiling.

"Hey, congrats on making the cut!" Mark finally remembered. "Lauren's here. You made the cut!"

"Yep. Barely. Good night, Mark." Brad smiled.

"Good night and hey! Keep it down in there. I need my rest," Mark said as they shut the door.

Chapter 36

It would be the first time Lauren had ever seen Brad hit a golf ball. It would be her first tournament as well. She met her father by the practice area. Walker had watched her kiss him right before he entered the secured area. Her smile exuded one of pure joy, and he could see it as easily from where he stood as he could if they were sitting across from each other at the office. She was in love with Brad, and in spite of his initial concern, the happiness she was feeling took his concern away.

Mark would join them shortly, and the three would walk along and pray for the miracle round Brad needed. He was eight shots behind and had little hope of winning, but as difficult as the United States Open became on Saturday and Sunday, if Brad could muster a couple of rounds of par, he would pass a lot of players. They kept their distance and would all day. Walker thought it best served Brad if they did.

"I was thinking, Carson ..." Brad paused, looking down at his little friend who was walking feverously to keep up. "We don't have a thing to lose, do we?"

"No, sir. I guess not," Carson replied.

"What I mean is we made the cut, and we both get some money, so why play scared? Nothing dumb, just not afraid," Brad said.

"Sounds good to me." Carson had been a caddie for less than a week, but he knew it was best to agree with the guy actually hitting the shots and never give him a reason to doubt his ability.

"Good. If I look timid or tense, you just tell me to trust myself," Brad said.

"How will I know?" Carson asked.

"Because I always back off when I get that way," he replied.

"I can do that," Carson said, smiling.

When the television coverage started, Brad had only three holes left. A ticker ran across the bottom of the television, and the players came up in alphabetical order. Bill and John would have to wait until it came around again. They sat and waited.

"Plus six when he started?" Bill McKnight asked, and John Hicks confirmed it for him.

"He's three with four to play," John Hicks announced. "If he finishes three, he'll be in the top ten."

"He's still three with three. Damn, they could show him," Bill added.

Brad stood with Carson in the sixteenth fairway. What was normally a par five was now a hellish par four that Brad bogeyed the first two days. He could not afford another bogey now. When he reached into his bag, he noticed Carson panting.

"Are you okay?" Brad asked.

"Yes, sir, just nervous. I promise," he whispered back.

"Well, don't be. Me and this hole have a score to settle," Brad told him.

Brad stood behind the ball and closed his eyes. He pictured the shot and cleared his mind. Carson couldn't watch; he simply looked at the ground and waited for the sound of impact.

Carson looked when he heard the sound he was hoping for.

"It's a good one, isn't it?" Carson asked.

"It's the best I've got, Carson," Brad told him.

Lauren stood next to her dad and Mark near the green. She covered her sunglasses with a scorecard she had been using to keep Brad's score and asked her father question after question, her favorite one being "That's good, right?"

"What a shot!" Walker exclaimed as Brad's ball stopped four feet from the hole.

Lauren finally looked after her father pulled her hands down and told her to look. She couldn't stop thinking about Brad. The one thing she had noticed watching Brad play golf was that he was different—confident, sure of his abilities—and it excited her. He had been the same way in bed last night, and that had been a pleasant surprise.

Brad confidently rolled his ball into the hole for another birdie and made a routine par on seventeen. He and Carson climbed a small hill, and each grabbed a bottle of water. He was four under, and one more par would give him the lowest round of the tournament, and that was his only thought as he hit his final tee shot. Brad rolled his eyes as he watched his ball head for the right rough. Carson's head dropped, as did Mark's and Walker's.

Lauren wanted to know what was wrong.

"He can't get to the green. He can only chip out to the fairway. He's probably going to make bogey," her father told her. Lauren frowned. Brad and Carson made their way to his offline tee shot.

A spotter was standing beside his, which had settled to the bottom of deep, course Bermuda grass. Carson shook his head while Brad walked up, checking his yardage. He could still manage a par, but he had to get back to the fairway and not have it go through.

He reached into his bag, pulled out his sand wedge, and backed several feet away. He made a couple of swings. He took his stance and violently gouged at the ball, and with it, a large swath of turf flew forward twenty feet before falling downward. Brad watched anxiously as the ball finally came back into view. He shook his left hand. The impact had jarred his wrists, but he was okay. The ball barely cleared the rough and rolled to a stop in the right side of the fairway.

He wanted to get it close, but it was more important not to make another mistake. Brad was nervous, out of sorts.

"Take a deep breath and trust yourself," Carson said.

"Thank you, Carson. That's just what I needed to hear." Brad did his best to do what Carson said as he looked at the gallery that had completely filled the stands around the green.

His unsteady hands drew the club back, and the club clicked at impact and then held his abrupt finish. The ball landed short and left of the flag, rolling to a stop fifteen away. The putt would be fast, downhill, and breaking to his right. Brad marked his ball and handed it to Carson, who cleaned it with the towel he had draped around his neck.

"I haven't made one of these in three days," Brad whispered to Carson as he waited for his competitor to finish.

"Yeah, I know," Carson whispered back, and Brad smiled at his caddy's candor.

"Okay, wise ass ..." Brad smiled. "Show me the line I should hit it on."

Carson walked to the other side of the hole and then back. "Right here, that's the spot. Do you see it? Your speed is good. Trust my read," Carson reminded him.

Brad gave Carson a nod and spotted his ball and began lining it up. Everything was still and quiet as he pulled his putter back and tapped his ball, and now his ball was rolling, passing over the very place Carson pointed to. As it did, Carson began walking to the hole, pumping his small fist back and forth, and when it found the hole, he jumped straight into the air as the crowd bellowed its approval. Brad bent over and pulled the ball from the cup. "Nice read," he said, and Carson smiled proudly. They exchanged handshakes with the other player and his caddy and started making their way to the scoring tent.

Walker, Mark, and Lauren were waiting for them, along with Carson's mom and dad.

Brad smiled at Lauren, and they kissed.

"I love you," she said.

"Love you too."

He turned to Carson's parents. "Did you see Carson read that last putt?" Brad asked. "I'd missed every left-to-right putt, so I got him to read it," Brad said as he saw Wallace Fay approaching.

"Terrific round," Wallace greeted Brad.

"Thank you."

"I hate to interrupt, but could I have a moment?"

"Is there a problem?" It was Brad's favorite question to ask.

"No, just want to ask a favor if I could," Wallace answered, and Brad knew what he wanted.

"I need to take care of my scorecard, and the answer is still no."

"What's the question?" Lauren asked.

"Mr. Fay wants me to go to the media center."

"I'll go with you," Lauren replied.

"You don't understand, Lauren. They're going to ask questions that I don't want to answer—questions about the past, and they're that, in the past." He went to the scoring tent and exchanged cards with the guy he had played with and finally signed it.

"Brad, just do it," Lauren said when he was done. "Get it over with and don't answer questions you feel are personal." Brad relented because Lauren asked him to.

Lauren stayed behind a curtain as Wallace Fay led Brad to the stage. Camera's clicked away, and television lights made the room more than warm as beads of sweat ran down Brad's face. He removed his hat and sat it by his name card.

"Welcome, Brad. Brad shot sixty-six today, leaving him two over and currently in the top ten. Congratulations on a fine round," Wallace said.

"Thank you."

"Before we open for questions, tell us about your round," Fay said.

"Not much to say really. I was fortunate enough to not make any mistakes until eighteen and got away with that one."

"Questions for Brad?" Wallace asked.

"How does it feel to be back playing and playing so well?"

"Great. I'd like to thank Mr. Fay and the USGA for the exemption to play, and I'm grateful I made the cut and justified their decision," Brad said, leaning forward and crossing his arms on the table.

"Can you tell us about your caddy?"

Brad smiled and began to brag about Carson. "He's eleven years old, I think twelve next week. He's the son of the PGA member Jerry Beaman, who's the head professional at Silver Lakes Country club where I play. We practice and play a lot of golf together. He'll play in the Open one day," Brad said.

"What have you done for the past seven years?"

"Do you have a golf question?" Brad asked back.

"No," the reporter answered.

"Don't ask me another question. You used up your chance. Who's next?" Brad asked.

Four straight questions followed by prying into the past. Brad looked over at Wallace Fay.

"I'm sorry, but this is the United States Open, our national championship, and you guys want to talk about the past. I've had seven years to talk about it if I had wanted to, but I haven't, and that hasn't changed. I'm playing golf, and I had a good round." Brad stood and grabbed his hat and walked off stage. "Let's get out of here," he said to Lauren.

"Are you mad?" she asked.

"Not at you, Lauren. At least you got to see what it's like."

When Brad finished his shower, he walked into the den and found Lauren curled up on the sofa next to the armrest. She looked distracted, distant, and void of emotion. She stared blankly ahead.

"What's wrong?" he asked. She shook her head as if to indicate nothing was wrong, but Brad knew better.

"Talk to me," he said.

"I was flipping through the channels and saw your press conference and then ..." She paused and looked away from Brad.

"Then what?" Brad asked.

"They showed the news coverage." Lauren finally broke down. "I understand," she said through her tears.

"Understand what?" Brad asked her.

"If you, I just need to know ..." Tears ran down her cheeks, and Brad knew.

"I would have never told you I love you, never been with you, if I wasn't past it. I needed to know that I could love you as much if not more than Susan. I know that now. I just didn't want to go back there so a reporter gets a story. You're everything to me, and I love you and only you." He wiped the tears from her cheeks and kissed her, and she knew he loved her.

Chapter 37

The second he woke up, Brad checked his alarm clock. He had slept so hard he feared he had missed his tee time. The green LED lights showed the time to be 7:00 a.m., and he let out a huge sigh of relief. He rubbed his eyes a moment and felt Lauren nuzzle closer and reach for him. He slipped back under the covers, and she slid one of her willowy legs over him and then pulled herself on top of him. She kissed him and rested her head on his shoulder. He smiled contently.

"How would you like some coffee?" he asked her.

"I would love some."

While waiting for the pot to brew, he grabbed his laptop and sat back down on the bed. He pulled up the USGA website to check his tee time and pairing. Brad had vaulted up the leaderboard and was now tied for sixth place but still five shots behind the leader who seemed unstoppable and had the experience of having already won the United States Open. He sent an e-mail to all of his friends, thanking them for thinking about him and all the support. He promised to touch base when he finally got back home.

He spent the morning trying not to think about how important this round would be. Yes it was the national championship of American golf, but there were numerous benefits Brad could reap with a good finish. His head spun thinking of them—exemptions into the Masters, British Open, the PGA Championship, and most importantly his tour card. He could finally be a member of the PGA tour.

"Let's go for a walk. I need to get out of here for a bit," Brad told her.

"Okay," Lauren replied. "Is everything okay?"

"Yes, sweetie, just thinking too much already."

They both dressed quickly. Lauren grabbed one of Brad's hats to cover up her tangled, blonde locks, and they walked out the back of the condo, which sat beside one of Sandhill's eight courses. The fourth, as it was known, was eerily quiet. As they walked, a golf cart drove toward them and stopped.

"Hey, sorry to bother you ... you didn't happen to see a ball over here?" the man driving the cart said.

"Yes, sir, it's just right of the path. It had a pig on it like the grocery store chain," Brad said.

"Hey, Sandra," the man said to the woman sitting next to him, "he looks like the guy from the news last night, doesn't he?"

"Yes, he does," she answered.

"Are you the guy ... oh what the hell's his name?"

"Brad Ford?" Lauren asked.

"Yes, that's his name," he answered.

"Yes, sir, I am," Brad replied.

"Well, son of a gun, Sandra, this guy's got a chance to win the tournament."

"Could we get a picture, dear?" Sandra asked. Brad looked at Lauren, who smiled.

"Give me the camera. I'll take it," Lauren said. Brad stood between them, and Lauren took a picture. "How's that look?" Lauren asked, handing the camera back.

"Oh, that's perfect. Do you mind signing an autograph?" the man asked.

"Uh, sure. Pen?" Brad asked.

"I have one right here."

"What would you like me to sign?" Brad asked.

"Oh, your hat, Brad. Sign your hat," Lauren offered as she took her cap off, handing it to Brad. She began fluffing her hair as Brad took the pen and signed the bill of the cap and handed it and the pen back to the older couple.

"We better get going. Hope you both play well. It was nice meeting you," Brad said, shaking their hands.

"Nice meeting you too. Good luck, Brad."

They walked quietly for just a minute or so.

"How's Trot?" Brad asked.

"He's doing great, having a blast with Mom. I'm sure she's spoiling him rotten, but he's been keeping up with you." Lauren smiled.

"He's a good boy. I know you're proud."

"But of course." Lauren blushed with pride.

"I'm ready to tell him when you are," Brad said, stopping and turning toward Lauren.

Brad started getting himself ready when he remembered something from the past. It took him a couple of minutes to find the number, and then he sat down on the edge of his bed and began dialing. Lauren came in, surprised to see Brad on the phone.

"Thought you were ready to leave?"

"Give me a second." He then spoke into the phone. "Yes, I was hoping you could connect me to the men's locker room?"

"One moment please," the operator answered.

"I met this great old man named Malcolm Jefferson ... Hold on, it's ringing." Brad smiled.

"Could I speak with Malcolm Jefferson please?" Brad asked, and then listened. "Really? When? How?" Brad' shoulders slumped. "I'm sorry too. He was a fine man." Brad hung the phone up.

"He died a month ago." His hand covered his eyes as he told Lauren about the kind old man he met in San Francisco and his kind words before he played and how it was like hearing his father's encouragement.

"I just wanted to let him know I was thinking about him. I should've done that a long time ago," he said.

Chapter 38

Brad and Carson were greeted with overwhelming encouragement as they made their way to the practice area where the crowd stood and applauded. Carson blushed at all the attention, and Brad tugged the bill of his cap. He instructed Carson to go to the end of the range where they warmed up every day. Brad stopped for practice balls, and Roger Smead approached him. He was the lead on-course reporter who had been assigned to his group.

"Brad, could I have a minute?" Roger Smead said, introducing himself.

"Sure."

"Just a couple of questions. I'll tell them you agreed, and then I'll say, 'Thanks, guys,' and we'll be live."

"Okay, sounds good to me," Brad said. Roger nodded to Brad, giving him the heads up.

"Thanks, guys. I'm here with Brad Ford. Sixty-six yesterday helps you move up fifty-plus spots and now tied for sixth, just a terrific round. How are you feeling?" Roger asked.

"Pretty good ... nervous, but I find that's not a bad thing." Brad smiled.

"This is your home state, United States Open. You're an incredible story, and do you think you can pull this off?" Roger asked.

"That's a great question, but I'm five behind a guy who came here thinking he could win, has already won the US Open, and honestly, I came here hoping to make the cut."

"How does it feel to play on such a big stage?" Roger asked.

"It's an incredible experience. Mentally, the challenge is almost more than you think you can stand. The really great thing is seeing if you can control yourself until the end. If I don't play well, it won't be my swing, it'll be my nerves," Brad responded openly.

"Well said. Thanks for taking some time for us and good luck today."

"You bet. Thanks." Brad shook Roger's hand and walked down to where Carson was waiting patiently.

"Did they interview you?" Carson asked.

"Yeah ..." Brad answered, embarrassed a bit.

"That's so cool. Mom and Dad are recording it for me." Carson glowed.

"Did you sleep well last night?" Brad asked.

"Yes, sir. I was so tired. This caddying stuff is hard work."

"I know it is, and I really appreciate you doing it for me."

"This has been the greatest week of my life," Carson answered.

"Well, when we get home, I'll caddy for you at your next junior tournament if you want me to," Brad told him.

"Really? That would be awesome." Carson's toothy smile flashed back at Brad.

"Just don't ask me to read any putts for you," Brad said, and Carson smiled.

He started thirty minutes ahead of the leaders, and before Brad hit his first shot, he made Carson promise not to look at anything that would indicate their position until he told him, and Carson agreed reluctantly.

His steady play on the front had been rewarded with one under par score of thirty-four, and he told Carson as they walked to the tenth hole that he could look if he wished, but Carson could see nothing. Roger Smead was near them, so he motioned for Roger to come over.

"Are the leaders still lighting it up?" Brad asked.

"Do you really want to know?" Roger asked.

"No, but my caddy might have a nervous breakdown if he doesn't find out," Brad said, and Roger laughed quietly.

"Well, Brad, you're in a three-way tie for first," Roger informed him.

"Come again?" Brad asked.

"You're in a three-way tie for first ... now get back to work," Roger said.

"A tie with who?" Brad asked.

"Trevor Caufield and Ridley Dowell. Dowell and Gerkins have blown up. Now go play golf," Roger told him.

Brad's face showed his disbelief as he walked over to his bag and Carson, who stood silent and pale. He heard the swelling mass talking among themselves, creating a drowning noise. Brad placed his hand on Carson's shoulder and left it until he felt Carson's heartbeat calm.

"Can you believe we're tied for the lead?" Brad leaned down and whispered to Carson.

"I know. Are you feeling okay?" Carson asked.

"Great. How about you?" Brad asked.

"Not so good."

"Would you feel better if I messed up?" Brad asked.

"No, sir."

"Okay then, let's have some fun," Brad answered.

Lauren, her father, and Mark were so nervous they could hardly watch.

"What did do you do to him last night?" Mark whispered to Lauren.

"I made sure he knew how much I loved him," she answered. Mark smiled and relaxed.

The next five holes were uneventful for Brad. Five straight pars were normally great but not today on the last nine holes of a major championship. While Ridley Dowell and Jed Gerkins were no longer factors, Trevor Caufield birded ten and twelve and was two ahead of Brad, and Thomas Hagen, the world's number-one player, had caught Brad with birdies on ten, eleven, and fifteen.

When Brad reached the tee on sixteen after yet another par, he learned Hagen bogeyed the hole he was about to play. Still two shots back but alone in second by a shot.

Lauren was a wreck. She knew the pressure that came along with competitive individual sports, but watching helplessly was a new experience. She wasn't alone. Walker and Mark were used to it, but it didn't make it any easier. The Barneses, who knew nothing about golf, watched every shot. Bill, Tom, and John watched, drinking steadily, trying to cope with it. Thomas Hagen bogeyed seventeen. Brad was now two clear of him after his par at sixteen. Brad waited for the eighteenth tee to clear before hitting his tee shot to the par three, and while doing so, he convinced himself to take one less club. He could feel the adrenalin surging through his body. Carson just turned away, knowing Brad didn't have enough club, and Roger Smead noticed.

"Guys, I know his caddy's an eleven-year-old, but he doesn't like the club Brad just pulled."

The sound of impact was as expected. Brad held his finish, his hands over his left shoulder, staring at the ball and its towering flight that seemed enhanced by the nearly thirty-foot drop in elevation from Brad down to the green, which sat in solitude. It was shaped like a bowl sitting upside down, with its edges running to shaved grass areas where balls collected like insects on a bug strip. Brad's ball landed on one of those edges, much to his dismay. Ten more feet, three more normal steps, and his ball would find a plateau of sorts that would feed the ball within twenty feet of the hole. Instead of bouncing forward and staying on the slick, unpredictable surface, the ball crept back to Brad, off the green well below its surface, making par virtually impossible.

"Carson, why on earth as golfers do we hit shots we know we shouldn't even try?" Brad asked.

"I didn't hit that shot, and you never asked me what I thought," Carson said, and Brad laughed.

Roger Smead walked beside them. "Caufield made par on fifteen. Dowell and Gerkins cannot catch either of you. Three-horse race, and Caufield needs to help you and Thomas a lot."

Caufield accommodated them, missing his tee shot left into the rough, causing the crowd in the area to groan collectively. Carson caught Brad looking at the gallery as they pointed and gawked at the awful position.

Brad stalked what he had left for par, paying a lot of attention to where the ball needed to land. The spot could not be more than a two-foot-by-two-foot square. If he hit his pitch short of the square, the ball would come back to him, and too long or left of that spot, and it would be more difficult shots because if Brad had one thing in his favor, at least he had some room to work with where he was.

Trevor Caufield had no choice but to hit his ball back to the fairway, and after his approach shot, he putted from twenty feet. With the lead and his closet foe in trouble, Caufield made the right play.

While Brad and Caufield struggled, Thomas Harvey did what great players do. He finished his last hole with a birdie and at two over par was now the lowest player who had finished the tournament, but he trailed Caufield by two.

Brad's pitch shot landed near the spot he hoped for, bouncing forward, and it began rolling toward the flag. As much as the crowd urged it on, it slowed much faster than Brad, Carson, or the masses could have imagined, stopping ten feet short—and with it the hopes for Brad and an impossible dream.

Carson handed Brad his putter, nearly in tears. Carson felt that any chance Brad might have had ended. The bogey would put Brad two behind again. Carson couldn't watch; he turned away, looking for Lauren, his parents, anybody or anything other than the putt. Trevor Caufield stood by the tee and observed, knowing his lead was only one. Brad addressed his putt, his head tilted to the hole, and as it returned to the ball, he released his deep breath and made his stroke.

Carson couldn't watch, preferring to wait. His concern lasted until the moment the crowd cheered as the ball somehow made it to the bottom of the hole. Carson hopped all over the place as Brad pulled the ball from the cup.

Brad marched to the last tee and spent little time before hitting a tee shot that blasted from his club straight to the middle of the fairway. Brad handed his club back to Carson, who squeezed the Wake Forest "Mr. Deacon" head cover over the club head and followed Brad.

Thousands of spectators followed, but more stayed behind to watch Caufield's tee shot. As they reached Brad's ball, a ground-moving roar came from behind them, and Brad knew Trevor Caufield had hit it close, and he was four feet from another two-shot lead with only one hole left.

Brad knew birdie was his only hope. He smiled and put his hand atop Carson's hat, which was soaking wet.

"He's gonna make birdie, I guess?" Carson asked.

"Not our problem, little buddy. This shot is all that matters, okay?"

"Yes, sir." Carson's voice was dejected still.

Brad pulled out his eight iron and set himself up to the ball when another roar rose from behind them.

"Well, that answers that, huh?" Brad said to Carson, who couldn't muster a word.

Brad reset and reminded himself not to rush. Another crisp blow, and the ground surrounding the green screamed for the ball to get close, but Brad knew better. Halfway there, the ball quit turning.

"I stood up on it, Carson," Brad admitted.

The crowd still applauded loudly as the ball found the green thirty feet away. The two marched up the hill, and Brad removed his hat.

"What should I do?" Carson asked.

"You walk by my side, right here," Brad answered as the patrons who had been sitting in the grandstands rose, showing their appreciation while Brad nodded a thank-you.

Lauren was watching with Walker, Mark, and Carson's parents five deep in the crowd when Wallace Fay approached them.

"Follow me," he instructed.

He led them around the stand and through the security point just off the back of the green for a close-up look.

Ben Thorton tapped in for his par and a round of seventy-five and then looked at Brad and then to the hole and smiled. He stood by the caddy.

Carson stood behind the green as Brad continued studying his putt. He took his time, hoping he could calm his shaky, sweating hands. He walked to Carson, wiped his hands on the towel, and returned to his ball, which rested in front of a dime he always marked his ball with.

Brad's stroke was as pure as any he had ever made. The crowd stood again as the ball rolled. He stared at it desperately, knowing it was an inch ... one inch farther right than it needed to be. He watched helplessly as it grazed the edge of the hole, refusing to go in. Brad crouched down, sitting like a catcher awaiting a pitch as he watched the ball stop, still able to see it.

He stood slowly and walked to the ball, pausing for a moment before tapping it into the hole. The crowd stood again as Brad met Ben Thorton to exchange handshakes.

"You can keep this if you want it," Brad said to Carson as he handed him the ball.

"Yes, sir. Thank you." Carson fought back his tears. Lauren walked over and kissed Brad, and he shook hands with Walker, Mark, and Carson's parents.

She held his hand tightly as she walked with him to turn his scorecard in.

"Stay here with me. We can watch on the monitor." She stood behind and rested her hands on his shoulders.

Brad signed his card, and they watched as Trevor Caufield pitched his ball safely on the green, and two putts later, Trevor Caufield won his first major by one shot.

Brad waited for him.

"Congratulations. Well played," Brad told him.

"You're a hard man to put away, Brad," Trevor answered. "I told my caddie you were like trying to beat a bloody bulldog."

"I guess I am," Brad replied, smiling.

"Yes you are, and I love you for that," Lauren said. "I'm sorry you didn't win."

"Oh, I won, and what I won was more important than winning this would ever be." Brad smiled and kissed Lauren.

Chapter 39

Ten months had passed since Brad Ford finished second in the United States Open. He had just played in his first Masters, and it had been everything he dreamed it would be and more. He made the cut, and as each round seemed to get more difficult for the rest of the players, Brad became more comfortable, and his scores improved each day. Just like in the Open, he had the lowest combined score for Saturday and Sunday, and he finished alone in eighth place. He would get to play again next year. That thought left his mind as Brad watched his clubs get loaded into the trunk of his caddie's car.

"I'll see you Tuesday. I booked you a room at the place you asked for starting today, so all you have to do is get there," Brad told him.

"Thanks, man. You said Tuesday, right?"

"Yeah, Tuesday is good. I played it before, got the book on it, so rest up and have some fun. Just don't get in trouble. I've got too many things to worry about, and getting me to bail you out of jail isn't going to happen this week," Brad replied. His caddie nodded, knowing just how big this week was for his boss. Brad drove his rental car from Augusta to Atlanta, dropped it off, and boarded his flight to Raleigh.

The flight lasted less than an hour, and he made his way to the baggage claim, quickly grabbing his suitcase. He hopped on the shuttle the nearby hotel provided and took the short ride. He stepped off quickly and went into the lobby and checked himself in.

"Mr. Ford, here's your key, and your friend has already arrived," the manager said. Brad nodded his thanks.

When the elevator doors opened, room-number signs directed him. He slid his key card in, watched as the green light blinked, and turned the handle. The room smelled of her, and before he could put his bag down, Lauren was kissing him, his long day now worth every second. He smiled, dropped his bag down on the top of the small dresser next to the TV, and opened it up. He pulled his clothes off, and Lauren gazed and smiled.

"I need a quick shower," he said.

"I'll be in bed waiting," Lauren replied.

He dried off in the bathroom, wrapped the towel around his waist, and walked over to the bed. Lauren's arm reached from under the covers and pulled his towel to the floor. She raised the sheets, exposing her body, both of them in an equal state of undress. He slid into bed, and they held each other like they hadn't seen each other in several weeks, not just one.

The phone rang, the computerized message telling him it was their wake-up call. He made coffee and woke Lauren. She looked as good this morning as she'd looked last night when he arrived.

"Good morning." He kissed her, and she sat up, the covers tucked under her arms. He handed her the coffee cup. "I'm gonna get cleaned up while you enjoy your coffee." Lauren smiled.

The shower roared, the water steamed, and Brad washed quickly from head to toe. He finished shaving and was brushing his teeth when she walked in, still naked. Brad smiled.

"What?" Lauren asked, smiling from ear to ear. "You do realize moments like this will be few and far between when Trot's with us twenty-four hours a day," she reminded him.

"Yes, I most certainly do, but let's agree to steal a moment for just the two of us when we can?" he asked.

"Yes, I agree."

"Promise?" Brad asked.

"Always," she answered.

Chris Baker was waiting for them. To Brad, he looked the same eight years later. He introduced Lauren, and they boarded the same private jet he had come home in from San Francisco.

"Brad, I know it's early, but Mr. and Mrs. Hicks sent a bottle of champagne, and the refrigerator is full, so make yourselves at home,"

Chris said. Lauren smiled, and Brad went and got some orange juice to make Lauren a mimosa. They taxied to the runway, and in minutes they were near their cruising altitude.

"That was so nice of them to do this for us," Lauren said as she sipped her drink.

They landed and called the rental-car company to pick them, and after the papers were signed, they headed to the courthouse and the office of the clerk of courts. Lauren, the lawyer, had called and made sure they both would have all the documents needed in order to get a South Carolina wedding license. Less than thirty minutes later, they were off to the hotel.

They checked in and went to their room. Brad placed their bags on the sofa while Lauren sat on the edge of the bed and called her parents.

"Hi, Mom. We're here," she said. "Okay, we'll be right down."

They left again and took the stairs instead of waiting for the elevator. Two floors later, they knocked on the door. Walker White answered and hugged and kissed his smiling daughter. Trot squealed as he shouted, "Mommy!" He bolted to his mother and jumped into her arms, and she held him tight.

Walker and Brad exchanged a manly greeting. Walker was a happy man. Lynn White was more excited than anyone. Lauren had let her mother make all the plans, and Brad expected the worst. Lynn picked out the outfits, and Lauren handed Trot to Brad. Trot wrapped himself to Brad the best he could, and Brad just smiled. Lynn showed Lauren her dress and Brad's clothes. Lauren gushed; she had expected her mother to go overboard, but she had not. Everything was perfect.

Lauren and Brad decided Wednesday afternoon would be the best day. Tuesday would be his only chance to practice, which was the last thing on his mind. The course would be closed Wednesday for the pro-am regular tour events held for sponsors and their guests. Brad and his caddie would go out early, and then the rest of the day would be left for her and Trot, and whatever they wanted to do was fine with him. He just wanted to spend it with them.

That Tuesday afternoon flew by, with shopping and more shopping, lunch, and dinner. And a most curious young man had exhausted them both. They fell asleep without a thought.

Chapter 40

No alarm was needed Wednesday morning. Brad was the first to wake up. He went to the kitchen and started the coffeemaker. He walked to the balcony and opened the sliding glass door to the subtle sounds of the coast and a perfect breeze. The weather could not have been more perfect as the sun made its way up above the Atlantic Ocean, making the water glisten. His hands were resting on the rail, oblivious to the world, when Lauren's hands snuggled around him from behind, her head resting against his back.

"Good morning," Lauren said.

"Good morning to you as well," he replied as he turned to her.

They ordered room service and spent a quiet morning together. Brad pulled the outfit Lynn White had chosen for him out and laid it on the bed: beige linen slacks and a white pinpoint oxford shirt, along with a woven leather belt. He was still a bit surprised that Lynn hadn't gotten more carried away. He showered and shaved quickly and started dressing under Lauren's watchful eye. Once he finished, she came over and adjusted everything to suit her, and he didn't mind. He wanted to look exactly the way she wanted him to.

He left Lauren to get ready and met Trot and Lynn in the lobby. The three of them made their way to the beach to meet the minister. Lynn, armed with her digital camera, reminded him to keep it short and sweet, and then she clicked off several pictures of Brad and Trot, who had wrapped himself around Brad's waist, smiling all the while.

"I like the beach. Don't you?" Trot asked Brad.

"Yes, I do, Trot," he replied.

The swirling breezes announced her presence, as her perfume carried gently down to them. Lynn smiled and then started taking pictures of her beautiful daughter as her father escorted her onto the soft sand.

Lauren's blonde hair floated about her shoulders, and the hem of her cream-colored sundress swayed back and forth at her knees. She smiled almost shyly, looking at Brad with Trot still clinging to him. Trot reached into his pocket and pulled out the ring his mother would soon be wearing. Lynn had Brad's ring hooked on one of her fingers.

When Lauren reached Brad, Walker gave his daughter a kiss on the cheek and moved out of his way. She turned to Brad, and together they turned to the minister.

Printed in the United States
By Bookmasters